PRAISE FOR JANICE CANTORE

"This timely police procedural from a twenty-two-year veteran of the Long Beach, Calif., police satisfies."

PUBLISHERS WEEKLY on *Code of Courage*

"*Code of Courage* by Janice Cantore is an exciting romantic thriller. . . . I guarantee you will not be able to put this book down! It is a thrilling and inspirational read and one I highly recommend for anyone who enjoys romantic suspense."

CHRISTIAN NOVEL REVIEW

"Another fantastic police procedural from one of the best. [*Code of Courage*] is completely satisfying and downright enjoyable!"

WRITE READ LIFE

"Cantore's fast-paced and unpredictable suspense kept me burning the midnight oil for the next page and the next. Romantic suspense doesn't get better than this."

DIANN MILLS, bestselling author of *Airborne* and *Fatal Strike*, on *Breach of Honor*

"*Breach of Honor* is one of the best stories I've read in a long time! Pulling on her years of expertise in law enforcement, Janice takes the reader on an edge-of-the-seat journey that makes you willing to lose sleep to find out what happens next! This one is on my keeper list and I'm eagerly awaiting the next book from Janice."

LYNETTE EASON, bestselling, award-winning author of the Danger Never Sleeps series

T0006008

"I can't remember the last time I've been so invested in the outcome of a story or so satisfied with its conclusion. With *Breach of Honor*, Janice Cantore has crafted an adventure filled with brutal crimes, heartbreaking injustice, shocking twists, a gentle romance, and hard-won faith. Words like *page turning*, *breath stealing*, and *pulse racing*, while accurate, don't begin to do it justice."

LYNN H. BLACKBURN, award-winning author of the Dive Team Investigations series

"In *Breach of Honor*, Janice Cantore tells a complex tale of deceit and backroom deals that leaves you wondering who the good guys actually are. . . . I could not wait to get to the end and see how it all tied together."

HALLEE BRIDGEMAN, bestselling author of the Song of Suspense series

"A fast-paced thriller with a strong Christian message . . . [*Cold Aim*] is an exciting and thought-provoking book."

CHRISTIAN NOVEL REVIEW

"A complex tale of murder, deceit, and faith challenges, complete with multifaceted characterizations, authentic details, and action scenes, even a subtle hint of romance . . . [all] well integrated into a suspenseful story line that keeps pages turning until the end."

MIDWEST BOOK REVIEW on *Lethal Target*

"Well-drawn characters and steady action make for a fun read."

WORLD magazine on *Lethal Target*

"Readers who crave suspense will devour Cantore's engaging crime drama while savoring the sweet romantic swirl. . . . *Crisis Shot* kicks off this latest series with a literal bang."

ROMANTIC TIMES

"A gripping crime story filled with complex and interesting characters and a plot filled with twists and turns."

THE SUSPENSE ZONE on *Crisis Shot*

"A pulsing crime drama with quick beats and a plot that pulls the reader in . . . [and] probably one of the most relevant books I've read in a while. . . . This is a suspenseful read ripped from the front page and the latest crime drama. I highly recommend."

RADIANT LIT on *Crisis Shot*

"Cantore, a retired police officer, shares her love for suspense, while her experience on the force lends credibility and depth to her writing. Her characters instantly become the reader's friends."

CBA CHRISTIAN MARKET on *Crisis Shot*

"An intriguing story that could be pulled from today's headlines."

MIDWEST BOOK REVIEW on *Crisis Shot*

"The final volume of Cantore's Cold Case Justice trilogy wraps the series with a gripping thriller that brings readers into the mind of a police officer involved in a fatal shooting case. . . . Cantore offers true-to-life stories that are relevant to today's news."

LIBRARY JOURNAL on *Catching Heat*

"Cantore manages to balance quick-paced action scenes with developed, introspective characters to keep the story moving along steadily. The issue of faith arises naturally, growing out of the characters' struggles and history. Their romantic relationship is handled with a very light touch . . . but the police action and mystery solving shine."

PUBLISHERS WEEKLY on *Catching Heat*

"Questions of faith shape the well-woven details, the taut action scenes, and the complex characters in Cantore's riveting mystery."

BOOKLIST on *Burning Proof*

"[In] the second book in Cantore's Cold Case Justice series . . . the romantic tension between Abby and Luke seems to be growing stronger, which creates anticipation for the next installment."

ROMANTIC TIMES on *Burning Proof*

"This is the start of a smart new series for retired police officer–turned–author Cantore. Interesting procedural details, multilayered characters, lots of action, and intertwined mysteries offer plenty of appeal."

BOOKLIST on *Drawing Fire*

"Cantore's well-drawn characters employ Christian values and spirituality to navigate them through tragedy, challenges, and loss. However, layered upon the underlying basis of faith is a riveting police-crime drama infused with ratcheting suspense and surprising plot twists."

SHELF AWARENESS on *Drawing Fire*

ONE
FINAL
TARGET

JANICE CANTORE

Tyndale House Publishers
Carol Stream, Illinois

Visit Tyndale online at tyndale.com.

Visit Janice Cantore's website at janicecantore.com.

Tyndale and Tyndale's quill logo are registered trademarks of Tyndale House Ministries.

One Final Target

Cover designed by Dean H. Renninger

Published in association with the literary agency of Books & Such Literary Management, 52 Mission Circle, Suite 122, PMB 170, Santa Rosa, CA 95409.

One Final Target is a work of fiction. Where real people, events, establishments, organizations, or locales appear, they are used fictitiously. All other elements of the novel are drawn from the author's imagination.

For information about special discounts for bulk purchases, please contact Tyndale House Publishers at csresponse@tyndale.com, or call 1-855-277-9400.

Library of Congress Cataloging-in-Publication Data

A catalog record for this book is available from the Library of Congress.

ISBN 978-1-4964-5760-8

Printed in the United States of America

30	29	28	27	26	25	24
7	6	5	4	3	2	1

Dedicated to first responders who face trauma on a daily basis yet continue to work at helping people

*It is jolting when all of a sudden your life has been impacted
by trauma. It may feel like your reality and the person you once
were is not the person you are after trauma. Survivors of trauma
often feel out of control of their self, their mind, and their body.*

BETH SHAW, *Psychology Today* BLOG

*Whenever our heart convicts us [in guilt] . . . God is
greater than our heart and He knows all things [nothing
is hidden from Him because we are in His hands].*

1 JOHN 3:20

CHAPTER 1

SERGEANT JODIE KING TAPPED the butt of her handgun with her index and second fingers, an outward sign of inward anxiousness. She figured when she stopped being anxious about serving a warrant, it was time to do something else. Unease would keep her on her toes.

Adding to the unease—the frigid predawn temp. *Cold* and *fidgety* described her team. Everyone was ready to move. Snow had fallen earlier and was threatening again. Jodie checked her team and saw four determined expressions and four spirals of icy breath swirling up into the air.

A beach girl at heart, Jodie felt out of her element in the mountain cold. But the target was here, and they would take him into custody. She and her officers—affectionately called RAT, an acronym for recidivist apprehension team—were staged beside a vacant home, on the west side of the target address. Paramedics were present just in case, and since they weren't in the city but in the county's jurisdiction, a deputy sheriff also stood by, monitoring the situation.

"Ready?" she asked.

"You bet, Chief," Tiny Peters answered first. At six-five and 250 pounds, the ex–football player held the universal key, the battering ram they'd use on the door. Convinced Jodie would be chief one day, he never called her sergeant.

Gail Shyler nodded, her cop expression firmly in place.

Tim Evers popped his bubble gum as a way of saying yes.

Gus Perkins gave his trademark thumbs-up.

Of course they were ready. RAT consisted of the best of the best. Jodie would accept nothing less. She ignored the hitch in her thought process that reminded her they were one day early and one man short. Proper planning would compensate for the change. Time to go.

"All right. Let's do it."

Jodie moved her people as a unit from the staging van across the neighboring yard to the overgrown, completely unkempt front yard of their target.

She and Gus trotted to the left side of the door. Tiny stepped to the right side. Shyler and Evers were the entry pair.

Tiny gave the announcement. "Norman Hayes, Long Beach PD. We have a warrant. Open the door." He repeated the phrase twice more.

No response. One practiced swing and the door splintered apart, leaving a gaping opening.

Shyler and Evers, weapons at the ready, moved in first, going left. Jodie and Gus were directly behind them, moving right. In short order, the efficient twosomes cleared the small two-bedroom, one-bath mountain cabin.

Jodie took a breath as disappointment hit like a punch. This was supposed to be a sure thing. Norman Hayes had two felony warrants out of Long Beach and numerous connections here in San Bernardino. Besides her confidential informant, the sheriff's office had confirmed Hayes was living in the house.

Holstering her weapon, Jodie surveyed the living room, conscious of a few odd things: the smell of fresh paint, the warmth of the room from a heater, and the neat and tidy nature of the inside. While the outside of the house was obviously neglected, the living room was decidedly minimalist and even cozy.

"See what you can find. I can't believe Jukebox was so completely off."

"I don't know why you have so much faith in Juke," Gus said as he walked into the kitchen. "He's too many fries short of a Happy Meal."

"But he's from here and he hears things." Jodie frowned as she looked at the cozy room. "Someone has been living here. And recently." Glancing at Gus, she saw dismay on his face. "What do you see?"

"Coffee is warm."

"Shower is wet," Shyler called from the bathroom.

Tiny stopped his progress toward the back of the house, cocking his head, listening. He and Jodie both circled back and ended up at the front door.

Jodie put her hand on her service weapon. "He must still be here. What did we miss?" She looked up, wondering about an attic.

A loud click sounded in the kitchen, like a big switch being pulled. This was followed by a hissing of released air or gas.

Gus looked down at his feet, then raised his head, eyes wide. Jodie turned toward Tiny and saw a look of absolute horror on his face.

"It's a trap! Everyone out!" Tiny grabbed Jodie by the shoulders. She resisted, wanting more of an explanation. In a split second, he physically lifted her up and carried her out the door.

"What—?" The question died in her throat as Tiny literally threw her into the yard.

"Get clear," he yelled as he strode back into the house, calling for Gail and Tim to get out.

Momentum from Tiny's toss propelled her across the yard, but Jodie couldn't flee. *I have to save my friends.*

Catching her breath, she rolled to her feet and pivoted to go back in—too late. The horrific boom of the blast obliterated Tiny's yells and exploded chaos in Jodie's frantic thoughts. A punch of hot air, much stronger than Tiny, lifted her from the ground as if she were a rag doll and pitched her across the yard again.

Jodie's stomach lurched, her eardrums popped, and pain screamed up her right arm as it took the full force of her landing, the thin layer of snow doing nothing to cushion her fall. All around, the sky rained flaming debris. Scrambling to her left side, she pushed herself to her knees, ignoring the bits of jagged glass abrading her palm.

The house she'd just been inside became a fireball.

Heat hit her face in a wave, and Jodie watched in horror as angry flames consumed the house and her coworkers. Staggering to her feet and holding her good arm in front of her face to shield it from the heat, she stumbled toward the inferno, screaming for Tiny, Gus—*anyone.*

Voices clamored behind her.

"Sergeant King, get back, get back!"

Someone grabbed her.

"My guys! They're still in there." She tried to pull away, but the arms were strong.

"No one could have survived that blast," the voice said as the man dragged her back.

Another explosion rocked the house, and a wave of searing, noxious heat rolled over them.

The foul smoke from the burning log home brought hot tears that stung her eyes. Coughing and fighting, Jodie could not prevent herself from being dragged to safety. The paramedics forced her behind the waiting ambulance as fast-approaching sirens from alerted fire personnel drowned out her complaints. A swirling cloud of black smoke snaked across the cloudy sky, smearing it like ink.

As darkness closed in, one thought ran through Jodie's mind: *How did something so routine go so horribly wrong?*

CHAPTER 2

"A memorial plaque and four blue spruce pines, dedicated to your team."

Jonah Bennett meant well by offering to plant a memorial to the dead somewhere on the mountain, but when Jodie parked her car and stared at the still-desolate square footage where they'd lost their lives, realization dawned—she'd have to say no to the offer. At least for now. A memorial honored something that was finished, over. Nothing about the case was over for Jodie, not by a long shot.

She got out of the car, a shiver running through her when the cold wind assaulted her face. Who knew it was cold in hell?

She knelt in front of the charred foundation, unsteady, nearly bowled over by the intensity of the emotion vibrating through her. Coming back to the scene hurt more than she'd imagined it would.

Fueled by a busted gas line and open propane tanks, the fire had obliterated the house. A black smudge on the ground pierced Jodie as a sharp reminder of all she'd lost.

Jodie was no stranger to loss, having been orphaned at eight. As devastating as losing her parents had been, she survived. Now, losing her team made her feel orphaned all over again. More than Jodie's arm and wrist had broken because of the blast. She felt as if she were Humpty-Dumpty, broken in pieces by the memories hounding her day after day. Surely no one—not all the king's horses nor all the king's men—could put her back together again.

But God.

Those two words gave Jodie comfort and stabbing pain at the same time. With all her heart, she believed God was present and in control. Yet she could not climb out of the pit she found herself in. The valley walls surrounding her kept her from God's line of sight.

A cold wind sent an involuntary shiver down her spine. She hugged her arms to her chest when an eerie snapping sound drew her gaze to the lot boundary. The remnants of yellow crime scene tape popped and cracked as it twisted in the frigid breeze.

Closing her eyes, she saw the fire, smelled the acrid smoke, and grieved for her lost teammates and friends. Tiny appeared in her mind's eye, bloodied and charred, expression accusing.

"You let us down, Chief."

She jerked to her feet, running her palms across her cheeks to wipe away the tears, as grief threatened to overwhelm her. Would the tears ever stop? For a few minutes she stood still, hoping her legs didn't give way beneath her. When her thoughts cleared, she hugged her arms to her chest as tight as she could, wishing she'd wake up from this nightmare.

Even in her grief and pain, Jodie wanted to move from this place, this mire she found herself in. She just didn't know how. She had tried. After the last funeral, days morphed into weeks, weeks into months. Slowly, feeling as if maybe time helped ease the heavy crush of pain and loss, she'd resolved to take steps forward, to return to the land of the living. The removal of her cast signaled it was time to go back to work. She tried.

Two weeks ago, while still in physical therapy for her wrist, she accepted an administrative position. Jodie sat at a desk reviewing arrest reports. She lasted only a week before turning in her badge and filing for early retirement, against the advice of her friends and the department psychologist.

Her team had been multijurisdictional. Gail hailed from Seal Beach PD, Tim from El Monte PD. Gus and Tiny were from her department, and the station seemed filled with ghostly memories: Tiny working out in the basement gym. Gus boasting about the retirement home he had planned. Gail pretending she didn't notice Tim was sweet on her and working up the courage to ask her out.

And there was one who wasn't a ghost: Ian Hunter, Jodie's second-in-command on RAT. Because Jodie had chosen to go a day early and he had to be with his wife, who was having surgery, Ian wasn't there during the raid. Every chance he got, he reminded Jodie that she had rushed things. *"You should have waited."*

In the days before returning to work, Jodie had smiled through the pain. *"I'm ready, back on my feet. I want to go back to work."* Those words now rang hollow in her memory as empty lies. Jodie did not know how to go back to life as a police officer—not without her friends and colleagues.

Doc Bass begged her to be patient. *"Allow yourself time to grieve. Emotional wounds don't heal as fast as physical ones. Stop looking at this as your responsibility. Focus on the cause of the explosion: Hayes. Not you. Forgive yourself. The deaths of your friends were not your fault.*"

"Four good cops died on my watch. They. Were. My. Responsibility."

Jodie couldn't forgive, and she couldn't blame anyone but herself. She'd missed something in the weeks leading up to the warrant service, something she should have seen.

I should have known.

Norman Hayes was still missing. Once the fire was out and forensics responded, they discovered a partially collapsed tunnel leading from the target address to the lot behind, where an unoccupied vacation home had been burglarized. Someone *had* been in the cabin, ostensibly Hayes, and fled, probably after the first knock. This prompted a huge manhunt—which came up empty.

Investigators theorized Hayes fled the residence through the passageway to the vacant home, escaping before the blast, eventually finding a way off the mountain and possibly out of the country.

Jodie didn't buy it. Her CI, the man who'd given her the tip about the cabin, was also missing. A local lifeguard, Jukebox had no criminal record. It was inconceivable to her to think he was part of this heinous ambush. She'd stayed quiet and let the investigation run its course, and here she was, three months later, with no satisfactory resolution.

There had to be a way to discover what really happened and who was responsible. Jodie vowed to find it.

She kicked a piece of burnt wood and watched it disintegrate into black flakes. "I'm finished crying. I will find out the truth somehow."

No echo bounced back. Her words faded in the chilly wind.

She jerked a therapy ball out of her pocket and squeezed it in her right hand. Her injuries had healed slowly. The therapy ball became a nervous habit. Frustration fueled each squeeze.

She'd lived while the people she supervised went up in smoke in the blink of an eye. Guilt kept telling her she shouldn't be alive while her whole team had perished. Her knuckles turned white around the ball. She wondered if she'd pulverize it.

Another shiver ran through her, as much from the memory as from the wind, which seemed to get colder with every gust.

The sound of an approaching vehicle caught her attention. Turning, she saw a late-model black Jeep cruising slowly up the drive toward where she had parked, the crunch and snap of large off-road tires rolling over gravel loud. The vehicle was unfamiliar. She could see a man in the driver's seat, but he, too, was someone she didn't know. Tensing, Jodie wondered who else would have business here, at this lot, which was essentially a graveyard now.

Suddenly the Jeep leaped forward, straight toward her, and the man laid on the horn. Startled, Jodie lurched from his path and sprinted for her car just as the sound of gunfire destroyed the mountain morning quiet.

CHAPTER 3

SAM HIT THE SEARCH BUTTON on the radio, listening as the tuner roved up the dial, looking for a strong signal. It pinged through talk, country, rap, and finally settled on a worship station. He listened for a moment, then turned the radio off. He'd not been able to worship for a while and was not ready to try now. His mind was like the search mode, bouncing around for a solid signal but not finding what it needed to stay tuned to. The radio could be silenced, but his thoughts were not as easy to turn off.

So many things were on his mind. He'd just finished moving into his new home, a two-bedroom, one-bath cabin on Canyon Drive in the small mountain community of Green Valley Lake. Fittingly, it was perched on the side of the canyon, and he'd drunk his first cup of coffee sitting on the deck this morning, despite the cool temperatures. The mountain communities were experiencing a late spring cold snap promising more snow. He'd stayed in his deck chair for an hour, taking in the scenery and watching his breath and steam from the coffee rise in the frigid air.

While he sat, he'd contemplated the injuries that almost ended his law enforcement career, the fight he'd had to get his job back, and the ongoing battle he was having with the department psychologist. Weeks after passing all the requirements to return to patrol, Sam was itching to get out from behind a desk.

In all his life, Sam had never failed. He succeeded at everything he'd ever attempted—except pulling his partner out of the burning car and being able to tell Doc Roe he'd processed everything about the incident.

He couldn't tell him that because Sam couldn't lie.

But yesterday had been different.

"Have I completely forgiven myself? No, I haven't. But I'm moving forward. I'm accepting things I can't change. To quote you, 'Healing from trauma doesn't happen in an instant.' I'm healing slowly but surely. Right now, all I'm doing is pushing paper. I need to be more active, more involved in doing what I became a police officer to do."

He didn't get patrol, but he got moved to a more active detail—homicide. The move surprised him, but he wasn't about to look a gift horse in the mouth. Rather than argue and try to figure out what motive was behind the offer, he said yes and then decided to charge in, full speed ahead.

Sam stopped at the intersection where Green Valley Lake Road met Highway 18. As downhill traffic passed, he absentmindedly flexed his right hand. Scaly, marred, and blemished from the burns and the skin grafts, it was still tight, painful at times. So was his elbow and, to a lesser extent, his shoulder. But the hand worked, and Sam would never stop rehabbing it, trying to get as close as he could to 100 percent.

His destination this morning was a friend's house, but he had a stop to make first.

He made the turn to the small hamlet of Arrowbear, wound around on quiet streets, passed his friend's street, and then turned left where a sign proclaimed No Outlet. Sam continued to the end of the street, arching his eyebrows in surprise when he saw a small SUV on the parking pad in front of the burned-out house. Slowing, he scanned the area and spotted a woman standing near the blackest portion of the foundation, blonde hair pulled back in a ponytail, erect, alert posture.

Something like a lightning bolt hit him square in the chest as he recognized her. Sergeant Jodie King. The case file he'd been given in homicide was filled with photos of her and her team. She was the reason he'd been given the plum position in homicide. Doc Roe used Sam's Army experience as a bomb technician to argue that Sam was perfect for the gig. His expertise could help solve King's case.

Though he technically didn't start in homicide until Monday, he'd already read through all the paperwork and the input from federal agencies. The next task on his list was setting up an interview with King herself. The shock at seeing her in the flesh took him aback.

A flicker up and off to his left caught his attention. For a split second Sam couldn't process what he saw, but he'd been under fire in Afghanistan too often to be in denial for long. There was just enough sunlight on the cloudy day to reflect off the barrel of a gun. Someone was on the ridge with a rifle, aiming at the woman in front of him.

Sam reacted by stomping on the gas, determined to get between Jodie King and the shooter. He pressed down on the horn, hoping to distract the gunman enough to cause him to miss.

In his peripheral vision he realized he'd startled King. She lurched away, toward her vehicle. Good.

Then the man on the ridge began firing. *Bang, bang, bang.* The gunman squeezed off three controlled rounds.

Sam saw the dirt kicked up by bullets on King's heels.

He jammed the Jeep to a stop as soon as he was between the ridge and King, then rolled out and drew his weapon, thankful he'd worn his shoulder rig today.

Using his door as cover, he fired his weapon toward the ridge, near where he'd seen the flash. Since he couldn't see the shooter, the man on an elevated position had all the advantage.

After capping off four rounds, Sam backpedaled to the rear of his vehicle. He moved slowly up the passenger side, now using the entire Jeep as cover, keeping his gun up, and scanning the ridge. But the firing had stopped.

At the sound of footsteps, he glanced back. King was at his side, crouched, automatic handgun in a two-handed grip, pointed down.

"What on earth?" she asked calmly, no panic, and when Sam caught her eye, he saw only alertness, no fear. Yet there were dark shadows under her eyes.

"I saw the glint from a gun up there. He had a bead on you." Sam turned his attention back to the ridge.

Suddenly it sounded as if the man switched his weapon to fully automatic.

Rat-a-tat-tat-tat-tat-tat. The hillside gunman strafed the ground in front of Sam's Jeep, then the hood. A tire exploded; the front windshield spiderwebbed in several places. Sam ducked and turned, grabbing King and pulling her down and back, all the way behind the vehicle, even as he felt the searing whoosh of bullets zipping past his head.

"Get down, get down!" He dragged her down to the ground, shielding her body with his as the fusillade of bullets continued for what seemed an eternity.

When it stopped, Sam rolled off King, sat up on his knees. "You okay?" he asked, hand on her shoulder, ears ringing from the gunfire.

She pushed herself to a sitting position. "I think so."

For a minute, silence reigned; not even an echo of the gunfire sounded in his ringing ears. Then he heard a motor start on the ridge, sounding like a motorcycle or an ATV.

"He's splitting." Jumping up, Sam hurried around the now-listing Jeep and sprinted up the ridge toward the retreating sound of the motor.

"Hey, be careful," King called out.

Sam's blood was up, pulse racing. Someone had just tried to kill him, and he was not about to let go of that bone. But when he reached the top of the ridge, all he saw was the back of a subject on an ATV, climbing up the hill, out of range of his .45 auto.

Lowering the weapon, Sam calmed his breathing. The guy disappeared into the forest wilderness behind Arrowbear. He'd have to come out somewhere between here and Big Bear. His trail would be easy to follow in the snow. Sam's attention was drawn to the area where the subject had been hiding. He saw a pile of ejected shell casings, as well as a green camo blanket, energy drink cans, and other trash indicating the shooter had been here for a while.

Sam holstered his weapon and studied the scene. He wondered

who on earth would be targeting Jodie King. Her whole team had died three months ago, assassinated in a bomb blast. Nothing in all the reports he'd read gave a clue as to why someone would be here, now, trying to kill her.

But someone had, and they'd come very close to hitting the bull's-eye.

CHAPTER 4

AFTER A MOMENTARY HESITATION, still processing gunshots and being thrown to the ground, Jodie sprinted up the ridge after her rescuer, her heart pounding.

When she'd twisted out of the path of the Jeep and the shooting started, she'd realized the Jeep's driver was trying to protect her, not hurt her.

And now another realization struck like a blow: the bullets were meant for her. *Why?*

The man who'd come to her rescue moved and acted like a cop, but she couldn't recall ever seeing him before. He was strong, his grip like iron. When he'd pulled her behind the car, she'd felt as weak as a child. But as strange and disconcerting as it was to have the man pull her to the ground, Jodie recognized that he was shielding her, protecting her at the risk of his own life. A mix of emotions swirled through her, jumbling her thoughts, filling her mind with questions.

When she reached the top of the ridge, her guardian angel faced up the hillside.

"He's gone?" she asked.

The man turned to her. "Yeah. I'm trying to figure out where he'd possibly be heading. I need to call this in." He pulled his phone from his pocket, and Jodie had a chance to look him over.

He was tall. Jodie stood almost six feet and he was at least a couple of inches taller than she was. Dark-red hair cut short, he was a little on the thin side, but he looked fit, wearing jeans and a blue flannel shirt over a dark-blue T-shirt. His shoulder holster was visible as the flannel shirt flapped open. It was cold—Jodie was in a jacket—but she figured, like most guys, the cold didn't seem to affect him.

From his side of the conversation, he was familiar with the area, and no doubt he was a cop. He was talking perimeters and search parameters.

He also wore only one glove, on his right hand, and she wondered why. Then she saw the right side of his face. Scarring ran up from his collar, along his neck, across his jaw to his ear. The ear itself was scarred, bent, and odd-looking. He'd obviously been seriously injured at one time, by fire, Jodie thought.

Something niggled at the edge of her memory, but she couldn't quite grasp the thought.

He finished his call and faced her. "The sheriff's department is notified and they're responding. They want us to sit tight. They've also notified the CHP. Are you okay?"

His eyes took her attention away from the scars. They were

warm pale-green eyes, but they were also alert and intelligent, his gaze piercing. She doubted this man missed much. He'd already proved his prowess by spotting a sniper on a dull, overcast day.

"I'm fine, thanks to you."

"I'm glad I pulled up when I did. What are you doing here?"

"I could ask you the same thing."

"Oh, sorry, we haven't been properly introduced. I'm Detective Sam Gresham, San Bernardino County Sheriff's office." He reached his gloved hand out.

The name was vaguely familiar to Jodie. The SBCS office had led the IED investigation—but she had no recollection of Sam Gresham.

"Detective Gresham?" She stared, trying to place him, pull on the thread of a memory, as she extended her hand. "I know all the deputies on the investigative team . . ."

"And you've never met me." He released her hand and nodded. "I've just been assigned to homicide." He pointed to the blanket, effectively changing the subject. "This guy was prepared to be here for a while. I don't know how long you've been here, but did you hear him drive up?"

Jodie thought back to her arrival. Had she heard anything? After a moment she shook her head. "All I heard was the wind."

She walked toward the blanket, careful where she stepped, cognizant of evidence lying all around. She decided this must be how a victim of a burglary felt, coming home to find her house trashed, leaving her vulnerable, exposed. When she looked toward where she'd been standing mere seconds ago, she could see how clear a shot this guy had from the ridge.

But who and why?

"I only just got here. I—" She swallowed, turning back to

Gresham. "At most I've been here five minutes. I heard nothing out of the ordinary." She'd been lost in her own thoughts.

Gresham nodded and studied the pile of casings, eyebrows knit together tight. After a few seconds, he waved a hand around the area. "Let's walk back down the ridge. A uniform should be here soon. I've got my radio in the Jeep. I'd like to hear what's going on."

Jodie nodded and followed Gresham back to the cars.

"Wow," she said, noting his listing vehicle. "He killed your car. Guess I'm responsible for this."

Sam inspected the damage. "You're not responsible for anything; only the shooter is. This will be a test of my insurance policy for sure."

He opened the driver's door and reached inside, coming out with a police radio in his hand. He switched it on, and Jodie listened to a cacophony of radio traffic. It took just a second for her ears to sort everything out and then understand what was happening. Officers were en route to their location and on the lookout for the man on the ATV. Gresham got on the air and suggested they try Snow Valley, a ski resort a few miles farther up Highway 18.

"Man," he said, "I'd like to be in on this search."

Jodie agreed. Who else could the shooter have been other than the person who set the IED? The thought of finally catching the person responsible for killing her friends had her struggling to keep from grabbing the radio, jumping in her car, and speeding away to join the search.

"You said you've just been assigned to my case." She still struggled to remember why his name was familiar. "Where were you before? And why now?"

"Yeah, I guess I should explain." He put the radio on the hood of the Jeep and shoved his ungloved hand in his pocket. Jodie noticed the wind had picked up.

"A couple of months before this happened—" he waved his gloved hand around the blackened foundation—"I was injured on duty. A drunk driver obliterated my patrol vehicle." He brought the hand to his scarred cheek and gave her a crooked smile. "Just a bit of the lasting mementos from the crash. I want to go back to patrol, but the department psych is resistant. For the past month I've been pushing papers. Being moved to your case is a promotion of sorts."

Recognition sparked. Now Jodie remembered reading about what had happened to Sam Gresham. Rick Farmer was the name she remembered, Gresham's partner. It had been a horrific accident; Gresham barely survived, but Farmer expired on scene. Many members of her department attended the funeral. She hadn't been able to because her task force was working in Antelope Valley at the time.

Besides, Jodie hated funerals. More so now.

"Oh, I remember. Your patrol car caught fire and your partner didn't make it."

. . .

"Your partner didn't make it."

Sam kept his expression blank, surprised at how those last five words could still pierce him so completely. He'd worked his body back into shape physically, but he couldn't stop the way his mind jolted when images of the crash blasted through his consciousness every time the accident was mentioned. Would those images ever stop?

"Yep, I'm the guy who survived."

Genuine sorrow crossed her features. "I know what it feels like to survive."

Sam cleared his throat, struck by her statement, *What it feels like to survive.* He'd learned survival wasn't always all it was cracked up to be. It was painful, dreadful, shameful, excruciating—and he'd only lost one partner. Jodie King had lost four. The impact of that realization hit Sam, shaking him to the core.

Her entire team was gone. How did she still stand? He noticed the haunted eyes and could almost feel the pain radiating from her. Could she do the same with him? Did they share a burden of grief? *Don't go there.*

"Of course you do," he said, looking down the road in the direction the dispatched units would come. He needed to talk. Silence would make him think, remember.

"I was an explosives technician in the Army and on the sheriff's bomb squad before the accident. Since this involved an IED, they assigned me to Detective Smiley. I'll do my very best to find Hayes, if he is indeed the man responsible for this."

An odd expression crossed her features—pain, Sam thought— but then it was gone, and she looked away, eyes raking the blackened foundation. King was a shell of the image he'd seen in photographs. She was thin, almost gaunt, and the darkness under her eyes was unmistakable.

"I wouldn't think there's much left here for you to investigate. The Feds don't think so anymore. They put Hayes on the most wanted list and then left the cleanup to Detective Smiley." Bitterness dripped from the last sentence like acid.

"It's still open in our shop. Smiley's still searching. But in a way, you're right. I've sifted through all the reports already written. This was my first chance to get up here and view the scene. I like to try and put myself in the bad guy's shoes. Sometimes the scene helps me visualize. What were you doing here?"

She shook her head. "A friend wants to do a memorial planting. I planned on checking out the site he picked. It's further up the highway." A half shrug. "It's my first time back since . . ." Her eyes surveyed the foundation.

Sam could see her struggle; he recognized his own struggle in her eyes. Driving past the spot on the freeway where Rick died . . . well, it was never easy. Rick's family had erected a temporary memorial to him near the spot. The county let it stay, and now Rick's dad had a petition going to make it permanent. To Sam, seeing the memorial was like lemon juice on an open cut.

"I get it," he said, hoping to unstick her mind from three months ago. "I'd planned on visiting a friend who lives in Arrowbear and thought I'd stop here first."

He followed her gaze even as his thoughts tumbled back to the night of his crash like water tumbling down a waterfall.

He'd been out of the car when the drunk struck. He and Rick had stopped to help at the scene of an earlier accident. The fire department and paramedics hadn't arrived but were on their way. While Sam dealt with the people involved in the first crash on the shoulder of the freeway, Rick sat in the passenger seat of the patrol car running the license plates of the vehicles. His head was down, reading the computer screen, when the drunk slammed into the car at sixty-five miles an hour without any braking. Momentum from the crash carried the wreck forward and barely missed Sam and the couple he was talking to.

Fire erupted almost immediately. Sam tried with all his might to pull Rick from the wreckage, ignoring his own burning flesh, until the firefighters dragged him away. His best efforts weren't enough to save his partner and best friend.

"You have to forgive yourself." Doc Roe's words came back to him. *"Guilt is a destructive emotion, Sam. It weighs on you—I can tell."*

Sam could agree with Doc Roe on that point. Sometimes the guilt pressed so hard he couldn't breathe. At this moment though, he could admit there was truth in the statement *Time heals all wounds.* Still, time moved at a snail's pace when it came to healing.

Through the experience of his own grief journey, he could see that King was not nearly as far along as he was. Sighing, he prayed this shooting would not set her back as he returned his attention to the here and now. *Lord, if there is a way for me to help her, show me.*

He switched gears to King and her case. Though he'd only recently received the case file, he had it memorized.

"The guy who set this device three months ago was a pro. It wasn't a garage hobby special; it was professional. He wanted maximum damage."

King nodded. "The why is the issue I'm still grappling with. Hayes had three narcotics warrants. According to the Feds, the IED was overkill. Hayes is an opportunistic criminal, not a planner."

Just then a highway patrol vehicle came screaming up the drive. Sam started for the driver's window, King on his heels.

The officer held a hand up as he listened to a transmission on the radio. Sam only caught a couple of words.

When it finished, the officer turned toward him. "Everyone okay here?"

"We're good," Sam said.

"Okay, a deputy came across a stolen ATV up at Snow Valley, hot, so just dumped. We have a description of a vehicle speeding away."

"Great." Sam turned to King, who had perked up noticeably. She jammed a fist into her palm. "Oh, catch him, please."

"I'm on my way to help there," the CHP officer said. "Someone will be here shortly to take the paper on this—can you wait?"

"I can wait for good news," King said.

Sam was happy to see light in her eyes. "I agree. Go get him."

The officer nodded. "Okay. Hopefully, I'll intercept this guy on 330."

"We have the advantage," Sam told Jodie as the CHP officer punctuated his statement by activating his siren and speeding off. Sam was familiar with the area, having grown up in Big Bear Lake, with the San Bernardino Mountains as his backyard. When his dad was alive, they hiked and fished from Big Bear to Crestline for years. "There aren't a lot of ways off the mountain. Unless this guy is Houdini, I'm guessing he'll be in cuffs before long."

CHAPTER 5

AS JODIE WATCHED THE CHIPPIE DRIVE AWAY, she prayed for success. To be this close to catching the shooter had her as on edge as if she'd mainlined a shot of espresso.

She listened to the radio traffic, her practiced ear filtering out the static. A non-cop friend she'd taken for a ride-along once called radio traffic "so much gibberish." But to a cop on patrol, it was a lifeline, something you never wanted broken. If you needed help or heard a call for help, the radio was indispensable.

An older-model white Honda sedan was seen leaving the ski area at a high rate of speed. A sheriff's deputy was in pursuit on Highway 18 while the highway patrol officer cut through Running Springs to Highway 330, the only two ways out of the mountain communities since the car wasn't apparently traveling north, toward Big Bear.

Jodie tapped her fists together, her mind chewing on the who. Turning to Gresham, she said, "The FBI concluded that all the evidence pointed to Norman Hayes setting the IED trap to avoid capture. If my team died because Hayes wanted to get away, why is someone trying to kill me now?"

"You don't think it was Hayes shooting at you?" Gresham answered her question with a question.

Jodie stared at him. In all the chaos, she'd never considered Hayes as the shooter. It just felt wrong.

"No. I don't see it, not at all."

"If not Hayes, then who?" There was genuine curiosity in his tone, no mocking condescension, which she felt like she got from a couple of the FBI agents.

"I don't know. You said the IED was complex. Nothing in Hayes's background suggests he could put together such a device. He's a drug dealer, and that's what the warrants were about. No gun or explosive charges. What beef could he have with me? Everyone is stuck on him, to the exclusion of anything else," Jodie said through gritted teeth.

Gresham's eyebrows arched. "You're right. I've been through the reports, backwards and forwards. Except for Archie Radio—"

"Jukebox."

He nodded. "Your CI—I haven't seen the names of any other viable suspects."

"Jukebox is not a killer." Jodie felt her face flush and worked to control the frustrated rage bubbling to the surface. She wasn't certain if it was coming to the surface now because she'd just come close to being shot or because she'd stuffed it down for so long.

"This all feels so personal. The IED was premeditated. Whoever planned that day had a personal reason for so deadly an attack." She pounded her fist into her hand to emphasize her point. Her voice rose as anger festered, then spilled out like flaming liquid.

"My team and I were never threatened beyond the normal stuff you get when you arrest a bad actor. I've told everyone who will listen that I know the explosion was personal. The FBI and the ATF said there was no evidence to support my 'gut feeling.'" She held her hands up to make air quotes.

"They tore apart everyone's life, took phones, laptops, everything, and said they found no reason for any single member of the team to be the sole target. In their minds it had to be the whole team. Because we were so high profile, Hayes did it to prove he was the baddest of the bad. I believe there are other possibilities they just ignored."

She saw Gresham flinch and realized he shouldn't be a target for any of her frustration or anger.

Deep breath. "Sorry. For months, ever since the last funeral, I haven't been able to wrap my head around Hayes doing this. Even now. There is something else at work here—there must be. Assuming Hayes acted alone reads like a bad B movie." Her voice broke and she swallowed, fighting to regain her composure and a little embarrassed at having nearly lost it.

But Gresham did just the right thing. He stepped forward and looked her in the eye. "Sergeant King, I never assume anything. And I know what it's like to lose a trusted partner. I've been trained to look for facts and evidence. Evidence should fit without someone having to take a hammer and pound it into place. Detective Smiley is sharp, and I trust him. We will find out who set the IED, who shot at you today, and why."

His gaze centered Jodie. Those sharp, clear eyes held hers, and Jodie felt a connection deep and strong. He could relate to her on a level no one else could. As their eyes held for a moment, oddly enough, a Bible passage came to mind. She couldn't quite place it, but it spoke about the apostle Nathanael as a man without guile. She believed the same was true about Sam Gresham.

Fortified, and with the first spark of hope she'd had in a long while, Jodie allowed herself half a smile. "Thank you, Detective Gresham. And please, it's Jodie. I officially took an early retirement a week ago."

She watched surprise cross his features. "Ah, sorry to hear you quit. I didn't realize you were hurt so badly."

Jodie said nothing. She wasn't badly hurt but she didn't want to go into her reasons for quitting.

Gresham continued. "Jodie, it's nice to finally meet you. Please call me Sam." He smiled, and it brought light to his eyes. He nodded toward her handgun. "It's hard to give up the sidearm, isn't it?"

"Yes. I have a CCW permit. At least the shrink didn't deem me crazy or suicidal."

Just then a San Bernardino sheriff's car pulled up and a stocky deputy stepped out. Jodie recognized him from the day of the explosion. Bob Takano had been the standby deputy. He was a good man; he'd steadied her, as much as she could be steadied after watching her team go up in smoke.

Takano knew Sam right away. But while Takano appeared genuinely happy to see Sam, Sam seemed to stiffen and become uncomfortable and guarded.

"Sam." Takano reached out his hand. "I heard you were working inside nowadays. What gives?"

"As of yesterday, they let me out of the admin slot. I jumped through all the hoops. Cleared for full duty. Assigned to this IED case."

"Great to hear. Really good to have you back in the field. What just happened? Someone shot at you?"

"Not me. Sergeant King." He gestured to Jodie.

"Just Jodie King now. I recognize you from the day of the explosion, Deputy Takano," Jodie said.

Takano nodded her way. Sorrow crossed his features briefly. "Yep, I'll never forget that day. It's Bob." He turned back to Sam. "How did you end up here?"

"I was on my way to visit George. This was a detour," Sam said.

Jodie listened as Sam explained what had happened. She noticed he downplayed his actions. He'd also relaxed a bit. He probably didn't know how Takano would react to him, Jodie thought. Losing a partner had its own special stigma. Of course, the circumstances mattered, but in Jodie's experience, sometimes other cops didn't know how to react to her. It was probably the same for Sam.

Today, Sam had placed himself in real jeopardy to protect her, but he didn't emphasize it. This man was no showboat. He'd just about summed everything up when the deputy's radio came alive.

Takano turned it up. "Sounds like there's going to be a car stop of a possible match. Deputy picked up the vehicle at the turn-off for Lake Arrowhead. It was heading down 18. He's following, approaching Crestline."

Sam turned down his radio so they could all listen to Takano's. The deputy's voice came over the air. He'd activated his emergency lights and the vehicle stopped. He recited the license plate number.

Seconds later, return on the plate came back 10-29 Victor—stolen.

Another voice, a backup officer, said he was ten minutes away. Timing was everything. Jodie tensed; she hoped the first deputy would wait for backup. In the city, if she stopped a stolen car, she'd wait for a lot of backup units.

"I have to go." Takano hurried back to his vehicle. "I'm more than ten away but I need to be there."

Jodie and Sam stepped back as Takano burned rubber to get to the highway.

They continued to listen on Sam's radio. For several minutes, all seemed routine, and Jodie hoped her worry was for naught. But then the radio went quiet.

The dispatcher tried to raise the deputy, but there was no response.

Jodie felt fear grip her insides as if someone had put her in a vise.

Suddenly another officer came on the air, voice breathless.

"Officer down, officer down! Suspect vehicle is gone. I need paramedics now."

CHAPTER 6

CHAOS ENSUED ON THE RADIO after the *officer down* call went out. Sam felt the tension with every fiber of his soul. He leaned against King's SUV, knees weak at the knowledge that another officer's life hung in the balance. He'd heard the call sign but didn't know to whom it had been assigned. He was certain he would know the man.

His radio volume was up again, but there was limited traffic now. The air was being kept clear for emergency traffic.

King paced. "I can't believe he tried to stop the guy on his own," she said.

"You know as well as I do that adrenaline sometimes gets the better of us."

She turned toward him, seemingly ready to say something

when she looked over his shoulder. "Who is this?" she asked, hand on her weapon.

Sam turned and saw a pickup truck moving slowly toward them. "Ah, a friend," he said. "George Upton, my first training officer. He retired and moved here. I was going to visit him after I came here."

His explanation satisfied King; Sam saw her relax.

"What is going on with all the sirens?" George pulled closer and leaned out the window. "I heard gunshots."

Sam felt Jodie follow him as he stepped close to speak to the man. "It's a long story. It spawned a pursuit down Highway 18 and a deputy just got shot."

George closed his eyes and ran his hand over his face. "Heavens, I pray it's not fatal." When he opened his eyes, he focused on King. "You look familiar."

"George, this is Jodie King. Jodie, this is George Upton, the finest cop I ever had the pleasure of working with."

George opened the door and climbed out. He extended his hand. "I remember Sergeant King." They shook. "I was here the day of the explosion. Thank God you survived."

"It's difficult to thank God when my team didn't." Ice dripped from her tone as frosty as the air. Sam heard the sudden animosity. He understood anger but was surprised, nonetheless.

George didn't seem surprised or offended, though. His tone went soft, conciliatory. "I'm sorry. It wasn't my intent to poke an old wound. The painful things in life are the hardest to reconcile with what we know about God, aren't they, Sergeant King?"

Sam winced. George was always direct, too direct maybe, he thought as he watched Jodie give a tense nod.

"But it's only if we forget that above all, he is a good God,"

George continued. "Trust what you do know, not what you can't see."

"I can't see any reason to justify what happened to my people." Jaw set, Jodie said, "What I do know and can see is that an evil killer is still loose and needs to be stopped."

"What happened was pure evil. Yet even with that, I believe with my whole heart that God can turn any evil into good. A horrible loss is difficult to get over, I agree. Grieve—it's necessary—but don't waste your life staying in the past. Trust me, you can't honor their memories by staying put. Move on at your own pace, but move on."

"I don't need your pity or your advice—"

The rest of King's sharp response was cut off when a sheriff's vehicle roared up the road. It was a supervisor's vehicle, not Takano. Sam guessed Takano was likely tied up at the scene with the stolen car.

As the sergeant got out of the car, Sam recognized the guy and noted his grim expression.

"Who was it, and how is he?" Sam asked, stepping between George and Jodie.

"Chad Logan. Shot in the face but stable right now. The shooter got clean away."

■ ■ ■

Jodie swallowed and glowered at the old cop. He might as well have had *Retired Cop* tattooed on his forehead, he looked so much like one. Guarded posture, balanced stance, prepared for any threat, he still had a full head of gray hair cut in a neat crew cut and his expression said, *"I see through all lies."*

Upton had hit a raw nerve. Anger smoldered. She found herself opening and closing her fists, her shoulders knotted with tension. The temperature seemed to have dropped ten degrees in the last five minutes. She stepped away and took several deep breaths.

She watched as the three men shook hands all the way around. The old cop knew the supervisor well, from what she could see.

All she could think was *How dare he?* He had no idea what kind of losses she'd dealt with her whole life.

"I lost my parents when I was eight, you buffoon," she wanted to scream.

Sam stepped toward her. "You okay?"

His gaze and his words snapped her out of the pit she felt herself toppling into. "Yeah, um, just processing this morning."

He nodded. "Take your time. George can be direct. He means well. I'll walk through everything for the boss, that good with you?"

"It is, thanks." She felt her shoulders relax a tad. The three men walked to Sam's car; Jodie could hear them talking in low tones. She wanted to hold on to her anger, but she'd learned in the last few months how exhausting that was. Her thoughts drifted back to her parents. Dedicated missionaries, they died in a plane crash taking them back to their calling.

After their deaths, she heard about "God's plan" from every adult she encountered. At eight she really didn't understand; all she wanted was Mom and Dad back. But with time, recognizing that somehow there was a reason behind their deaths, Jodie stopped questioning and started believing in "God's plan" and his care in all circumstances. Until her team died in front of her eyes.

Three months later she couldn't deny that the blast had certainly done a number on her faith. Jodie felt as though she was limping along on the fragments of what she grew up believing.

Another saying Jodie had heard was: If tragedy could destroy a person's faith, then the faith was not worth keeping. True enough. She couldn't say she'd lost her faith completely. Jodie still believed in a God who was sovereign. But that belief felt wobbly and anemic. The why question tormented her. The absence of a clear answer rubbed like a raw blister. She had no choice but to keep asking.

"You'd better believe I'm stuck in the past!" she'd wanted to yell at the man. But as the seconds ticked by and her anger faded, she conceded to herself that he shouldn't be a target for her anger. She grudgingly admitted to herself that she understood every word he'd said. Before the blast, she probably would've said the same thing to him if their roles were reversed. She'd grown up in church and knew all the Christian platitudes tossed at people when they faced hard, painful situations. The debate with herself was did she truly believe them now?

The old cop wasn't responsible for the blast three months ago or the shooter today.

Jodie worked to refocus her thoughts. Sam and the supervisor were walking through the scene, marking evidence. A sheriff's lab unit pulled up. With the snow beginning to fall harder, they would need help to collect everything quickly.

Jodie stepped forward to help. She didn't want to be mired in a pit of self-pity any more than she wanted to be stuck back at the day of the explosion.

Everyone pitched in, following the direction of a sheriff's lab tech. They started by carefully developing a perimeter. Shell casings were dispersed about the area, ejected when the shooter sprayed bullets in her direction. From the looks of it, he moved as he fired. Some casings were several feet away, and the team didn't want to miss anything. Next came the energy drink cans, trash, and blanket. They moved as quickly as they could, to ensure that nothing got too wet before it was carefully packaged. The work helped to ease Jodie's anxiety. She held out hope that what the shooter left behind would lead them to the identity of the man.

"As scary as it is to have someone shoot at me," she told Sam as they put the last of the evidence bags into the lab vehicle, "I hope this opens the investigation back up."

Everyone's breath hung in the air, the temperature dropping as daylight waned and the snow fell harder and faster. A layer of flakes had built up on Sam's shoulders. He nodded in agreement and some snow flaked off.

Jodie continued. "No one in custody for what happened is like an open wound. I can't help but think I should have known, or I should have done—"

"What a twisted path, Jodie. It's fruitless to stew about things we can't change."

She stared at him. "You sound like Dr. Bass."

Sam smiled. It was sincere and warm, and it caused Jodie to relax, unclench her fists.

"Wish I had you on tape, prove to my Doc Roe that what he's been telling me has sunk in."

"I want someone held accountable. True, it can't undo what's been done, but . . ." Her voice trailed off because Jodie couldn't articulate exactly what closing the case would mean or do for her—yet.

The smile faded, and she saw the detective mask slip back over his features. "Believe me, I understand."

CHAPTER 7

SAM WONDERED if he really did understand Jodie. She lost her team through no fault of her own. His struggle with his own feelings of guilt about Rick made placing blame a sensitive subject. Doc Roe would say he was comparing apples to oranges. Rick's death was a tragic accident. The loss of Jodie's team was premeditated murder. Yet they were both tortured by what they should have done differently.

He thought about the situation with Chad Logan, praying the deputy would be okay. The trouble with this job was how easy it was to second-guess—Monday-morning quarterback. Jodie was right: Chad probably should have waited for backup.

Maybe I should have too. If I'd waited for the fire department before getting out of the car, maybe I would have seen the drunk in the rearview mirror and moved the car out of the way.

The truth he'd just spouted to Jodie pierced. Nothing could be changed now.

Sam worked to concentrate on the task at hand. He thought about Jodie's admission that the loss of her team was an open wound. It grated because she didn't know who rigged the IED. His open wound grated because he did. George believed there was a plan in everything. *"God can't be God if there's something he doesn't control,"* he would say. And Sam believed the same. He just didn't feel it where Rick was concerned.

A part of him wondered if God's back was turned the night of the accident.

"Sam?"

"What?" Sam willed his thoughts back to the present, untangling the feelings of guilt and loss.

Jodie was talking to him. "My uncle is here to escort me off the mountain before the roads get too bad."

She turned and an older man stepped up. He was a tad shorter than Sam, and his light hair looked white with the snow falling on it. Deep-blue eyes met his gaze and Sam knew he was being sized up. He also saw the resemblance to Jodie in those eyes.

"Sam Gresham?" He held his hand out. "Mike King."

They shook.

"I remember your name from the reports. Nice to meet you."

"Likewise. I can't thank you enough for what you did for my niece."

"I happened to be at the right place at the right time."

"You've been assigned to the investigation?"

"Yes, I was supposed to start Monday morning. Guess I'm getting an early start."

"Will Smiley be coming?"

"No, he had a family emergency. He asked me to record Jodie's statement for him to hear. So can I have a few minutes with her before you leave? I should have pinned her down earlier. I'm still getting back in the swing of things."

"I understand." King reached out and touched his niece's hand, gesturing toward his car. "I'll be waiting just over there. You can follow me down the road. Sound okay?"

"It does." Jodie nodded.

Mike left for his car, shaking snowflakes off his head as he went.

Sam returned his attention to Jodie. "Let's sit in your car. I'll record your statement on my phone. I'm sure I've got most of it anyway."

"You do. But recordings often help."

She unlocked the SUV and he climbed into the passenger seat. Once they were out of the elements, Jodie told him everything about the day, for the record. He let her talk without interruption, and then he asked a couple of questions to clarify and fill in some holes.

"Who knew you were coming here today?" Sam asked.

She seemed taken aback by the question. "Uh, no one. I only made the decision myself this morning. I . . ."

"What?"

"I'm trying to remember if I made an offhand comment to anyone." She shook her head. "No. I've been thinking about it for a couple of weeks. Jonah offered to come with me."

"Who?"

"Jonah Bennett. He's a friend of the family, a Realtor. He bought the lot to make a memorial to my team. He asked me to come with him to check it out a few weeks ago. I said no. I didn't tell him I was coming today. I didn't tell anyone. Maybe a couple of days ago I mentioned to the department psych I'd been considering a visit . . ." She stopped.

Sam got the feeling she didn't want to finish the thought.

"I think I sent Jonah an email insinuating I might come here today, but I don't remember how I worded it exactly. Honestly, until I got in the car, I wasn't certain where I was going," she finished.

"Hmm . . . Someone knew you were headed this way. That guy up there was waiting for you for at least a couple of hours, I'd bet. Someone is watching you, Jodie. Take this day as a warning to watch your back. For some reason, this guy is still after you. I'm just glad I pulled up when I did and stopped him. Now we'll catch him and get you your answers."

Sam held her gaze. Her striking blue eyes were clouded with pain and loss. Sam wished he could chase the clouds away. He wanted to reach forward, hold her hand, and tell her it would be okay. But only one resolution would make the situation okay—crime solved, bad guys caught.

It was time to go. Sam thanked her, then climbed out of her car, closed the door, and stepped back to watch her drive away, Jodie following her uncle carefully down the hill.

The day had started out so peacefully, with so much promise, then exploded into the attempted murder of Jodie King and the shooting of a deputy. A massive manhunt had turned up nothing. The suspect fled after shooting the officer, disappearing off the mountain. Last Sam had heard, Chad was hanging on after being shot in the face.

When Sam had done everything he could do at the site, and his shot-up Jeep was towed down the hill, George gave him a ride home.

"Sergeant King is in a lot of pain. It's still simmering," George commented as they neared Green Valley Lake.

"I thought so too," Sam said.

"I'll add her to the prayer chain."

"Thanks, George."

"I know you're still simmering as well."

Sam looked at George, a little surprised. "Hey, I'm back on my own two feet."

"True, but you've still got Rick on your shoulders. Careful, he's a heavy load to carry."

"You sound like Dr. Roe."

"Then you have two of us to listen to. Forgive yourself, Sam. Guilt will drag you down like concrete." He pulled into Sam's parking space.

Even though it was 10 p.m. and he'd had a long day, Sam stayed seated. This was the core of his problem with Dr. Roe.

"You're rife with grief over the loss of your partner. And in denial about the magnitude of grief. If you're in a patrol car facing another life-threatening situation, I fear you will put yourself at unnecessary risk, subconsciously considering self-sacrifice as a way to assuage your guilt."

Sam thought it was a doublespeak way to say that Roe feared he was suicidal.

"I'm working on it." He got out of the car and headed for his front door, hoping George would drop it. He didn't.

"Are you?" George asked as Sam stepped into his entryway and flipped on the light.

"I haven't stopped praying." He dropped his keys in their dish. "Sometimes I feel as if everything hits the ceiling." He picked up his spare key, hoping to change the subject. "Here's my spare key.

I'd like you to have it, in case something happens or you need to get into the house for some reason." He held the key out.

George took it. "Sure. One of these days I'll talk you into a security system."

Sam nodded. Walking into his living room, he sighed and fell back into his recliner.

George followed and sat on the couch. "You do know prayer is your first, best weapon, right?"

Sam sighed. The subject wasn't going to be dropped, so he had to keep thinking and talking about it.

"I know the only place to go is to the Lord," he said. "Sometimes I just feel like the widow pleading to the unjust judge who tries to ignore her."

"The widow petitioned the judge for what she needed. I'm not sure you know what you need. In any event, God is not an unjust judge."

"Fair enough. I'm okay, George. Don't worry."

"I won't. I know how useless worry is."

He looked around Sam's new house and they chatted about lighter subjects. After George left, Sam was tired yet wound up. The "Rick on your shoulders" comment had stung.

I'm not sure you know what you need.

Sam didn't even know what to think about his friend's observations.

His thoughts kept falling on Jodie King. Having an inkling of what she was going through made him feel close to her, though they'd just met. But at the same time, meeting her stirred up the legion of if-onlys in his own scenario: if only he'd parked the car differently, if only he'd seen the drunk sooner, if only he'd been in the car and not Rick . . .

Working to stop himself from dwelling on the accident, he realized he'd been assigned to Smiley's investigative team because his superiors didn't know what to do with him. He'd been so vocal about how boring administrative work was, he was certain they figured the almost-cold IED investigation was "safe." Only now he'd stepped into a hornet's nest with a lot more happening than they bargained for. There was a lot of police work left on Jodie's case, and he planned on being front and center.

Sam did what he'd told Jodie he wanted to do: he worked to put himself in the bad guy's shoes.

She was right to think this was personal. The Feds didn't see it the same way because there was no solid evidence singling out one person as the target. They had torn apart her life and the life of every team member, according to the forensic reports. Jodie King was a hard charger, a cop's cop. She'd earned her rank and the prestige of leading RAT by being conscientious and thorough. She had garnered threats, but none rose to the ranks of credible as far as all the alphabet agencies were concerned. From what he'd read, they had tunnel vision about Hayes, with the CI Archie Radio, aka Jukebox, as an accomplice.

Maybe it wasn't a criminal threat, Sam thought. Maybe it was much closer.

He shivered with an odd feeling. His mother called it the "someone walked across my grave" feeling. Somehow, someway, Jodie had affected this guy so much he'd gone to extraordinary lengths to kill her. He'd killed her team but wasn't satisfied. This was a powerful, malignant hate.

Would Hayes have hated her so much? King was simply executing a warrant on him. A judge issued the paper. Hayes had been arrested before; he was familiar with the drill. If he did set the IED to escape, well, he'd very nearly committed the perfect crime. Would he resurface three months later to again try to kill Jodie King?

It made no sense.

Jodie was the target of the IED three months ago, and she was still a target. A sniper setting up and shooting at her *now* was proof someone still wanted her dead.

Sam took in a deep breath and let it out slowly to calm down as a stark realization hit. Whoever wanted the woman dead knew her intimately and had a very personal score to settle.

He would have to dig. Somewhere in the reports, in the interviews, in the pile of paperwork related to King and the explosion, hid someone with a strong personal motive and animosity. And Sam was determined to throw the curtain back and find the individual. He'd make a list and research each person one by one.

His thoughts drifted back to his observations of the day, of the scene, and of who he now considered the target. Danger notwithstanding, Sam was captivated by Jodie King. Despite being shot at, she remained cool, calm, and collected, trying to help in any way she could, though she was way out of her jurisdiction and not even on the clock. Her professionalism told him she'd been a good cop, steady and thoughtful, not given to making emotional decisions.

Yet she'd quit and she'd lashed out at George. Indeed, from what he and George had observed, she was far from healed after the loss of her team. Sam never thought of quitting, even at his lowest. People told him he'd have to quit, and he was ornery enough to want to prove them wrong. Guilt still walked in lockstep with him, but somehow the thought of turning in his badge seemed a bigger betrayal of his friendship with Rick.

Sam wondered if he'd ever be in a place with Jodie where he could ask her why she left the PD. Maybe with time her anger and hurt would ease.

By the time King had followed her uncle down the mountain, Sam was chagrined to realize he also had a personal motive behind getting to know her better. He wanted to see more of the tall, blonde ex-sergeant with the amazing brilliant-blue eyes.

CHAPTER 8

"YOU'RE SURE YOU'RE OKAY?"

Jodie closed her eyes and tried hard not to fall apart. Uncle Mike didn't just escort her home; he came in with her, still worried about her and upset about the shooting.

"Yeah, not even a nick."

"I didn't mean just physically."

"I'm just tired. Please don't worry about me."

Mike grabbed her in a hug and Jodie felt her throat thicken. She didn't want to cry. She didn't want to think about the deputy who got shot because of her. She didn't want to think about anything.

"I'll always worry about you," he whispered.

If she moved, she'd lose it. Mike had taken her in when her

parents died—he was a father to her. He'd also been the reason she became a police officer, to follow in his footsteps. She didn't know how to ease his pain or his worry—she couldn't ease her own, much less anyone else's.

Once he was sure she was okay, Mike left. As she closed the door behind him, Jodie's energy faded. She didn't even have the energy to shower. She got into bed, closed her eyes, but could not sleep.

The day kept running through her mind: the shots, Gresham, the chase, the wounded deputy, and the encounter with George Upton. For some reason, anger with the old cop flared up again and she had trouble getting past it. He'd sounded like the department psychologist, Dr. Bass, who encouraged her to move on from the IED. The idea of moving on infuriated Jodie. *How do you move on when four good friends and officers are blown up on your watch?* It was not easily forgettable. The trouble was old cops and psychologists always thought they knew everything. At least in Jodie's experience.

She forced her thoughts to Sam Gresham, the only bright spot in the day. Jodie was glad she'd met him. But her last conversation with him had also stirred up something negative. He was right to ask who would have known she was going to visit the site.

I didn't even know until about thirty minutes before I got in the car.

The next morning, the conversation was still replaying in Jodie's head. *"Someone is watching you. . . . For some reason this guy is still after you."* She hadn't gotten much sleep, so now, with the dawn just breaking, she did what always seemed to calm and center her. Surf.

Jodie zipped up her wet suit, grabbed her board, and exited the garage area of her apartment complex to cross the street to the beach, probably checking the quiet street more carefully than she would have before the events of the previous day. She'd always felt safe here in Seal Beach. The small-town feel increased her sense of safety, and she loved the proximity to the ocean. She'd waited on a list for a year and a half before this apartment across the street from the Seal Beach pier and shoreline came available. Now she'd been here for a year and couldn't imagine living anywhere else. It was well worth the high rent.

It was also where she'd met Gail Shyler and decided she wanted the sharp officer on her team. Seal Beach PD had been as good to Jodie as her own department. It had been a good place to land and live after the tragedy.

In a few minutes Jodie was in the water and on her board paddling out beyond the break line. Several guys were already in the water, and she recognized a few. Since it was Sunday, the water could get crowded. This time of the morning it was all regulars, good swimmers and good surfers.

There was a swell coming in, some nice-size waves, and Jodie tried to empty her mind and concentrate only on the sea and her board. She tried to find the zone, the place where what mattered was her board and the wave, a peaceful place unencumbered by worry or angst.

It eluded her.

Sam Gresham and being shot at kept intruding on her thoughts. Realizing someone still wanted her dead sent ice through her veins. Something good came out of it, though. She'd thought a month ago that the investigation needed new eyes—now it had them.

Gresham's being on the case was a godsend for Jodie. He understood her need to find the truth behind the IED. Maybe he even understood a bit of the grief and guilt she still felt.

Jodie stayed in the water for a couple of hours. After catching some good waves, she made her way to shore and returned home for a shower and light breakfast. For the first time in months, she had enjoyed her time in the water, even though good feelings engendered guilt. Just about any pleasant feeling made her feel guilty.

While she ate, she fought to beat back the guilt and concentrate on something else. Checking news headlines online, Jodie was happy to see that the cop who got shot was in serious but stable condition. She scanned all the news sites for information about the manhunt. There wasn't much. Logan's shooter was still at large—he'd fled off the mountain. Where to? she wondered. The news brought up Hayes and then rehashed the IED and the loss of her team. She turned her computer off.

Smiley hadn't put out a description of the shooter yet. Maybe Logan was hurt more seriously than they'd said. Jodie never considered the shooter was Hayes because lying in wait did not fit what she knew of his MO. Hayes was an in-your-face thug, according to his rap sheet. Acting as a sniper would have been more out of character for him than the bomb.

Her phone pinged with a text. It was Tara Corson, asking if she felt up to lunch, then a walk on the pier.

After a couple of seconds, Jodie typed back, **Yeah, I do.**

Feeling more alert and refreshed after her ocean time, she dressed in shorts and a tank top, left home around noon, and headed for the Seal Beach pier. It had the distinction of being the second-longest wooden pier in California. Here, the weather was warm and springlike, unlike the cold and snow she'd experienced the day before in the mountains.

She'd just reached the street when her cell phone rang. A 909 number—San Bernardino. One of the investigators? she wondered as she answered the call.

"Hello?"

"Jodie, hello, it's Sam."

Gresham.

Surprise and hope sparked through Jodie—was there a breakthrough already?

"Sam. You have news?"

"Uh, no, I'm sorry. I didn't mean to give you a false impression. I just wondered how you were holding up today."

Spirits crashing, she took a second before answering. The department shrink asked the same question all the time, and Jodie often thought he doubted she was okay and he wanted to dig down into her feelings. But Sam wasn't the shrink.

"I'm fine. I read news online. The deputy's prognosis seems good."

"Yes. The bullet did damage but didn't hit anything vital."

Hope started to rise again in her chest. "Is he able to describe the suspect?"

"He's not talking yet. Smiley and I will speak to him as soon as he's ready."

"How are you doing? Did you get your Jeep squared away?"

"It's in the shop. Might be a total loss. Insurance will cover it."

"Sorry." Jodie looked both ways before crossing the street.

"It's just a car. I thought I'd call and check up on you. Kind of the result of having a mom who's a nurse. She always checks up, and I guess it rubbed off. I've already spoken to Detective Smiley about yesterday and he agrees this is personal. This case is no longer cold. Can you tell me more about Jonah Bennett?"

The question threw Jodie and she stopped on the sidewalk.

"Jonah? Like I said, he's a friend of the family. Kind of an uncle to me. Why do you ask?"

"You mentioned his name when I asked you about who knew you were going to the mountains."

"Because he's pushing the memorial."

"You're not on board with a memorial?"

"I'm not. Not now. Not until whoever killed my team has assumed room temperature." Her tone was sharper than she intended, and she hoped Gresham wouldn't notice. But he did.

"I didn't mean to upset you."

"And I didn't mean to snap at you. Jonah is like family. I've known him practically my whole life. Him, my uncle Mike, and Gus—they are lifelong buds."

The line went quiet for a bit and Jodie took a deep breath, centering her thoughts on the here and now, not the day before or three months ago. Sam's calm voice helped bring her back to a level place.

"You can snap at me whenever you want. Be real, Jodie. My shrink tells me it's the only way to heal."

"Thanks. Sometimes . . ." Her voice trailed off as she became somewhat guarded. True, she felt a connection with Sam, thought he understood her, but she'd only just met him. How many doors should she let him open?

"Sometimes what?"

"I think you understand my loss more than anyone else. Thank you, Sam, for your help."

"You're welcome. I will do my absolute best on this case."

"I believe that."

"Good. How are things down in the flatlands?"

"Warm. I'm enjoying the sun."

"Lucky you. We ended up with several inches of snow last night."

Jodie chuckled and arched a brow. "Wow, I don't know what to say."

"You don't have to say anything. I'm just glad you're doing okay. If you remember anything at all about who might have known you were going to the mountains, call me. You have my number now."

"You'll be the first person I call."

"Enjoy your day, Jodie, and don't worry about me up here shivering."

Jodie smiled as she signed off, marveling at the feeling of life being more normal in the last few minutes than it had been in the last three months. And someone had just tried to kill her. The fresh eyes Gresham brought to the case was a huge reason why she felt hope today. Walking in the sunshine of a beautiful day, her steps felt lighter. She saw Tara at the traffic signal.

"Wow, I don't think I've seen you smile in . . . well, I don't know how long. What's funny?"

Jodie had known Tara for her whole career, just not very well. They'd gone through the police academy competing against each other in just about every training module. Jodie won them all, and for a time she thought Tara, an intense, competitive person, had a chip on her shoulder. Once off probation, their career trajectories in Long Beach PD had gone in different directions, and they'd lost touch. Jodie's star rose quickly—patrol, detectives, promotion to sergeant and then task force leader—while Tara remained in patrol. They'd reconnected because of Tara's position as the Long Beach liaison for the multijurisdictional task force assigned to the IED investigation.

At first, Jodie questioned Tara's placement. She wanted

someone from LBPD with more investigative experience and Tara had only been assigned to violent crimes for a year. But she had proven herself able and sharp and Jodie now had no problem with her investigative skills.

Lately, because of the lack of leads and the disappearance of Hayes, only Detective Smiley and his jurisdiction had been actively involved. Smiley still updated Tara once a week with the status of the investigation. And Tara always updated Jodie.

"Nothing. Just something someone said."

Tara looked at Jodie's phone, then her face and made a humph sound. "You, my friend, cannot stay off the news," Tara said.

"You mean because cops seem to get hurt or die around me?"

Tara blanched. "No, uh, not at all."

Jodie sighed, regretting the lame joke and determined not to lose this good-mood feeling, something she'd not felt for what seemed an eternity. "Yeah, I know. Come on, let's eat. The Hangout?" She suggested the restaurant directly across from the pier.

"Perfect." As they waited for the light to change and then crossed the street, the sunshine warming them both, Jodie told her all about the incident in the mountains.

"Sam Gresham, wow. Guy's a superhero. Smiley mentioned he might join the team, but he wasn't certain when."

"Gresham said he was just cleared for full duty."

"What's he like?"

Jodie shrugged, remembering the intense, yet calm, cool, and collected man who'd steadied her with his professional manner.

"A good cop. He's focused, not a show-off. I think he'll add to the investigative team."

Tara gave her name and the pair sat out front to wait for a table. The area was busy with tourists and locals. Jodie absentmindedly watched the surfers across the street, alongside the pier, in the water. There were a lot more now. And a lot of barneys, or novices. The swell had lessened, and the waves were only ankle busters now. The swell was forecast to pick up again later in the afternoon.

"He knows bombs."

"From what I've heard he was a decorated bomb guy in the service before he became a cop," Tara said. "How bad were the scars?"

"Scars?" Jodie frowned. He was scarred, she remembered, but they hadn't dominated her thinking. "They didn't look so bad to me, just some puckering on his cheek and chin." Were there more scars? Jodie wondered. She'd been captivated by the man's eyes and manner, not by scarring.

"I tried to recollect the incident where he was burned, but I think I was out in Antelope Valley then."

Tara nodded. "I went to the funeral of his partner, Rick Farmer." She made a face. "I hate cop funerals. I've been to way too many. I asked one of the SB guys about the crash. Gresham and Farmer were stopped at the scene of an injury crash on the 10 freeway. Fire hadn't gotten there yet."

"I hate the 10 freeway even on good days," Jodie murmured.

"Yeah, me too. Gresham was out of the car checking on the two or three people involved in the crash. He glanced up at the last minute and saw the car coming and saved the lives of the people he was standing with. When the drunk hit the patrol car full speed, it pushed everything Gresham's way."

"Wow" was all Jodie could say. There was a saying in patrol about a flashing light bar on the freeway being a drunk driver magnet. When she was in patrol, she only made stops on the freeway if the violation was egregious.

Tara nodded. "Nightmare, huh? Gresham gets up and runs back to his patrol car, which now looks like a smart car. It bursts into flames with Farmer still in it. The SB guy said Farmer died instantly at impact anyway, but Gresham tried to pull him from the flames. The fire department arrived and pulled him away, but he was on fire. The right side of his body. Supposedly his ear melted off."

"His ear did look a bit odd, and he wore a glove on his right hand. But he fired his weapon with no problems. He saved my life."

Tara studied Jodie. "You attracted to the guy?"

Jodie felt her face flush. "You know my rule: I don't date cops."

"Rules were made to be broken."

"Hey, I just met him." She held her hands up.

Tara smiled. "Like I said, he's a superhero."

Jodie pondered the meaning of *superhero* for a long while.

CHAPTER 9

DESPITE BEING STIFF AND A BIT UNCOMFORTABLE in his new suit, Sam was glad to be back at the station. Because of the attempt on Jodie's life, he reported to work early on Sunday, instead of waiting until Monday. Even though the cop shop was Sunday quiet, Sam relished the sights, sounds, and smells of his once-upon-a-time second home.

Being here was bittersweet. Memories of Rick were everywhere. Not only had they worked together, but they'd also grown up together. Sam couldn't remember a time when he wasn't friends with Rick. They went to high school together, enlisted together, were only apart for a couple of years because Sam worked with bombs and Rick didn't want anything to do with them. Rick's greatest fear in life was being killed in an explosion.

Remembering the night they talked about career aspirations, Sam winced, the loss still raw.

They completed their military service, both in one piece, and joined the San Bernardino County Sheriff's Department together. Brotherly competition dominated their relationship, and they finished the academy one and two. Then Sam was Rick's best man when he married Gina. Rick had planned on returning the favor. Sam remembered talking right before the stop about his upcoming wedding to Vanessa Reilly.

Now, everything from that day was gone. Rick in the crash and Vanessa afterward.

"I can't do this. Gina is wrecked. I can't go through what she's dealing with. I can't marry you and then worry every night whether or not you'll come home from your shift."

She'd returned his ring while he was in the hospital. Losing Vanessa had stung—he'd never deny that. But Sam had made peace with it. She was honest enough to walk away. If she'd stayed quiet and they'd married, his work would have always been a source of conflict.

Sam shook the memory away and kept walking through the station. Another memory, this one fresher, took its place. He'd needed a ride to the rental car office and George was occupied. So Sam called his mother. Leslie Gresham was a neighbor of sorts, living in Lake Arrowhead, so coming to get him wasn't a big deal. Her four-wheel drive handled the freshly plowed roads without a problem. He explained about the incident with Jodie King. His mother made no comment, which, where she was concerned, was usually worse than if she read him the riot act. In the end, the conversation was brief, and she agreed to give him a ride down the hill.

"I like your new place," she said, gazing out the window at the thin layer of snow on his deck. "It's beautiful here."

He handed her a cup of coffee. "I like it too. Much quieter than it was in Redlands."

She sipped her coffee and Sam stayed quiet. He could tell she had something on her mind and it was best to wait her out. After about a minute, his mother looked at his workbag, sitting by the front door.

"Sam, are you sure you're ready to go back to fieldwork?" She faced him, frown on her face, probing his eyes.

He held her gaze. "Yes, Mom, it's time. I've had enough desk work."

"I don't doubt your ability to do the job. I'm concerned you haven't processed all that happened when Rick died."

Shades of Doc Roe and George Upton. Sam sighed. "I can't change the past. Neither can I sit around and rehash it over and over like you and Doc Roe seem to want. I needed to be back at work. I finally got Doc Roe to agree. I've been back at it a month without issue. What more do you want me to do?"

She didn't answer the question. "You have nothing to prove."

"It's not about proving anything. It's about doing my job. Can we talk about this in the car?"

The frown eased, but she kept looking at him. The mom face came, the expression that said, "No matter what, you're still my baby." "We can. And will you let me pray for you?"

Sam swallowed. His mom was a prayer warrior, something he also thought was important at one time. But since Rick's death, he felt as though his prayers had been bouncing off the ceiling. He still believed—his faith got him through rehab—but always in the background was the question why Rick and not him. Was his mother right? Did he have to be in the field to prove something—maybe that he deserved to live? Sam shook the thought away. He wrestled with so *many why questions for God, sometimes he thought his middle name should be Jacob.*

"Sure," *he said, setting his coffee cup in the sink and walking to retrieve his workbag.* "Better get going so I'm not late."

She'd prayed, asking the Lord to watch over Sam, keep him safe, and help him heal. Sam bowed his head and said amen when she did, but his heart wasn't in it, and he wondered if it ever would be again.

He pushed the conversation to the back of his mind when he reached the homicide office.

"Hey, Sam, good to have you back." Detective Smiley stood when Sam entered. He smiled and gripped Sam's hand in both of his, then gave him a quick hug, patting him on the shoulder. Smiley always reminded Sam of a basset hound, jowly cheeks with soulful eyes. Appearances were deceiving. Smiley was a bulldog when it came to working a case.

"I'm glad you decided to re-up. Especially after what happened yesterday."

"No choice. This is my career. I'm not ready to give it up."

Smiley squeezed his hand one more time before letting it go, gave him a nod, and pointed toward an empty desk. "Yours," he said as he checked out the scars. It didn't bother Sam; he was used to it. Everyone's eyes seemed drawn to the scars. Since ears were cartilage, and his right one had partially melted, it had been reshaped with skin grafts. Sound was a little muffled in the right ear now.

Sam set his bag on the desk, pausing before unpacking his stuff. "Want me to fill you in on yesterday?"

"You bet. Sorry I couldn't make it up there. My mother-in-law was in the ER for a bit."

"Is she okay?"

"Yeah, she just doesn't manage her diabetes very well." He gave a wave of his hand. "I've read all the reports. You and Deputy Takano did a good job. But it boggles the mind what you wandered into up there."

"Yeah, it does," Sam agreed. He told Smiley everything, even repeating what he was sure the boss had read in reports. He also included his and Jodie's conclusion about all of this being personal, directed at her and her alone.

Smiley nodded. "How is King?"

"She seemed okay, considering she was a target. She might have been shaken up a bit." He shrugged. "She wants to find the bad guy. This could be the lead we needed to find a hot trail."

"I agree. It surprises me, though."

"What does?"

"This killer just about committed the perfect crime. He's gone, we ran out of leads, yet he tries again." He rubbed his chin, pensive. "King have any ideas about who might still be after her?"

Sam shook his head. "Any more information on the shooter?" He didn't think there was and was happily surprised when Smiley nodded.

"I just got a call from dispatch as I was coming to work; a patrol unit found the Honda. It was dumped at the bottom of the hill."

"Seriously? Anyone see it get dumped?"

Smiley held his hand out flat and tilted it back and forth. "Still asking around. There's a lot of evidence to be processed. I've got uniformed officers sitting on it."

"Was it stolen from the ski area?"

"No, it was stolen yesterday morning from San Bernadino, not far from where it was dumped. The reporting party found it gone around six in the morning."

"The ATV?"

"Stolen from the ski area. It belonged to the maintenance detail. The rifle wasn't located, but there was a full clip for an AR-15 in the ATV. It had dropped down and wedged between the seat and the back cargo area. A lot of the evidence on the ridge was contaminated by snow, so the clip might be our best hope for prints. Might be a couple of days before we get anything concrete. I'd like to talk to Logan, but we might not be able to for a while."

"Has he been able to talk at all?"

"Once stable, they took him into surgery to repair his jaw. Not sure when he'll be able to speak. One or two people from Snow Valley offered vague descriptions of the guy speeding away in a white Honda with a green driver's door. Generic male white in a ball cap."

"What can we do now?"

"I want to go look at the stolen Honda before it gets to impound. Then I want to check in with the vehicle's owner, see if he can tell us anything else. With any luck there will be camera footage from somewhere. It's shoe leather time—you up for some snooping?"

"You bet."

CHAPTER 10

JODIE AND TARA ATE LUNCH at the Hangout. Jodie picked at her food and worked hard to keep her tone upbeat, hating it when Tara or Uncle Mike commented on her demeanor. *"You're frowning,"* *"What's wrong?"* and *"I really miss your smile and laughter"* were a few phrases she'd heard a lot since the IED blast, and she was tired of hearing them. She'd learned to wear a mask around people.

"Be real," Sam had said. She couldn't, not with people who didn't understand.

"So I have to say I'm impressed." Tara pushed her plate aside, breaking the silence.

"About what?"

"You. Cool as a cucumber. Someone shot at you yesterday."

"Being shot at doesn't come close to being blown up." Jodie

regretted the statement almost immediately. She set her fork down. "Sorry, I didn't mean to be flippant." She inhaled and let her breath out slowly. "I hate to say it, but I'm almost glad I got shot at. It breathes life into the investigation."

"I guess I can see where you're coming from. Did you make it to the memorial site?"

"No. It's not actually in Arrowbear. It's in Green Valley Lake. I'm not on board with the memorial."

"Why Green Valley Lake?" Tara asked.

"It's Jonah's memorial, his idea."

"You'd think he'd pick a place closer to where it happened."

Jodie shrugged. "A memorial is the last thing on my mind. The case is not over. The only thing I'm concerned with right now is catching the killer."

"I'm with you there, girlfriend." Tara raised her soda glass as a toast and Jodie tapped it with her glass of tea. The check came and Tara paid.

"You didn't have to."

"I wanted to. Let's walk the pier."

Together they crossed the street and for a bit, silence reigned as they strolled along the wooden slats.

"What are you going to do for the rest of the day?" Tara asked.

"I don't know. I'm still figuring out this not-going-to-work life." Jodie's Sundays used to be about resting up for the workweek to come. Surf if the waves were good, maybe go to the movies, or play volleyball with friends. Now, each empty day stretched into another empty day. Her voice betrayed none of the turmoil boiling inside over her status. Truth was, while she had no long-term plans, she had plans for the here and now. She just wasn't ready to share anything with Tara.

"It was a mistake to quit. How are you going to pay your rent? Half a pension won't cover it."

Jodie shrugged. "I have a trust fund, remember? The settlement from my parents' deaths. I can always tap those funds."

"Right." Tara slapped her forehead. "You actually can be a lady of leisure. Can we still be friends since I'll always be a working stiff?"

"Ha. I'll have to get back to you."

Tara smiled and stood. "Well, I'll make sure to fill you in on anything I hear from Smiley. Take care, Jodie."

They made their way back to the street and Tara left for her car while Jodie walked back to her apartment. She was a little amazed the trust fund idea had popped out. Yes, the fund would support her. After her parents' deaths, the airline had been found negligent in the plane's maintenance, so the settlement was generous. She hadn't tapped into the fund yet and hadn't made plans to. Jodie had moved in with her uncle Mike after the crash and had no reason to draw from the fund. And she hadn't thought about it until now. She just didn't want Tara, or anyone, to worry about her.

The trust fund money could make a lot of things easier for Jodie. Her rent would be paid, travel was possible—she could surf all over the world if she wanted. But leisure was the last thing on her mind. The money couldn't buy her the one thing she wanted more than anything: to find the person who killed her team.

"Why the frown?"

Jodie looked up, startled, and saw Ian Hunter sitting on the short rock wall bordering the outside of her complex. Jaw set, Jodie determined she wouldn't let him upset her. Ian had survivor's guilt on steroids. The rift between them broke her heart. In his anger and pain, he was pushing everyone away; she'd heard that his wife had left him.

When he showed up, it was neither pleasant nor welcome. But Jodie put up with it. He hurt. He lashed out, and she was his target.

"What are you doing here?"

"Hello, nice to see you too." There was an edge to his voice. While everyone else told her the IED was not her fault, Ian blamed Jodie for what happened.

"Sorry, Ian. I have a lot on my mind. I didn't mean to be so short with you."

He didn't look mollified. "Can you explain what happened yesterday?"

Jodie sighed. "No, I can't."

He stood and glared at her. "Why'd you go up there? Looks like you almost got another cop killed."

Jodie felt the words like a blow. She swallowed and kept any rancor out of her tone. "How was I to know I'd be the target of a sniper?"

"You're the boss," he sneered. "You know everything, don't you? When to schedule raids and when not to."

Jodie pinched the bridge of her nose, not having the energy to argue with Ian. He'd been her right-hand man on RAT. They'd worked well together for years and had been friends outside of work. But when he'd come to see her in the hospital, all he brought with him was blame. And she had no good reason why she hadn't waited a day—she was simply impatient to get the job done.

Dr. Bass explained Ian's behavior with the cliché "hurt people hurt people."

Uncle Mike asked her to make a formal complaint and tell IA about the harassment. Jodie couldn't. She listened to Ian; she took his barbs and arrows. Something inside said she deserved it.

"What happened this weekend has reopened the investigation. Maybe we'll get some real answers now."

He snorted derisively and kicked a rock from the pavement, looking over Jodie's head for a moment.

"Will it solve anything? Will it bring back all those remarkable people who died?" Ian directed his gaze back to her, pain in his eyes. "Why didn't you just wait twenty-four hours?" he whispered.

"We can't keep going through this. Maybe if you'd been there, nothing would have changed—have you thought of that?"

"Yeah, maybe not, but maybe I could have died with my friends. Maybe I should have."

She frowned. "Ian, please—"

He silenced her with a wave of his hand and sniffed. "No pity, just keep me in the loop if you find out something useful."

"I will."

He turned on his heel and strode to his car.

She watched him drive away, heart heavy. She understood his pain. How often had she felt like she should have died as well? She couldn't fault him for berating her and she wouldn't stop him.

After a few minutes, she went inside her apartment to the small alcove that served as her office. Here, she had a whiteboard set up. On it was every bit of information she had about the investigation into the IED. Jodie might have quit her job, but she had no intention of quitting the investigation. She checked her email even though it was too early for Tara to have sent her any new information.

She closed her email window and clicked to different news sites, stopping when she saw that the San Bernardino Sheriff's public information officer was giving a press conference. She didn't hear anything new.

Her phone interrupted the Q and A from reporters. From the caller ID she saw it was Dr. Bass, the department psychologist. Even though she'd quit, he'd kept in contact. He had certainly heard what happened. Jodie let the call go to voice mail, then closed her computer.

She wasn't interested in talking to Bass, exploring her future, and coming to terms with what had happened. All Jodie wanted was true resolution, which to her meant being able to avenge the deaths of her team, her friends.

Ian's visit left her feeling unsettled. It reminded her how different life was now. She flipped around the channels on the TV but couldn't sit still to watch anything. Peeking out the window, certain Ian's car was long gone, she decided to do something he would not have approved of. Jodie grabbed her keys and purse. She climbed into her car with two destinations in mind. The first was Huntington Beach. She'd been looking for her confidential informant Jukebox. His being missing was the most perplexing part of this.

At one time Jukebox had wanted to be a cop, which was how Jodie had met him. In the end, he was too laid-back for a career in law enforcement. But he lived in two worlds, following the waves in the summer and the snow in the winter. He'd become Jodie's informant when she was working narcotics because he saw and heard a lot. When Jodie left narcotics to lead the task force, she kept in touch with Jukebox.

Jodie usually tapped Jukebox for anything narcotics related. When Hayes's file came across her desk, checking in with Jukebox was natural. Jodie studied Hayes's rap sheet and saw another connection: he'd attended the same high school as Juke.

Where was the man now? If Jukebox had been in the mountains

the last couple of months, he should be back now. Since snow in the mountains of Southern California wasn't ever reliable, sometimes he went to Mammoth to ski. But Jodie was certain he would have told her if he was leaving. Besides, she'd expected to hear something from him after the IED. But there was silence. Because no one had heard from him, Smiley and Tara had put him in the possible suspect column. He had disappeared after the blast like Hayes, so they believed he might have been complicit.

Jodie disagreed. Jukebox wasn't a criminal mastermind. She'd started looking for him as soon as the cast came off her arm. No one had seen him, but she kept at it.

Once in Huntington Beach, she found a place to park. The regular surfers here were guys she called friends, and they all knew Jukebox. Most surfers tended to be a little on the unreliable side. Jodie didn't see it as a character flaw; rather, she saw it as a practical result of the fact that waves were unpredictable. When they happened, guys had to jump on them or they'd be gone. Jobs and relationships suffered. Jukebox was more grounded, more reliable. He was a fixture at the beach, not a skipping-out kind of guy.

As she walked and talked to the surfers, she wondered if the mild-mannered, often goofy guy could really have had something to do with the explosion. *No* screamed in her thoughts. Nothing so sinister was in him.

She'd reached the pier near the volleyball courts when she saw him. Not Jukebox but Finn, Jukebox's best friend. He'd been gone, certainly chasing the waves, for as long as Jukebox had. Brothers in the waves, Jukebox loved snowboarding as much as he loved surfing while Finn was strictly a surfer. Jukebox supported himself with odd jobs and taught skiing when he was in the mountains; Finn was a trust fund baby. Jodie had heard he survived on a monthly allowance large enough to comfortably support a family of five.

Her heart quickened in her chest. Finn would know where Jukebox was. She jogged to where he stood, surfboard at his feet, three or four bikini-clad ladies hanging on his every word. Finn was gorgeous—the only fitting way to describe him. Tall, tan, head topped with a striking mop of blond hair bleached by the sun, with a physique that looked sculpted, he could have stepped out of the pages of a movie magazine. He probably could have been an actor, if he had an attention span longer than a ten-year-old's.

"Finn," Jodie called.

He turned toward her, big grin splitting his face. "Jo-Jo, g'day!" he called back, affecting an Australian accent.

"Where have you been, buddy?"

"Down under. Just got off the plane. You know it's summer there when it's winter here. Sometimes I like to surf all year round. Where's your board? I hear the swell is pumping."

"I was in this morning. It was great. Hey, have you seen Jukebox?"

The grin faded and he scowled. "No, man, I haven't. He was supposed to go with me. I bought him a ticket and he never showed."

"He was supposed to go with you to Australia?" The excitement at finding Finn faded. Jukebox wasn't fickle, at least not when it came to surfing or skiing.

"Yeah, he'd never been. Totally flaked, man. Wait, uh . . ." His face scrunched together like he was trying to remember something. "He wanted me to tell you something."

"Tell me?"

"Yeah, it was strange. He said he was running late. Ah . . ." He threw down his hands. "I can't remember. It was like months ago."

"Try, Finn. It's important. Juke is missing."

"What?" He got serious and the fake accent fell away.

"True. I've been looking for him for three months."

He dug around in the pile of towels and clothes on the bench next to him and pulled out his phone. "I'll find his last text. It was from a different phone. No name showed up on my screen. I almost deleted it." After he scrolled for a moment, he handed the phone to Jodie.

She saw the thread. With the first text, it seemed Jukebox wanted to be certain he had the right number. He identified himself as Juke. Finn told him he did and asked where he was, since there wasn't much time for him to board the plane. She read the last entry Juke had typed. It was dated the day before the raid.

Sorry, Finn. Bad vibes. I might not make it. Can't tell you what's happening. Tell Jo-Jo it's a setup. Gonna try and stop it, not sure I can tell her. I'm sorry for the bad 411.

Jodie felt frozen in place. The world around her faded away. Clearly something had happened. Why didn't Jukebox call her? He had her number. Still holding the phone, she dropped her hands and looked up at Finn. He was watching her, a startled, serious look on his face.

"Was that bad? Did I mess up?"

She shook her head and handed him back the phone. "It's bad. You couldn't have known. Can you forward the text to me?" She gave him her number.

He sent the text and put a hand on her shoulder. "Is Juke in trouble?" His tone was so soft, sad, and caring she was tempted to give him a hug.

All she said was "I'm afraid so, Finn. I'm afraid so."

CHAPTER 11

THE SHOOTER HAD DUMPED THE VEHICLE at Forty-Fourth and Sierra Way. As they approached the location, Sam looked over a map, hoping for a clue as to where the suspect had headed.

"He took the first exit off of Waterman," he said to Smiley, "then drove right past where he stole the vehicle, continued a couple of blocks, turned a corner, parked, and left the vehicle."

"Yep."

Uniformed officers were waiting with a tow truck when Smiley and Sam arrived.

"Did you find anyone who saw anything?" Smiley asked.

"A worker from the fence company said he saw a guy get out of the car and climb into a waiting car. Then he drove south on Sierra."

"Another car?" Sam asked.

"Yeah, he didn't know what kind of car, said he only glanced at it. Blue four-door SUV was all he would commit to."

"Did he see the driver?"

The officer shook his head. "He thought the guy who dumped the Honda was a white male, but he wasn't sure. Like I said, it was only a passing glance. I leaned on him, but he just wasn't sure."

Sam and Smiley put on gloves. Sam took the driver's side, Smiley the passenger side. This model Honda was notoriously easy to steal. No windows were broken, and there was no sign of forced entry, so the thief probably had a key that worked in the door. As for the ignition, it had been punched, and there was a screwdriver in the steering column. Sam saw a steering wheel lock in the back seat behind the driver's seat. He checked it out. It had been expertly picked.

There was very little rubbish in the car. All of the upholstery was worn but clean. When he finished going through the car, he wasn't optimistic they'd get anything from it. Smiley put a *Hold for prints* sign on the hood and told the tow they could take the car. They then headed to the victim's address.

Doug Taylor's residence was on a triangular piece of land bordered by East Forty-Eighth Street, Sierra Way, and Leroy Street. East Forty-Eighth Street bisected North Waterman, which became Rim of the World Highway as it traversed Waterman Canyon and led up to the mountain resorts. Since the suspect apparently wanted quick access to the mountain, it made sense to steal a car from here.

Taylor was waiting for them when they parked. He approached as they got out of their car. "Hey, I got a call my car was recovered. When do I get it back?"

"Mr. Doug Taylor?" Smiley held his hand out.

"Right here." He grudgingly shook Smiley's hand. "I need my car. I'm going to school in Loma Linda to be a respiratory therapist. I can't miss. This is my shot at a good job."

Sam felt for the man. Loma Linda was about ten miles from here, not easy to traverse without a car.

"We're sorry, Mr. Taylor. Your vehicle is being processed for evidence."

"Yeah, I heard about the cop getting shot, and I'm sorry. But I did what I was supposed to do: I reported my car stolen. I'm the victim here—I need my car."

"We'll do what we can to get the car back to you as soon as possible," Sam said. "Can you show us where it was parked? Do you have any idea who would have stolen it?"

"Nah, man, if I knew who, I'd deal with it. It was parked in my assigned space—" he pointed—"back here behind the complex."

The three of them walked to the rear of the complex.

"Will your insurance spring for a rental?" Sam asked while he searched the area for cameras. He counted three in the lot by the time they reached the empty parking space, but none of the security cameras were trained directly on the spot where the Honda was usually parked.

Doug shook his head. "I just had the bare minimum. Been saving to put myself through school. I had a steering wheel lock, thought it would stop thieves. Guess not."

"No neighbors heard or saw anything?" Smiley asked.

"No one saw anything. Most people are probably afraid some gangster took it. They don't want to get involved if that's the case."

"Do you think a gangster took it?" Sam asked.

Doug held his gaze. "No, I don't. I keep my distance from the bad boys around here. I stay away from their stuff; they stay away from mine. Plus, an old beater Honda isn't high on the list of cars that would be parted out."

Sam nodded. True. The stolen vehicle trade trafficked in high-end vehicles they could strip and sell for parts. Or they just stole parts. The rise in thefts of catalytic converters from parked cars was astounding. No, the guy who took Doug's car needed it to get from point A to point B.

"I just had to get a rental." Sam pulled a card out of his pocket. "My friend works as a rental agent. Give him a call, tell him Sam sent you, and he'll give you a good deal. Hopefully the lab will only keep your car a couple of days."

Doug took the card. "It'd have to be a rock-bottom deal."

"It will be." He pointed toward one of the cameras. "There are surveillance cameras here. Did they film the theft?"

"They're always broken. I asked the manager; on one camera all you can see is the back of the car leaving the lot about an hour before I came down and found it gone."

"Turning left on East Forty-Eighth, toward Waterman?"

"Yep. Can I call the lab, make them speed it up?"

"You can try," Smiley said.

Doug kicked the dirt. "Yeah, I understand."

Sam and Smiley left him and walked to the end of the lot, where Doug indicated the car had turned.

"This is the part of the job I hate," Sam said.

"What, victims being victimized again by the system?"

"Yeah, that poor guy."

"Then I hope your rental agent friend will come through. And maybe we'll get lucky with camera footage. More and more people are investing in doorbell cameras, especially with the rise in porch pirates. There are probably a couple of houses on this street fitted with them."

They hit pay dirt at the third house on East Forty-Eighth. The resident had a top-level camera system at his front door and an unobstructed view of the street. He downloaded the footage for the last twenty-four hours to Smiley's phone.

Sam was happy to have something to search. He wanted to find this guy as much as he'd wanted to find anyone. For Logan, for Doug, and most of all for Jodie King.

CHAPTER 12

JODIE GOT HOME, threw her keys on the counter, and sat in her recliner, body numb. Jukebox was most likely dead. And she was second-guessing her use of confidential informants. He'd been willing. To Juke it was a big game, a fun diversion. Juke never would have seen the danger. Jodie should have. But serving the warrant on Hayes was routine. How could she have known he'd be put in mortal danger?

"Ahhh." She grabbed her head in both hands and rested her elbows on her knees. Her anguished heart cried out to God to answer the question he never seemed to answer.

Why?

She fell into a dark place, a place she'd been in the first week after the IED, a place where the guilt and grief were crushing, and all Jodie wanted was out. She should have died with her team. She'd been so cavalier with Jukebox's help, and she hadn't seen the risk, and it cut her like a carving knife.

I was so arrogant. Hayes wasn't terribly important, but I wanted another feather in my cap. Juke simply became a tool to help further my career, and he lost his life as a result. It was suddenly glaringly clear to Jodie that her job, her title, the feeling of having everything in her control, had been her god.

Acknowledging her failure only compounded her misery. Though the blast hadn't killed her, it had certainly taken almost everything she trusted in away from her.

Jodie lost track of time. Processing the probable loss of Jukebox was the straw breaking the camel's back. She wanted the pain to stop, wanted to be free of the accusing voices in her head and the ten-ton load of guilt.

She had a gun.

She'd told Gresham that the shrink didn't think she was crazy or suicidal. Was he right? she wondered now.

Just then a thought pinged in her brain as if she'd been pierced with an arrow. *If I die, then whoever set the IED will win.*

Jodie stiffened as soon as the thought entered her head.

"No, no," she whispered. "I won't quit. I refuse to let them win." Some of the guilt fizzled and burned away, incinerated by her anger.

The bad guy had to be held accountable. Seeing him locked up—or better yet dead—would be the only result Jodie could accept. She would never be free of all the guilt and the pain until the situation was resolved to her satisfaction.

She stood and picked up some paper and began tearing it into pieces, dwelling on all the bad she'd dealt with since the IED.

A knock at the door startled her. The last thing Jodie wanted was to socialize. In this dark space all she wanted to do was nurse the anger and the self-pity.

She opened the doorbell app on her phone and saw her uncle Mike. Conflicting emotions raged. Stay alone and stew or tell Mike what she'd discovered?

She needed to tell him about Jukebox. Hopefully this would take him off the suspect list.

But Jodie really didn't want company. Another side effect of the IED. Before, she had lived an extroverted life. She loved being with and around people. Now she'd transformed into an introvert, borderline shut-in. Mike probably came in person because she'd been ignoring his phone calls.

Jodie would have to deal with Mike being here without showing him how off she felt. Mask time.

Before going to the door, she covered her whiteboard and closed her laptop. She squared her shoulders, gritted her teeth, and pulled the door open. Mike's expression caught her off guard—he looked worried.

"Jodie."

"I told you last night I was fine." Jodie fought to keep her voice neutral.

"I know what you said. I thought I'd check up on you after you had some rest," Mike said before gathering her in a hug. "Can't an uncle come double-check on his niece after she narrowly misses being shot?"

"You're overstating," Jodie said. Still, she returned the hug. Once he let go, she backed away from the door to let him in.

"I don't think so." Mike closed the door behind him. He followed her to the kitchen. "I talked to Jonah this morning. He cut his business trip short and he's on his way back from Vegas."

"Why? I'm fine. You all need to stop fussing over me."

"It's fussing to ask why you went up there by yourself? Jonah said he offered to meet you at the memorial site. You've never been what I'd call reckless. Why start now?"

Jodie sat at the kitchen table and Mike sat across from her. Under the table her hands clenched into fists. *I hate being treated like a child.*

"I must be escorted everywhere? After everyone has decided Hayes is the only suspect and he fled the country? I didn't realize I was supposed to be afraid of something."

"You're twisting my words and my concern. Your mental state is fragile; you're not making clear decisions."

"I'm crazy?"

"I didn't say you're crazy." Frustration rippled through his tone, but Jodie did not want to make it any easier for him.

Mike sighed. "Jonah and I also lost a friend; in fact, Gus was like our brother. We get through the pain and loss by being together. You're doing the opposite. You're shutting out the people who care about you most."

She looked away and Mike continued.

"You stopped seeing Dr. Bass. You attend church sporadically, coming after it starts and leaving before it's over. You only hang out with Tara, and I know that's just to keep tabs on the investigation."

"So? Why shouldn't I keep tabs on the investigation? My team is dead. It was my fau—" She stopped, hating the threatening tears.

"It was not your fault!"

She stood and grabbed a glass, filling it with water at the sink. She drank half of it and turned to see Mike watching her.

"I don't want to go through this again. Please, Mike. I don't have the energy. I'm fine. Thanks to Gresham I'm fine."

"Thank God for Sam Gresham." Mike stood and put his hands on her shoulders. "Jodie, I'm your uncle. I raised you from eight years old. I consider you my daughter."

"I know." She put the glass down and crossed her arms. "Sometimes you smother me."

He dropped his hands. "Fair enough. Please, won't you go talk to Dr. Bass again or at least attend an entire church service, maybe talk to the pastor?"

She sighed. "I'll call Dr. Bass tomorrow. Fair enough?"

"Yes," Mike said. "If you'll do it."

Jodie gave a nod and swallowed, praying she could hold it together while she told him about Jukebox. "I found out something today, something about Jukebox."

"What?" Mike stared.

She had his full attention. She told him about the encounter with Finn, glad her voice didn't falter.

"You're kidding," Mike said, hands on hips, frown on his face.

"I wish I was." She showed him the text.

Mike held her phone and read the message a couple of times. He looked up and sighed. "I've always agreed with you on this. Jukebox was a lot of things, but killer isn't one of them."

Now Jodie couldn't speak. She swallowed a lump and nodded.

He handed back her phone. "I'll make sure Smiley gets this information. I'm so sorry, Jodie."

He turned to leave, then stopped and looked back at her. "Come to dinner tonight? We'd love to have you."

The *we* meant Mike's latest girlfriend. He'd never married, but he'd dated several nice women. At one time, Jodie thought he stayed single because of her, but now she realized Mike was, in fact, married to the job.

No part of Jodie felt like socializing. "I'm kind of tired. Maybe next week?"

"Sure. I'll keep asking until you say yes."

He left Jodie alone with her thoughts.

CHAPTER 13

BY MIDAFTERNOON MONDAY, Sam had finished studying the video from the doorbell camera. They got lucky. It yielded one good still of the car thief driving by in Doug's Honda. Sam held up the picture they were going to show to the press.

"This is so generic," he said, wishing the camera had captured a front view. Instead, they had a side view of a man in a ball cap and sunglasses.

"It's still a good shot, considering the darkness. Sheer luck the streetlight was so close. And even though it's generic, we can be certain of one thing: it's not Hayes."

"True," Sam agreed. Hayes was a big man; he'd been in prison before and had lots of tats and muscular arms. This image showed a small man. Since the vehicle was a compact Honda Civic, his height could be extrapolated from the man's position in the seat. This guy could almost be a teen. Who was he?

"More good news." Smiley walked over to Sam's desk. "Logan is awake. His jaw is wired but he can write. You up for a trip to the hospital?"

"Let's go."

Sam didn't really want to go to the hospital. Ever since his accident he had a strong aversion to them. He'd spent too many painful hours in one. He'd weather this visit by remembering who he was working for. He'd wanted to send Jodie the picture they had of the suspect but knew it wasn't his place. Smiley sent it to Mike King at LBPD. While it was a bit odd for Jodie's uncle Mike to be assigned to the IED task force, since he was family, it was ultimately the PD's decision, not the sheriff's. As far as Sam knew, Mike King had been an asset, so he had no reason to question the assignment.

When they arrived at St. Bernardine, there were cops everywhere, normal when a cop got shot. Walking through a mixture of deputy uniforms and San Bernardino city cops, Sam nodded here and there. A few of the faces were familiar brothers in blue.

As they reached the officer's room, there was a lot of brass outside, the people who usually surrounded the sheriff. As if on cue, the county sheriff exited the room. His gaze stuck on Sam.

"Deputy Gresham?"

Sam nodded. "Yes, sir."

"Good to see you up and at it after what happened on Saturday." He extended his hand and Sam took it. "You fought back, son, very admirably. The department and the community are better for you being on the job."

"Thank you, sir."

The sheriff turned to Smiley. "I know you both are on top of this. Catch this guy."

"Plan on it," Smiley said.

The sheriff and his entourage continued down the hall. Sam and Smiley entered the room and Sam recognized Detective Ezra Fenton at Logan's bedside. Since homicide handled officer-involved shootings, Ezra and his partner would handle Chad Logan's shooting. Sam and Rick had apprehended a suspect for Ezra Fenton once. The guy had killed his wife but tried to make it look like a home invasion robbery gone bad.

Fenton arched an eyebrow at Sam. "From pushing paper to jumping into the deep end of the pool, aren't you?"

"Yes, I am."

"So you said you have a photo," Fenton said to Smiley after handshakes.

"Yep." Smiley handed it to him. "It's not perfect, but it's something. We know it's our victim's car because of the different-colored door."

Fenton took the photo and studied it. He handed it to Logan. The deputy's face was swathed in bandages. All Sam could see was the man's right cheek and eye. The 9mm bullet had entered his face just below his left cheekbone and then took a downward trajectory and exited through his jaw. Luckily it missed all major arteries. Consequently, his most serious injury was a badly broken jaw. Doctors were likely going to do more surgery, but for now Chad could write answers to questions even though he couldn't speak.

Chad studied the photo with his good eye and nodded. Handing the picture back to Fenton, he picked up a writing pad and began to write. After a few minutes and about a paragraph, he handed the pad to Fenton.

"He says this could be the guy. The shooter was small, maybe five-five, 120 to 130. Short, light-brown hair. He got out of the car shooting. He was white, wearing gloves, a red Angels baseball cap, and sunglasses." He stopped. "There isn't much else. The kid took him by surprise, coming out of the car shooting."

Smiley rubbed his chin. "I'll have our artist draw a composite with the description. What kind of gloves did he have on?"

"Disposable gloves."

Sam hated hearing about gloves. "So we're not likely to get any prints off the car?" he asked.

Smiley shrugged. "Let's think positive. The lab is going over that car with a fine-tooth comb. We can hope the suspect wasn't careful every minute."

"If you say so," Sam said, trying not to sound too disappointed. He turned his attention to Chad. "The guy didn't say anything to you?"

Chad gave an almost-imperceptible shake of his head and winced.

"Do you really think this is connected to the IED explosion?" Fenton asked.

Sam saw Smiley's eyes widen in surprise. "We do. The shooting occurred at the IED scene, and the target happens to be the only surviving officer of the IED. What other conclusion would you draw?"

"The guy in the photo isn't Norman Hayes."

"No, he's not. But there is a connection somewhere and we will find it."

CHAPTER 14

MIDMORNING TUESDAY found Jodie staring at the photo Tara sent her. She also had the composite the San Bernardino sheriff's office had developed. Both were so generic it could be anyone. She wondered how much help composites really were. She remembered a sketch of D. B. Cooper, a hijacker from 1971. The sketch circulated everywhere, yet Cooper was never apprehended.

Frustrated, Jodie tossed the picture on her desk. Sketches weren't always 100 percent helpful. She found nothing familiar to her in the photo. She had mug shots of all the guys she'd arrested. She had mug shots of Hayes and all his known associates. This man driving a stolen car was not any of them. It made no sense, and it was crazy making.

She picked up one of her whiteboard pens, the red one, the

color she used for her questions. She no longer thought the attack was anything but personal. She had always been the target. Her being shot at proved that. The first question she scrawled:

Who hates me so much they'd go through all of this, a hate so strong it's lasted months after my team was killed?

1. Someone I arrested.

She had copies of all her arrest reports. She'd been threatened often in her career, but none of the arrestees who'd been vocal were viable suspects. There were two IA complaints in her file, both filed by mothers who insisted their sons didn't deserve to be arrested. Internal affairs had investigated both complaints and determined them to be unfounded.

2. Someone I offended.

How do you make a list of offenses? I've probably offended a lot of people in my career. What would it take to rachet up to mass murder? She tried to think of any personal conflicts—she'd had few—but nothing in her memory rose to a code red status in her mind. There were two cops working in her department she thought were lazy, and she'd told them as much in their performance reviews when she was a patrol sergeant. One had approached her, angry, but then two months later he was terminated for filing a false police report. He never could have put together the IED.

3. Just a random nutjob?

Random nutjobs rarely had focused anger, so focused they'd hit a target and then hit the same one three months later.

She looked over the list, restlessness and frustration growing. She thought the shooting would blow things wide-open. But they were still running in circles. She grabbed her car keys and decided to visit Hayes's stomping grounds. She'd run out of energy Sunday after encountering Finn. The funk had lasted all through Monday as well. Knowing that Juke was likely dead somewhere had sapped her strength. Today was as good a day as any to pick up where she left off.

Her doorbell rang and she groaned. Every fiber of her soul wanted to ignore the intrusion and stay still, hoping the person would just leave. She glanced at the phone and saw Jonah. She couldn't hide from him.

Setting her keys down, she went to the door. "Uncle Jonah," she said. Though he wasn't a blood uncle, she'd always considered him one.

"Jodie." He shook his head, sadness in his eyes, then hugged her tight. Jonah always wore a cologne Jodie loved, a scent that made her feel safe.

Her throat thickened, not so much because of Jonah, but because of the memories surrounding him. Much like the scent of his cologne, they were good memories. Mike, Gus, and Jonah had been friends since high school. Though from time to time, there were fights and bumps, as in any relationship, they called themselves the three amigos. They went through the police academy together thirty years ago, and even though Jonah left the job while Gus and Mike continued in law enforcement, they stayed lifelong friends. Jodie had known Jonah practically her whole life, but always as part of Mike-Gus-Jonah. Having him here alone brought home the point that Gus was dead and the three amigos were no more.

Jodie pushed free of his grasp. "You didn't have to cut your trip short because of me." She backed into her apartment, and he followed.

"There would be no more important reason to cut my trip short than because of you. I would have been here sooner, but I thought you needed time to decompress. You okay?"

"I'm fine." She hoped she sounded sure of herself, but when Jonah's gaze probed, she looked away.

"What on earth happened on Saturday?"

"I don't want to talk about it. I'm certain Mike told you. I'm fine, though. You guys don't need to worry about me."

"Honey, you can't stop us from worrying about you. We care." His eyes went to her desk and Jodie realized she'd forgotten to cover up her whiteboard. But he focused on the copy of the composite drawing of the suspect.

He stepped forward and picked it up. "This the guy who shot at you?"

"It's a composite of the description the wounded deputy gave of his assailant."

"Right. This dirtbag almost killed another cop." He looked from the photo to Jodie and back again. "He look familiar to you?"

She shook her head. "He could be anyone. The drawing is too generic."

Jonah shrugged. "Maybe. But it's a start. It was stupid and reckless for him to try to shoot you."

"I wish he'd been reckless enough to get caught."

He set the drawing down. "Jodie, I said I'd meet you at the

memorial lot. Please tell me if you want to see it. Don't go up there alone again. Please."

"Fine." She had no strength to argue with him. "I've learned my lesson. Let's talk about something else."

They chatted a bit, Jonah telling her about a woman he'd met at the conference in Vegas. Jonah had been married twice and liked to joke about always looking for his next ex. Sometimes she thought he was stuck in a country western song, looking for love in all the wrong places. There was a sadness in him, Jodie sensed. He really hadn't been the same man since his only son had died of a drug overdose. Jason was Jonah's pride and joy, and he'd boasted often about him, predicting the boy had a bright future. She remembered Jason fondly, younger than Jodie and a very bright kid, an honor student. Jonah figured him to be destined for great things. Sadly, it was not to be. His life was cut short at twenty-three because of one stupid decision.

While Jonah didn't stay very long, Jodie felt like she couldn't get him out of her house fast enough. He'd derailed her trip to look for Hayes and she wanted to get back on track. As soon as she saw his SUV drive away, she grabbed her car keys.

Norman Hayes ran with ESL, a large and dangerous street gang. A black-and-white in their neighborhood was just as likely to be shot at as hailed. Jodie would be in her own car. She'd stick out, but she didn't care. Her mission was to find Hayes. Or one of his associates. Mike would call her reckless and say what she was doing was too risky.

It will be worth any risk if I find the killer.

CHAPTER 15

SAM HAD HIS FIRST BAD SPELL Tuesday morning. Rick being gone hit him right between the eyes when he walked into the locker room and saw someone else at Rick's locker. He stopped, feeling as if the wind had been knocked out of him. He didn't think he'd been pretending Rick was just gone on vacation. But for some reason, seeing another officer at Rick's locker felt as if someone had stamped *finalized* on his forehead, and it took his breath away.

He put his hand over his mouth, bile rising, fearing he was going to vomit. Thankfully there was no one else in the bathroom. He rushed in there but didn't throw up. Instead, he rinsed his face with cold water. He put some water on a paper towel and pressed it to the back of his neck.

"I thought I was past this," he mumbled. After the pain of loss receded, the guilt roared back, full force. *I let my partner down.* This brought on the shaking, reminiscent of what had plagued him after the crash and in the hospital.

"Shaking or trembling after a traumatic event is normal," Doc Roe had told him. *"It's caused by the limbic system, the part of the brain responsible for emotions. It sends a signal that the danger has passed and the fight-or-flight response can turn off. The shaking is your body literally finishing the nervous system response to release the traumatic experience."*

Maybe, Sam thought, *but I'm months removed from the trauma. Why now?* It was a question he'd ask himself because he was loath to tell Roe about it.

Once he'd recovered and gotten his feet back under him, as his mother would say, Sam made it to the office. Sam turned on his computer and considered all that needed to be done with the investigation. Jonah Bennett came to mind. He punched the name into his computer and did a search. It wasn't long before the reason the name was familiar popped up.

Two years ago, Bennett's twenty-three-year-old son, Jason, died of a drug overdose. Sam remembered responding to the scene with Rick. They weren't the primary unit, so they hadn't dealt with Bennett, but he recalled the scene. The kid had been at a summer rave just outside Lake Arrowhead. Some bad pills had circulated, and ten young adults were hospitalized. Jason Bennett was the only fatality.

He leaned back and relaxed a bit. Bennett had experienced a tragedy, nothing sinister. In fact, other than one DUI, Bennett had no criminal record. He was a successful real estate agent with offices in Long Beach and the San Bernardino mountains. Nothing odd there. In Southern California having a second home in the mountain communities was common. Sam imagined Bennett probably had his own second home in the mountains and decided to expand his business.

"You sure are deep in thought."

Sam raised his head to see Smiley making a face at him.

"Yeah, you're right." He closed the page. "I went off on a tangent. I keep hoping something will jump out and knock me in the head, something we missed."

Just then Smiley's phone rang. He answered, listened, wrote something down on a piece of scratch paper, then nodded and hung up. "The lab got some usable prints from the car."

"Finally, progress." Sam was glad Smiley hadn't commented on how late he'd been this morning.

"Yes and no. They may all be Doug's and his friends'. I'm going to call and see how they're coming with the ATV and all those casings. I'm thinking the casings are our best hope."

"I agree," Sam said. The bad guy would be careful to wear gloves in the car or on the ATV, but he probably didn't think about it when loading the rifle.

They'd done the best they could to preserve the casings and other evidence before it snowed. Sam thought about the pile of evidence left up on the ridge. It was an amateurish move, despite the planning to maybe catch Jodie King up there.

Some live rounds had been mixed in with the spent ones, indicating a lot of nervousness on the part of the shooter. Sam also remembered the pause when the guy went from semiauto to fully auto. He certainly wasn't military trained. Could just be a low-level gangster. But the kid in the photo didn't look like a gangster. Yet, when the kid faced Logan, there was no hesitation at all.

So much was convoluted about this case.

Thinking about the investigation kept him from dwelling on the spell in the locker room. He hoped it was the last one he'd ever have. He prayed for peace regarding Rick's death and for no uncomfortable incidents to happen when he was out in the thick of things.

∎ ∎ ∎

Jodie had just climbed into her SUV when a familiar car pulled up to the curb and two people she knew well got out. Shannon and Tracy were women from church, both awesome beach volleyball players. Two years ago Jodie had played beside them for a city championship. At one time they were her best friends away from work. Before the IED, the people at church were family.

Each woman was carrying what looked like food. Jodie almost started her car and left, even though they'd seen her. *Why won't people just leave me alone?*

Her hand stayed on the key for a moment, then fell away. Seeing the women, she prayed a silent prayer. *Oh, Lord, why can't I be the same person they remember? Why can't I bounce out of the car and smile and laugh with them? Maybe I can't smile and laugh, but neither can I be rude.* She got out of the car.

"Hey, Jodie." Tracy spoke first. "Glad we caught you."

"We read about what happened Saturday and wanted to make sure you were okay."

"We didn't want to crowd you too soon."

"I hope today is good." Shannon grabbed Jodie in a tight hug before she could protest. "We miss you," she whispered in Jodie's ear.

When she let go, her eyes were moist. So were Jodie's. Jodie stepped back and ran a hand over her eyes, hoping Tracy didn't also want a hug. But Tracy wasn't the demonstrative type; Shannon was.

"Where you headed?" Tracy asked.

"Errands," Jodie said. She cleared her throat.

Tracy and Shannon shared a glance. "We brought you some food. I remembered how much you liked my southwest hamburger casserole," Shannon said. "I made a big batch. And Tracy made a carrot cake. Still your favorite, I hope."

Jodie swallowed. She hadn't had much of an appetite for anything since the explosion. Everything she made ended up half-eaten. She couldn't even finish a bowl of cereal. Food just didn't taste good anymore. But looking at these two women who had been such good friends through the years, she couldn't refuse the offer.

"Sure, sounds great." She gestured toward her door. "Let's put it inside."

The women followed Jodie inside. They chattered about church and Bible study, nervous chitchat. Jodie had gotten used to it from people by now. Right then she wished she could be the Jodie King these women used to know, happy-go-lucky, quick to joke. She thought about Sunday on the pier with Tara. She'd almost felt normal then. But the darkness returned when she realized the killer was still free.

She put the casserole and the cake in the fridge. "Thank you both. When I get back, I know what I'll have for dinner."

"It's our pleasure. We miss you, Jodie. I've only caught a glimpse of you at church once or twice. You're always gone when the service ends." Tracy was the blunt one.

Jodie looked at her friend. They'd done many Bible studies together, but Jodie didn't feel the connection they once had. She decided to be as blunt as Tracy. "I can't do this."

"What?"

"This friendship thing. I'm struggling with so much. I'm not in a good place where God is concerned." *Especially with what I just found out about Jukebox.* "Scripture verses aren't working. Church isn't working."

She expected them to move away. She wasn't one of them anymore; surely she'd be a leper to them.

Instead, she got another hug. Shannon wept.

"I can't imagine the trauma you've faced. All I can say is I'm so very happy you're alive and still with us. And we aren't here to push you into anything you're not ready for."

"We just miss you," Tracy said as Shannon let go and wiped her face.

"I miss me too," Jodie whispered. She wiped away her own tears.

Shannon nodded. "Please remember we care. We want to help. And we will keep praying. God is there. He's never left you. Keep talking to him; keep the dialogue open."

"I wish it were so simple."

"It is. I know it is. And I'll keep praying you come to realize just how simple it really is."

CHAPTER 16

THE LAB CALLED AGAIN AFTER LUNCH. Sam heard the excitement in his boss's voice, and he stopped what he was doing. The good news came when Smiley ended the call.

"The prints from the car didn't pan out to be anything but Doug and his girlfriend. But the lab pulled some good thumbprints from the live rounds left at the scene and from the rounds in the clip we recovered on the ATV. With those we got a hit through DMV records." He handed Sam a name written on a piece of paper and Sam read the name out loud.

"Dennis Marshall Collins." He looked up at Smiley. "His name hasn't come up anywhere else in the investigation."

"Plug it into the system."

Sam typed the details in. When the information came up, the DMV photo showed an average-looking white male in his midtwenties. At five-five, 120 pounds, he wasn't very big. He could be the kid seen in the photo driving the stolen car.

"He certainly isn't anyone on our radar," Smiley noted.

Sam ran Collins through wants and warrants. He came up with no record. "Guy's never been arrested. Not even a traffic ticket."

Smiley rubbed his chin. "If he didn't resemble the guy in the composite Logan and the sketch artist worked out, I'd think this was an odd glitch. Now we must see if there is any connection to Sergeant King or her team or Hayes. We'll have to dig into just who he is." He paused as if thinking about something, then said, "Run him everywhere and go after social media. Find out all you can about this kid. I'll call Long Beach and fill them in."

"I'm on it."

While Smiley made the call, Sam studied the DMV photo of Collins. The twenty-five-year-old wasn't anyone who'd stand out in a crowd. He had a plain, average face. Each police database turned up nothing. There were no guns of any kind registered to him, though he could have access to someone else's guns. Sam went to work checking Collins's social media accounts.

More of a picture emerged. The kid was smart; he'd graduated early at the top of his high school class. He received an under-graduate degree in computer science from Long Beach State and was doing graduate work at Caltech in Pasadena, a prominent engineering college. But there was no indication he'd finished or was still enrolled. Collins listed his current employment as a tech support company in Signal Hill. Sam pulled up their website and saw it was involved with all kinds of computer repair, networking support, and troubleshooting, just about anything tech related.

There wasn't much else on social media. The only platform Collins seemed to favor was Facebook. While people could lie on social media easily, Sam still believed he could get a feel for someone by what they did post, what was important to them. Collins hadn't posted anything in three months. Even three months ago, Collins didn't post a lot, and some of what he did post made no sense to Sam. There were equations, calculations, nothing overtly personal. He liked role-playing video games and talked a bit about different games. Nothing on social media mentioned parents, but Sam found a nod to a brother. Sam felt his pulse quicken. The brother was another avenue to investigate. Dennis posted a heart, saying he would miss his brother, Kent. End of post.

Digging into Kent turned out to be a bit more enlightening.

Big brother, Kent Collins, died a Marine, killed five years ago in Afghanistan in an IED explosion. Kent was someone Sam understood a little better. Patriotic, he enlisted because he felt it was his duty. He obviously loved the Marines and being a part of his unit. They obviously liked him. The remembrance posts after his death were moving. The guy died heroically, falling on an IED and saving the rest of his team. His fellow Marines kept his memory alive. They posted every year on the anniversary of his death.

Kent's social media page went back eight years and included more posts than Dennis's. There were old photos showing Kent, fit and strong, wrestling with his smaller brother and dominating him physically. Sam learned the brothers probably didn't get along very well. Kent referred to him as Dennis the Menace or Little Denny.

Waiting for Little Denny to get his act together. Smart kid but misdirected, face always in his phone.

Dennis the Menace, he hacked his own brother! He poked the bear!

"What do you have, Sam? You look pensive."

Sam told him. "He fits the definition of loner, wouldn't you say?" Sam handed Smiley his notes on Collins.

"Especially when it comes to social media, yeah."

Sam highlighted the number of friends on Collins's Facebook page—twenty-three. Most of them were involved in the same role-playing games Collins indicated he enjoyed. They posted science fiction stuff and memes about the games. Nothing was real world; some comments were edgy and disrespectful at times, but they all pertained to the games and the death and destruction therein. To Sam, they all appeared to be somewhat immature.

Tame stuff, really. He'd dealt with worse while on the job. He just had never gotten comfortable with any of it. Sam had been raised in church, taught to say "yes sir'" and "yes ma'am" and to respect others.

While the picture he developed of the kid was clearer, it shed no light on the investigation into who shot at Jodie King. What motive could Dennis Collins have to steal a car and attempt to kill a person?

"I just got off the phone with Detective Corson in Long Beach. Collins applied to be an officer there."

"What?" Sam's jaw went slack. Collins didn't appear at all interested in police work or becoming a cop.

"Yeah, a year ago. He wasn't selected." Smiley looked over his notes. "Collins went through the entire process with Long Beach. He qualified on the basics, but his background was weak, nothing horrible, but his overall score meant he wouldn't be hired. He was sent the 'thanks, no thanks' letter."

"Wait, are we thinking he's our guy because he wasn't selected for the academy over a year ago?"

"People have been shot at for less. But I'm with you. We need more. The PD will send us the whole background package. Did you come across any red flags in his social media?"

"I think he has problems, but no criminal red flags. I can't see him as a shooter. We're missing something."

Smiley looked down as his phone buzzed with a text. "Fenton is putting together a six-pack of photos to show to Logan. He's in surgery now, so he won't be able to look at it until tomorrow. The LBPD background packet should be in your email. Study it. I've got to go fill the sheriff in on how the investigation is progressing. They want a press release."

"Got it." Sam opened his email and found the packet.

Background investigations for police officers were long and detailed. People were interviewed, references checked, neighbors talked to. Applicants also had to fill out an in-depth background questionnaire. Sam read through Collins's. His parents were deceased; they both died two years after Kent. He wasn't in college at the time he applied to the PD but was already employed by the computer store.

His references were weak, vague. Sam understood why he scored so low. There wasn't enough information to predict whether or not the kid would successfully complete academy instruction and then field training. When Sam got to the interview section of the package, though, he stopped.

Long Beach did several interviews, one of them being a civil service interview with a sworn officer and a member of the community. Jodie King was the sworn officer at Collins's civil service interview. She'd given him exceedingly low marks.

Could this be the connection they were looking for?

CHAPTER 17

AFTER TRACY AND SHANNON LEFT, Jodie lost the impetus to go running around in Norman Hayes's neighborhood. She put her keys on their hook and sat down in front of her computer. The screen was dark and she saw a faint reflection of her face.

We see through a glass darkly. The phrase from the New Testament popped into her mind. It wasn't talking about grief. But she felt it applied to her anyway. It made her wonder if anything in her life would ever be clear again. Jodie couldn't see through a glass at all; she saw only darkness.

Just as Ian's visit the other day had reminded her of how broken she felt, Tracy and Shannon's did likewise. Church and her team had been the biggest parts of her life and her heart for years. They were both gone.

Shannon and Tracy wanted her back. Well, Mike had wanted her back at work, and she couldn't do it. Nothing in her said she'd be any more successful returning to church full-time. Not as long as she felt so disconnected from God. She kept asking and asking for clarity. The word stuck in her thoughts. God promised a lot in his Word: to guide, to protect, to never leave or forsake a believer. Try as she might, Jodie couldn't remember a verse that promised an answer to why.

But that is what I want to know. Why did they die? Why did I live? God stayed silent.

Jodie held her head in her hands. Sadness and grief often covered her like a shroud, coloring everything around her in shadows.

Wanting to get out of the pit of despair she found herself sinking into, Jodie stood and began to pace. Her thoughts returned to the only issue propelling her forward these days: finding the killer. She so wanted a name to go with the photo. Shannon and Tracy had said they'd pray for her.

Pray God answers me. Pray he answers my whys. Pray there is something redeemable in the loss of four good officers.

When the doorbell rang later in the afternoon and Jodie saw Mike again, she inwardly groaned and almost didn't answer. Lately all Uncle Mike seemed to do was lecture her. If it wasn't about why quitting was wrong, it was about why wasn't she back in church. Blah, blah, blah. But a closer look at her phone showed her he wasn't alone.

Tara was with him. Mike and Tara only worked together when on the task force. He'd been rotated back to homicide when it wound down. Had it been reactivated? Hoping this was the case and they were here with an update on the investigation, she pulled the door open.

"Looks like you two mean business. What's up?" she asked.

"It is an official visit. Can we come in?" Mike's tone rang formal.

"Sure." She stepped aside and they came in.

"Let's do this at the kitchen table," he said, using his homicide investigator voice.

"Wow, what did I do?"

Tara smiled as if trying to put her at ease. "It's a lead. Your case might have just been blown wide-open."

Jodie stared at her, wide-eyed, pulse racing. "Did we find Hayes? Or do you have a real suspect?"

They reached the table, where Mike sat, placed his briefcase on the table, and opened it.

Tara pointed to a chair. "Have a seat. We'll tell you everything. We have a name."

"A name to go with the picture?" On high alert now, Jodie didn't want to sit. She wanted to pace, plan. Instead, she sat to listen to what they had to say, holding her hands in her lap to keep from fidgeting.

"Yep. While we got nothing from the spent casings or energy cans, San Bernardino pulled a couple of prints off some of the rounds collected from the stolen ATV," Mike said. "They belong to a Dennis Marshall Collins."

"Do you recognize the name?" Tara asked.

Opening and closing her fists, Jodie shook her head. "It's vaguely familiar, but I don't know why."

"You interviewed him about a year ago. Remember when you covered for me at civil service interviews?" Mike asked. He pulled out a file she recognized as a background packet.

Jodie did remember. She hated doing civil service interviews, but Mike had been sick, so she covered one day. The process for new hires at the PD was long, and there were any number of hoops for a new applicant to jump through.

"A skinny little white kid."

Tara nodded. "You barely passed him, but the civilian gave him high marks."

Mike took a pile of papers out of the file. He laid the papers out like a deck of cards, singled out one form, and pushed it toward her. Each interviewer filled out such a form about the candidate after each interview. She scanned it as everything about the interview came back to her.

"You didn't like the guy," Tara said.

Jodie shook her head. "He said the right things, but something was off. I wanted to outright fail him, but the civilian thought I was being too hard. I figured the rest of his background would bear me out. I settled for just giving him the lowest score possible."

"Why didn't you like him?" Mike asked. "The civilian loved him."

"He condescended to us. I got the distinct impression he thought he was smarter than anyone and he wouldn't be teachable. Plus, he sounded so rehearsed. I can't explain my feelings any better. I felt as if he were saying what we wanted to hear and he didn't believe any of it. I know she liked him. I couldn't explain to her why I had the reservations I had." She reached for more of the papers, scanning each.

"He wasn't hired. You were spot-on with your reservations. All the endorsements in his background were weak. Nothing stood out about him as a candidate to be a police officer."

She snapped her fingers. "Then I was right." She frowned; something wasn't adding up. "Wait, he decided to kill my team because we didn't hire him a year ago? As much as I want to get the guy who killed my team, Collins is a stretch."

"We're not certain of anything yet. But his prints were on the bullets—one dot—and he has a tenuous connection to you—another dot. At the very least he loaded the rifle used to shoot at you. Still another dot. Odd coincidence, wouldn't you say?"

"I don't believe in coincidence."

"Neither do I. Smiley is on his way to talk to him as we speak. All we wanted was to get your read on the guy," Mike said.

"I thought he was a little liar, unteachable, not psychotic." Jodie reviewed the information in the background package. Nothing stood out; nothing said Collins would make a good cop. He barely passed the other portions of the application. The actual psych exam was sealed, but Dr. Bass didn't consider Collins a viable candidate.

"Because of the strange connection," Tara said, "right now he's our best lead."

"Any association with Hayes?"

"None we've found so far."

"All of this is certainly odd." Jodie leafed through the paperwork. Neighbors saying Collins was quiet, a good neighbor, yet they didn't know him well enough to offer an opinion. The candidate's own statement saying he wanted to serve his community and believed law enforcement suited him. There were deficiencies, however. Some classmates said he was a little weird, but they didn't elaborate. The hardest part about conducting a background investigation was getting people to be open and honest about the applicant. Either these people really didn't know Collins, or they did and didn't want to say.

He worked from home so had limited contact with anyone at

his job. His work history contained the most positives. He'd been with his employer for seven years, since his teens. His supervisor gave him high marks, said he completed every assignment thoroughly and on time. He wasn't sure Collins had the right temperament to be a police officer. That comment had been highlighted, probably by the selection committee.

Then Jodie keyed on Collins's address and memorized it. She wanted to contact the kid again, get her own feeling for him all over again. Mike would never sanction her having any contact with a suspect since she no longer worked for the PD.

Mike moved to take the background paperwork from her and put everything away. "It doesn't make sense. Maybe he's not the guy who set the bomb. But for some odd reason he handled those bullets. He could lead us to the shooter."

"Then again, it wouldn't be the first time a weirdo acted out because he was rejected." Jodie said the words without conviction. How would a little misfit like Collins have managed to take out her whole team and then disappear?

"If you think of anything, let us know," Tara said as she and Mike made their way out.

When the door shut behind them, Jodie uncovered her whiteboard and wrote down Collins's address before she forgot it. It was in Lakewood, an area bordering East Long Beach, about twenty minutes away from where she lived. She holstered her concealed carry weapon, and then, almost as an afterthought, she shoved her old city ID card into her pocket. It wouldn't hurt to take it, and like the gun, she might need it.

If Dennis Marshall Collins was her man, then Jodie planned on getting justice sooner than later.

CHAPTER 18

SAM HAD BEEN WORKING DILIGENTLY since he'd gotten the name Dennis Collins, digging up as much information as he could about the man. He'd discovered something new in real estate records.

"I found out information not in the background packet," he told Smiley. "Collins sold the family home and moved from Lakewood to Long Beach a year ago, about a month after his rejection."

"Really?"

"According to public records. However, he never changed his mailing address on anything I can find, and he didn't update his address with the DMV."

"Oversight?"

"Maybe."

Smiley and Sam were preparing for the ninety-minute drive to Long Beach to interview Collins. Smiley had called Tara Corson to give her a heads-up. From what Sam heard of Smiley's side of the conversation, Corson was trying to talk him out of pouncing on Collins so soon. Smiley argued he wasn't pouncing. He wanted to feel Collins out. He was convinced that if the kid was involved—and in Smiley's mind, it was a big if—he could lead them to bigger fish.

"I just want to talk to the guy, face-to-face, in a low-key manner. At his home so he feels comfortable, not threatened," Smiley told Corson on the phone while Sam listened. He'd already contacted Collins's place of business. The boss said Collins was working from home.

Sam didn't completely agree with Smiley's approach. He wanted as much intel as possible on Collins first. But he wasn't in charge, and Smiley had been working the case a lot longer than he had. It was also Smiley's style. He read people well and had a reputation for getting information out of the toughest suspects. It made sense for Smiley to want to hear what Collins would say when asked specific questions.

Corson also wanted to be with them when they talked to Collins, but Smiley nixed her suggestion.

"Too many cooks," he said. "Both the IED and the shooting occurred in our jurisdiction. I don't want to pull rank. I'm just giving you a courtesy call really. I'll text you when we're at the house."

They left the station, Sam running a finger around his collar, not really used to the shirt and tie.

"I'm spitballing here," Smiley said as they reached the parking lot. "Nothing about this case makes sense. But in a world where kids can be killed for sneakers, what if Collins was mad he didn't get hired and is acting out?" His phone rang and he stopped to answer it.

Acting out? Sam thought about the phrase. It said a lot and nothing at the same time. The IED blast had killed four good, solid cops—nothing "acting" about it. Did this guy have the wherewithal to do such a thing?

Smiley finished his conversation, telling his wife he wasn't sure when he'd be home.

"How do you want to do this?" Sam asked as Smiley directed the car to the freeway.

"Start off gentle. Just get a feel for the kid. Pin him down about how his prints could have ended up on those bullets."

"I'd like to hear an excuse for the fingerprints."

"Me too."

This tactic was Police Work 101. A cop always wanted to get a suspect to commit, make a statement that contradicted the facts. Once that happened, a good interviewer could usually force errors and incriminating remarks. If the suspect lied and, later in the investigation, tried to change his story, they had leverage; pressure could be applied. If Collins wasn't involved in the shooting, he should have a plausible reason for handling the bullets.

"If Collins is our guy, what are the chances he's working alone?" Sam asked.

"Good question. The Feds considered the operation a one-man show. I'm on the fence. What says the bomb guy?"

"I lean toward more than one. Which opens up a whole can of worms. The Feds couldn't see past Hayes."

"They were frustrated. And anyone can get tunnel vision."

Sam waited a moment; he could sense Smiley had more to say. "Anything else on your mind?"

"A little off topic. Are you sure your head is in the game? Doc Roe is concerned. He called me earlier."

Sam took a deep breath, irritated Doc Roe would say anything at all to Smiley.

"I'm fine, Bruce. Roe was never a cop. He can't truly relate to me or what I've been through."

Smiley turned; Sam could feel his eyes on him for a few seconds before he focused back on the road. "Yeah, I guess I can agree with you. But, Sam, I hope you know and believe, nobody blames you for Rick's death. There wasn't anything you could have done."

Nothing I could have done.

"I hear you."

"Good. Glad you're on the team. Everything from here on out is on topic."

Sam stayed quiet for the rest of the ride, but his mind was active and questioning. Ever since he'd read the file on the IED and Jodie's team, there was one big "how" no one had answered to his satisfaction: How did the killer know the time and day her team would be serving the warrant? Or who they were serving the warrant on? Only cops knew those details. Sam hadn't seen any indication of a dirty cop. The only bit different from other warrant services was the reliance on Jukebox, Jodie's CI. He'd fed Jodie a lot of information on Hayes, some of which ended up in the warrant paperwork.

Yet from what Smiley had heard from Mike King, Jodie recently learned about a cryptic text from Jukebox, who indicated everything was a setup. He hadn't been able to reach Jodie to warn her in time. Sam could only imagine how the news affected Jodie.

Oh, Lord, he prayed, *I know Jodie is hurting. Please ease her spirit.*

The irony didn't escape Sam. It wasn't Jodie's fault her team was murdered; there was nothing she could have done to prevent it. Yet when it came to what happened to Rick, though Smiley and others kept telling him he was not to blame, he couldn't believe it, not completely. Sometimes the guilt felt like a weight on his soul. How on earth did Jodie function feeling the same kind of guilt times four—five now?

CHAPTER 19

THE ADDRESS FOR DENNIS COLLINS Jodie copied was in a residential section of Lakewood, just over the border of Long Beach on a street called Adenmoor Avenue. From Seal Beach Jodie made her way to Bellflower Boulevard, which ran through Long Beach and into Lakewood. Crossing over Carson Street in the east part of the city put her in Lakewood. A few blocks after entering the city, Jodie turned onto Centralia and then onto Adenmoor.

A planned city, Lakewood had been built in the 1950s, cookie-cutter homes for growing post-WWII families. Jodie drove through a cozy residential neighborhood, with mature trees and neatly kept yards. It was a pleasant Tuesday afternoon. Kids had probably just gotten home from school; several were playing basketball in a driveway. There was a man mowing the yard at Collins's address. Not Collins. A gardener maybe?

She parked and sat for a moment, realizing how far over the line she was about to step. Even if she were still in uniform, she would not be investigating the IED or the CHP shooting. If Mike discovered her stepping out like this, and she were still employed, a suspension would not be out of the realm of possibility. As a private citizen she wasn't certain what the penalty would be.

Still . . . whatever the penalty was would be worth it if she caught the person responsible for so much bloodshed. In for a penny, in for a pound.

Jodie got out of the car about the same time the man stopped to empty the lawn mower bag.

"Excuse me," she called out.

He turned toward her. "Yes?"

"Sorry to bother you, but I'm looking for Dennis. Is he home?"

The man pulled a rag from his pocket and mopped his forehead. "He doesn't live here anymore. We bought this house from him a year ago."

Taken aback, Jodie scrambled. "Oh, um, would you happen to have a forwarding address?"

"Who are you?"

She'd have to tell a white lie and hope he swallowed it. "Sorry, I'm Sergeant King, Long Beach PD. Dennis applied to be an officer. I interviewed him."

"Interviewed him for the PD? No kidding."

"No, uh, yes. I'm simply following up."

He hesitated for a moment. "You have ID?"

Jodie pulled out her expired city ID and hoped the man didn't look too closely.

He glanced at it and said, "I thought you looked familiar. You've been on the news a lot. Give me a second. I'll get the address for you." He fiddled with the mower, then stopped. Jodie feared her ruse had failed. But he said, "The guy never put in a forwarding address with the post office. We're always sending him his mail. He doesn't get a lot, but I do have a few pieces now. Can I give you the latest packet?"

"Uh, certainly. I'll get it to him. Thanks."

He shoved the rag back in his pocket and left the lawn mower to go into his house. A few minutes later he returned with a full manila envelope addressed to Collins.

"He didn't move far."

Jodie took the item. "Thanks again."

"I don't know about you, but I'm old-school. I saw Collins once; he didn't really seem to be police officer material. He was kind of small."

"We're an equal opportunity employer."

She left for her car, not checking the address until she sat behind the wheel. When she did read it, she froze. She reread the address three times. One year ago, Dennis Collins had moved from Lakewood to Long Beach and now lived three doors down from Gus Perkins's house.

Jodie didn't need directions to his new neighborhood. Before she'd lost her team, she'd visited Gus's house often. In her mind, Dennis Collins became a more viable suspect.

If Gus knew the guy, Jodie couldn't remember him ever saying the name. At a stop sign she stayed motionless, racking her memory for every conversation she had with Gus before his death. His favorite topic of conversation was his impending retirement. He and Estella, his wife, were planning on selling and moving to Arizona.

A honk sounded behind her and Jodie shoved the envelope into her backpack and hit the gas.

Gus had raised his family in East Long Beach, on the other side of Carson Street. Besides being friends with Gus and visiting his house often, Jodie had worked patrol in East Long Beach both as an officer and a sergeant. Collins's and Gus's addresses were on Chatwin Avenue, another quiet residential street. In truth, it was difficult on the surface to tell where Lakewood ended and Long Beach began. The residential streets were much the same.

As she cruised toward the Perkins house, she passed the Collins place. She'd never noticed it before, and she'd been to Gus's house often. It was unremarkable, even plain, appearing vacant. There were no cars in the driveway and the blinds were closed. The yard was neatly maintained. A year ago, according to his background paperwork, Collins was single and lived alone.

Jodie decided she'd talk to Estella first and continued down to Gus's house. Estella's car was in the driveway, along with a second car. Jodie groaned. It belonged to Gus's son, Levi. She was loath to face the whole family, loath to stand before them guilty of killing Gus. But she had no choice. Estella certainly knew her neighbors. She would bring welcome gifts, food if you were sick, and she paid attention to what went on in the neighborhood. Estella's read on Collins would tell Jodie a lot. If Collins was their man, she wanted to know ASAP.

She parked and got out of the car. Estella had a very strong faith, much stronger than Jodie's. Gus had been the same way. Jodie stopped and looked up. She'd been praying and hearing nothing. Right now she needed help and there was only one place she could go, even with the silence.

Please help me to get through this, to not see Gus at every corner.
She continued to the front door.
Levi answered and surprise showed in his face. "Hi, uh, Jodie."

He used to look a lot like Gus, but when Levi developed a receding hairline, he'd opted to shave his head and grow a beard, covering up the resemblance. She could still see Gus in Levi's eyes.

Jodie swallowed, willing her voice to stay level. "Hey, Levi, how are you doing?"

"Okay, I guess. Helping my mom pack." He kept the door partly closed, seemingly eyeing Jodie warily. Jodie knew there were dogs in the house, so she tried not to take it personally.

From inside the house Jodie heard Estella call out, "Who's at the door, Levi?"

He turned. "It's Jodie, Ma."

The door jerked from Levi's hand and opened wide. Estella appeared. She held a small dog in her arms, and at her feet were three more. They were stray dogs Gus had brought home. He always had a heart for strays.

"Jodie!" Estella stepped out, and before Jodie could protest, the older woman pulled her into a tight hug, the dog off to the side. "It's good to see you. I've missed you," she whispered in Jodie's ear.

Throat thick, Jodie had no choice but to return the hug, realizing she had missed Estella. How she wished Gus were here as well.

When Estella let go, she sniffled and looked Jodie in the eye. "I haven't seen you at church in so long. I saw what happened over the weekend on the news. Jodie, what is going on?"

She swallowed a lump. "I don't know. I wish I did, but I don't."

For a minute Estella just looked at Jodie. Jodie felt tight in the chest, claustrophobic almost, but stayed still.

"I'm glad you stopped by," Estella said finally. "I've wanted to call you for days. We haven't talked since the celebration of life. It's just been crazy." She looped her arm in Jodie's. "Come on in. I've got some coffee on."

The tension in her body left and Jodie almost smiled. Gus and Estella always liked their afternoon cup. It never kept either of them awake, or so Gus always claimed. Estella put the dog down and walked Jodie into the house, the dogs at their heels. One mutt caught her eye. Gus had acquired him a couple of searches ago, a stray in a drug house. He'd wanted Jodie to take the dog, but pets weren't allowed in her apartment complex. She remembered his name: Macnut. Gus said the dog was the color of a macadamia nut, hence the name. The little guy looked up at her with the sweetest brown eyes. Jodie wanted to scoop him up and cuddle him. There was something calming in petting a dog.

All around the house Jodie saw evidence of Estella's upcoming move. There were boxes everywhere, but it didn't appear as if they'd started packing in the kitchen yet.

"I just brewed this pot," Estella said as Levi followed them into the kitchen.

He put two cups on the counter, then left the room.

"Still black?" Estella asked.

Jodie nodded and took the cup, glad for something to steady her nerves. "Thanks, but I didn't want to put you to any trouble." When she sat, Macnut put his head on her thigh, and she scratched between his ears.

"No trouble. Like I said, I've missed you, my friend. Why haven't you been at church?"

The question was asked without any acrimony, but Jodie couldn't look Estella in the eye.

She shrugged. "I've been to church."

"You come late and leave early," Estella said matter-of-factly, without accusation.

"It's just hard." Jodie swallowed before her voice broke.

"Because Gus and Tony aren't around?" Estella put her hand on Jodie's. "God is still around."

Jodie forced a half smile, determined not to break down. Being here in this kitchen brought back so many memories, each one stabbing at her heart like a dagger.

"Can we change the subject? I came here to ask you something." The words came out sharper than she intended, but Estella didn't seem to notice.

"Of course. What's going on with you?"

Jodie took a sip of coffee, then set the cup down, trying to frame the question the right way. "I was wondering about a neighbor of yours, down the street a couple of doors. Dennis Collins."

Estella frowned. "I don't recognize the name. And I know all my neighbors. Which house?"

Jodie recited the numbers.

"Kent lives there. I don't know his last name. Kent was best buds with Gus. He helped out a lot over here."

The hairs on the back of Jodie's neck stood up. Dennis had lied about his name.

"Kent. Did you like him?"

"I think I only ever said a couple of words to him. He was shy around women, at least Gus said so. Gus felt sorry for him. You know Gus and strays. He thought the guy needed male guidance. Why are you asking?"

"His name came up in the investigation. I don't think it's anything. He applied to be a cop at one time. I just thought I'd ask if you knew him." She tried to sound nonchalant and drank more coffee.

"A cop? Not Kent." She waved her hand dismissively. "You're mistaken. He's too timid. Though he was a big help to Gus in fixing things. He was good with technology. He's been gone for a few days now."

"He moved?"

"No, but he had to go back east to take care of his sick mother. Been gone, uh—" Estella looked up and tapped on her chin—"since Thursday or Friday. You know the days all run together. He asked his next-door neighbor to keep an eye on the house."

"Hmm" was all Jodie said. On the background packet he'd listed his parents as deceased. She sipped her coffee again and changed the subject. "You're getting ready to leave?"

Estella nodded and looked around at the mess. "Yes, I am. Slowly. We started the process before . . ." Her voice trailed off. "Anyway, the house in Arizona will be finished in a month. I didn't want to cancel. I'm moving on with the plans we made. Gus and I. Levi has been a big help."

"I'm glad to hear it." Jodie swallowed more coffee and stood. "I'm sorry to have interrupted."

"Oh, Jodie, you're never an interruption. I hope you'll come spend some time with me before I go."

Jodie managed a weak nod. When she moved away from the table, Macnut jumped up and pawed at her thigh.

"Oh, Mackie, you know better," Estella said, and the dog got down, but he stayed close to Jodie.

"I know Gus saved him," Estella said as she walked her to the door, "but Mackie has always loved you." She stopped at the door. "Can I pray for you?" she asked.

Jodie's voice caught in her throat, rendering her unable to speak.

Estella took her hand in both of hers and began to pray. "Oh, Lord, I lift up my friend to you. She's still hurting—her pain is obvious—and I pray you will comfort her. Heal her heart. Most of all, show her in some way that Gus would never blame her for what happened. Amen."

Before Jodie could bolt, Estella gripped her in a tight hug, tears rolling down her face.

"Gus would never blame you," she sobbed in Jodie's ear.

Jodie broke. It was all she could do to push Estella away and stumble off the porch to hurry toward her car, wiping at the tears streaming down her face. She climbed into the driver's seat and sat there for a minute, pulling herself together, wondering if she would ever believe those words.

Blame.

The blame most certainly belonged to her. She. Was. In. Charge.

CHAPTER 20

ONCE BACK IN CONTROL, Jodie got out of her car, leaving it parked at Estella's, and walked to Dennis Collins's address. She was tired, emotionally drained with zero patience. A certainty brewed in her chest that the darkness in her life would lift only when Collins was dead. A similar realization also blazed in her thoughts—she was way over the line now. The prudent thing to do would be to call Mike or Tara or Smiley or Sam and step back, let them do their jobs. But she couldn't. Instead, she increased her pace.

Jodie knocked on the front door and got no response. After a few minutes she backed off the porch.

"He's not home."

Jodie turned. A man in the next yard stood watching her. Estella had said "Kent" asked the neighbor to watch the house.

"Got it," Jodie said. "Do you know where he is?"

"Are you a relative?"

"Cousin," Jodie lied, a bit chagrined at how easily they seemed to fall off her lips today. "I just got into town and thought I'd look Dennis up."

The neighbor stepped over a small hedge. "You call him by his first name?"

"Yeah, always."

"He hates Dennis. We always called him Kent, his middle name."

Hmm, Jodie thought, *one mystery solved.* "Do you know where he is?"

"He said he was going back east to take care of his mother, your aunt?"

"My father is his dad's brother. I guess I'm out of the loop. Maybe I'll leave him a note."

The man folded his arms and frowned. Jodie was afraid he didn't believe her.

"Could you do me a favor first?"

"Sure, what?"

Now he looked ill at ease. "Well, I know Kent left—I saw him drive away and he asked me to watch his house, but . . ."

"But what?"

He motioned toward his backyard. "Let me show you."

Jodie followed the man over the small hedge and then through the back gate. She hadn't gone far when she smelled an unmistakable odor.

"You smell something?" the man asked.

"I do."

"It's coming from his house. I don't think he had any pets, but something large has died in there. Maybe a stray dog?"

"How long have you smelled this?"

"Just started yesterday. I almost called the cops, but I'd be embarrassed if it were just a stray animal. Is there any way you can check and see what's happening? Maybe call Kent?"

"I can. But you know, he often left a key under a flowerpot in the back. I'll go have a look around." Surprised again at how easily the lies came, Jodie hoped there were flowerpots in the backyard.

"Thank you. It's unpleasant to be in my backyard. Every time a breeze comes up, so does the odor."

"I'll bet," Jodie said as she left the neighbor's yard and stepped back over the hedge.

Collins's backyard gate was on the other side of his house. Jodie walked across the front yard and, happy to find the gate unlocked, let herself into the back. Once inside, she drew her handgun and followed a narrow concrete path. The further she traveled across the yard, the stronger the odor became. The stench emanated from a rear bedroom, she guessed, the unmistakable aroma of death. Jodie slowly walked to the other side of the house, where the odor was strongest. The windows facing the complaining homeowner were open. Collins obviously didn't fear break-ins.

The logical thing to do was call the police and have them do a "check the well." But Jodie wasn't about to wait for a police officer. She made her way to the back door. Sadly, there were no flowerpots. She turned over a couple of stones. No key. Collins wouldn't make it easy.

Confident no one could see her, Jodie took her gun and smashed a small window next to the door. She winced at the noise and hoped no one heard. Then she reached through the break and opened the door.

Most of the houses in this neighborhood had similar floor plans. This one was no different from Gus's. The back door led to a laundry room and then to the kitchen. There would be two small bedrooms on the left, a small living room in front, and a larger bedroom on the right. The smell was overpowering inside the house, and Jodie tried to breathe through her mouth. She was well acquainted with the odor, but it was something you never got used to. At least she hadn't.

Weapon in hand, she tiptoed past the kitchen, aiming for the door on the left where the offending aroma seemed to be emanating from. She opened the bedroom door, pinched her nose closed with her thumb and forefinger, and stepped one foot into the room. What she saw made no sense.

With the open windows and daylight, she could see a large rectangular freezer in the center of the room. No bed, no dresser, just the freezer. No sound of a motor, so it obviously wasn't running. The lid stood open, and Jodie guessed this was the source of the smell.

Could it simply be rotting food? A lot of it, by the size of the freezer. Jodie had to be sure. She stepped into the room and peered into the freezer. A bloated, discolored human face stared back at her.

"Uggh." She put a hand over her mouth and left the room, closing the door behind her.

Who was it? The neighbor said he saw Collins leave. Jodie doubted the body was him. Eyes watering from the odor, she stood still, wanting to investigate further but also recognizing she could possibly contaminate evidence. In the end, the obedient side of her nature won.

Jodie was caught now. She had to call the PD and face Mike's wrath for breaking into the house. Her only saving grace here was the improbability of Collins pressing charges against her.

She walked through the living room into the kitchen, intending to use her phone where it would be easier to breathe. When she reached the middle of the kitchen, she stepped on a soft part of the floor and heard a click. Not as loud, but the same kind of click she'd heard in the mountain cabin the day the IED exploded and killed her team.

CHAPTER 21

BY THE TIME THEY REACHED LONG BEACH, Sam's stomach was growling. It made him think of an old-school cop he'd met during his rookie days. *"A good cop never gets wet or goes hungry,"* the seasoned officer had told him.

Sam had been rained on and missed many meals working in law enforcement. He wished he could run into the old-school guy again so he could tell the man he was wrong.

He probably should have eaten a bigger lunch. Besides hunger, the hour-and-a-half drive had him stiff and wanting to stretch, especially his right arm and shoulder. Ever since the accident, he stiffened up quickly.

When they reached Chatwin Avenue, Sam was ready to get out of the car. He shifted in his seat and checked the GPS when they finally exited the freeway.

"Collins didn't move very far away. His old house on Adenmoor is probably less than a mile away from the new one on Chatwin."

"He moved from Lakewood to Long Beach," Smiley said. "I wonder why. From what I've seen, this neighborhood is similar to Lakewood. He certainly didn't move for new scenery."

What Smiley said was true. But Sam liked the neighborhood. It looked calm, safe. A family neighborhood, not unlike where Sam used to live in Redlands. Kids were playing in yards and driveways; people were washing cars, mowing lawns. He would have stayed in Redlands if Vanessa hadn't called everything off. When they got engaged, they agreed that the neighborhood in Redlands would be a perfect place to raise kids. After the crash and losing Vanessa, Sam saw no reason to stay and was glad he'd moved back to the mountains.

The afternoon weather was pleasant for spring. Still getting used to the suit and tie, Sam ran his finger around the collar and loosened his tie a bit. He'd really wanted to be back in uniform. But now, being a part of this investigation, Sam decided he'd be fine getting used to suits.

He almost smiled when he heard his mother's voice in his head: *God works in mysterious ways.* But then the smile died. He was here because Rick was gone.

Why did the crash have to happen?

Smiley stopped the car and Sam shook his head to bring himself back to the present. He got out of the car first and automatically surveyed the area, his eyes resting on a familiar vehicle. He was almost certain it belonged to Jodie. He'd sat in her front seat for a few minutes while they were in the mountains. But he could be wrong; it was a popular-style SUV. He wrestled with what to say to Smiley.

"That SUV looks like King's car," he said.

Smiley followed his gaze. "You sure?"

"Not 100 percent. But it's close."

"Do you know where she lives?"

"Exactly? No, I don't. But if she lives here, and Collins moved here . . . creepy."

"True. Hmph. I'll give LBPD a call, let them know we've arrived," Smiley said. "I'm calling Mike King. He'll know if it's her car and where she lives."

Sam said nothing. He had a bad feeling it was Jodie's car. Jodie wanted to find the killer more than anything. She could have gotten the address the same way he did. Why was she here? He considered logical reasons and didn't like any of them because they all involved confronting a possible suspect. Sam hoped Collins wasn't their guy. *Oh, Lord,* he prayed, *I hope Jodie didn't get more than she bargained for.*

"Mike King is on his way," Smiley said after he ended the call. "Jodie doesn't live here but according to him, the plate says the car belongs to her. I'll tell you who used to live in this neighborhood." He pointed to the house Jodie's car was parked in front of. "Gus Perkins."

"A member of her team?"

Smiley nodded.

"Wow, this is not good." Sam felt a heavy foreboding deep in his soul.

"Any suggestions on how to proceed?"

"King didn't want us to wait for him, did he?"

"No."

Sam peered at the house. "I don't see Jo—King. In fact, it doesn't look like anyone's home."

"Yeah, yet her car is still here."

Sam nodded. "She could be at Gus's house."

"I hope she is. I think we need to contact Mr. Collins."

"Let's go."

Together they walked toward the house. Sam noticed the man next door watching them as they walked up to the front door and knocked. There was no response. When they stepped back to check the windows for any kind of reaction, the man who'd been watching approached them.

"His cousin just went into the backyard looking for a key."

"His cousin?" Smiley asked.

"Yeah, just a couple of minutes ago. Who are you?"

"San Bernardino County Sheriff." Smiley held out his badge. "We wanted to speak to Mr. Collins."

"He's gone back east. Like I said, his cousin just went around back to check out a smell coming from the house. She must have gotten inside because she never returned." He started to walk around toward the gate.

Sam stopped him, all his cop instincts on high alert. "Don't bother. We'll check on her. Can you describe her?"

"Tall, blonde. She said Kent often left a key under a flowerpot."

Kent.

Sam and Smiley exchanged a glance.

"We'll handle this," Smiley said. "Thanks for your help."

"Of course." The man nodded and went back to his yard.

Sam led the way through the gate, drawing his weapon once he was in the yard.

"Collins have a cousin?" Smiley asked.

"None noted in anything I read," Sam responded, wondering what in the world Jodie King had found.

They reached the back door and saw the broken glass. The door was ajar. Sam moved forward and pushed the door open.

"Hello? San Bernardino SD. Anyone there?"

"Stay back! Get out of here!"

The panicked yell pierced Sam. It was Jodie. He disregarded the warning and kept moving forward.

She came into view, standing in the kitchen, both hands up, as if she wanted to push him out of the house, eyes wide with fear.

"Please. Get out! The floor clicked. *Please!* I don't want to kill anyone else."

Their eyes locked. Sam knew immediately what she was saying. She'd walked into a death trap, and they had followed.

CHAPTER 22

JODIE HAD NEARLY JUMPED OFF THE FLOOR when the first knock banged on the door. Torn, she first feared it was the neighbor, checking up on her progress. She didn't want him coming around to the back. But she couldn't stand on this spot forever. Someone had to be told where she was and what was up. She had her phone, but she couldn't bring herself to dial 911. What a conundrum—she needed to tell someone she was here, but anyone who came here might die with her.

Sweat beaded on her forehead. Terror had her heart pounding. *What can I do?*

She pictured all the people who'd been out and about in the neighborhood when she drove through. How many would die if the house exploded? Closing her eyes, fists in tight balls, she prayed. Though lately she didn't believe God heard her anymore, it was all she could grab on to.

You never listen to me anymore, but please, please, don't let anyone else die because of me. Please. Not again.

The knocking stopped and she held her breath. But then she heard the footsteps, feet crushing broken glass. A voice she recognized called out.

When Sam stepped into view, fear ratcheted up.

"I don't want to kill you, Sam. I don't want to kill anyone. Please just leave. Evacuate people, please." Her body shook with panic.

Sam held her eyes, his gaze soothing in the electricity of the moment. "Jodie, calm down. You haven't killed anyone and you're not going to start now."

His voice penetrated her panic, and she took a deep breath. "I heard the click. I know I'm standing on something bad."

"If you are, it's your lucky day. I am familiar with every kind of explosive device known to man. I can fix this." He holstered his weapon. "Now, calmly and carefully, tell me everything that happened once you walked into this house."

His voice, his confident manner, worked to steady Jodie. She told him in a measured tone what she'd done since breaking the back window.

When she finished, he told Smiley to call the PD and explain the situation.

"Should you be in here?" Smiley asked.

"Yes" was all Sam said; then he turned back to Jodie. "You felt the floor give?"

"Yeah, it sank a little."

"Do you see any wires? I don't from here."

Jodie looked all around the floor as carefully as she dared, cognizant of Sam watching her.

"No, I don't."

* * *

Sam looked around the room for himself, mind churning with IED building methods and remembering the device in the mountains. The FBI had reconstructed the device and determined how it had been set. It had been in the kitchen, in the stove and nearby cabinets. The bomber had replaced part of a floorboard with the trigger switch. The trigger switch cut the gas line when Gus stepped on it, and as soon as Gus lifted his foot, a spark ignited the gas. The first explosion ignited two more propane tanks, ensuring the blast would be deadly to anyone in the house.

Sam looked for any visible indications, anything to give him a clue about this device. He saw nothing except that this kitchen was all electric—no gas line here.

"How long do you think you've been here?"

"Maybe fifteen, twenty minutes."

The floor was a solid piece of linoleum. Jodie had been standing on the switch for at least fifteen minutes. He felt his own panic starting, knowing they didn't have much time. But he couldn't rush; he couldn't give in to the panic.

Lord, guide my steps, he prayed silently.

"These houses have crawl spaces under the floor?"

She nodded. "As far as I know."

"And you walked down the hall and entered the kitchen from the other door." He pointed.

"Yes."

"Okay. I'm coming toward you to give you something."

"Are you sure it's safe?" Panic started to rise in her voice again.

"Trust me, Jodie. I'm betting he cut the floor joist to place the switch. Me coming around the way you already walked is not going to change anything."

Sam walked down the hall, holding his breath against the smell of death.

"You saw bodies in there?" he asked, trying to put her mind in cop mode. He stopped at a spot where he could hold out his arm and hand Jodie something. She would have to reach as well but not far. He didn't want to interrupt the pressure on the switch.

"Yeah. At least one, in a freezer." Her voice steadied.

"A freezer?" Sam frowned.

"Yep, a big one."

"Wow," he said as he pulled a booklet out of his pocket and held it out for Jodie. "Take this." He carried it with him everywhere.

She took it from his hand, read the cover. "Psalms? Sam, I don't get answers anymore."

"Jodie, I don't need answers. I need you to be calm and steady. I want you to have something to read, to calm you down, give you peace. I'm going under the house to defuse this thing. You need to stay still. Don't shift your weight."

He saw her chest swell; a tear fell down one cheek. Voice shaking again, she said, "I don't want to be responsible for your death."

"Stop. I know what I'm doing. Trust me."

She clutched the booklet to her chest. "I don't have a choice. You're my only hope."

"I'm *a* hope. Read Psalm 46. It's my favorite. And I'll want the book back when I'm finished." He turned and went out the back door.

Smiley was waiting for him. "LBPD wants you to back off.

Mike King is here with a black-and-white. They are already evacuating the houses on either side. A bomb squad will arrive in twenty minutes."

"Not sure we have twenty minutes," Sam hissed, voice low. "I've got a bad feeling about this thing. I can't explain it any better." He undid his tie and jerked it from his neck. Then he took off his coat and laid them both on a hose reel.

"If this is the same type of device as in the mountains, Jodie staying still has kept it from detonating. But my guess is this guy wouldn't stop there. She could have set off a delay timer. Who knows how long Collins set the delay for?" He unbuttoned his cuffs and rolled up his sleeves, then turned to look for the crawl space opening.

"Sam." Smiley grabbed his arm. "I could order you back."

"You could, and I'd disobey. Look, I know this stuff. I can stop it. Get back if you don't believe me. But I'm not going to let Jodie blow up. I'm not." He stared at Smiley.

Finally his boss released his arm and looked away. "Okay, how can I help?"

"Help me find the crawl space."

In short order they found a small hatch over the opening to the crawl space. It was obvious someone had been in and out of it often, and there was even a tool kit just inside.

"Nice of him to leave this here," Sam said when he poked his head in. He removed a set of wire clippers from the kit and shoved them into his pocket.

"He probably didn't expect anyone to be poking around here," Smiley said, eyeing the opening. "Can you fit?"

"It will be tight. You might have to drag me back out by my ankles."

He flipped on his small flashlight, got down on his knees, and slid into the opening. The space was tight. Collins was quite a bit smaller than Sam. The flashlight illuminated dirt, spiderwebs, and the support structure of the home. Sam shone it in the direction of the kitchen and soon found what he was looking for: a mound of what looked like C-4.

He blew out a breath, wondering how on earth Collins got his hands on so much. He fought his own rising fear, knowing what a mass of explosives like this could do. All the surrounding houses were in danger. Gritting his teeth, he concentrated on the task at hand. He couldn't afford to be distracted. He had to keep his mind clear and calm, or he would make a mistake. He'd trained for this.

He moved toward it, pushing through the dirt with his elbows, certainly destroying his new shirt, and maybe his pants, to look for the detonator. IEDs were made up of four parts. He remembered the simple acronym PIES: power supply, initiator, explosive, and switch. The initiator was what caused the explosion and the switch set off the initiator. His mind centered on defeating the IED. He had to interfere with the initiating mechanism.

Suddenly thoughts of Rick took over, and it felt as if he couldn't breathe. Sweat rolled between his shoulder blades, and he began to shake. A voice rang in his head: *You let your partner die. Now this woman will die and it's all your fault.*

He froze for an instant, paralyzed by fear. What if he were responsible for more deaths? Then he forced a breath, which caused a puff of dust to rise from the crawl space floor. *Is this what Doc Roe was really afraid of? That I'll freeze and get more people killed?*

"No, no, no," Sam repeated over and over in a harsh whisper. Then he cried out in a stressed voice, "*Lord, I need you. I can't do this on my own.*"

A phrase rang out in his panicked thoughts.

"Be still, and know that I am God."

He clung to those eight words, willing them to drown out the doubt and the fear. More deep breaths and slowly the shaking eased. He began to move again, pushing himself forward with his elbows and knees, this time shutting out all but the IED in front of him and the need to render it safe.

The explosive was piled up under the kitchen floor. When he reached the perimeter of the device, he surveyed every inch with his light. Then he saw the timer. Fifty seconds left—49, 48 . . .

Yanking the wire cutters from his pocket, he scrambled for the wires attached to the battery. Defusing a bomb was disconnecting the explosive from the ignition source.

"Oh, Lord," he prayed under his breath, "with your help, all my training has to count for something." He prayed Collins hadn't gotten tricky with the device.

Sweat ran down his face into his eyes, and he wiped at it with the back of his hand. The device was not nearly as complex as the one in the mountains had been. Sam guessed it was because Collins had taken more time with the first one. This one looked more hastily put together, basic.

He studied it for as long as he dared, then clipped several wires, carefully pulling the detonator away from the C-4. The timer clicked down to 0 and nothing happened.

Sam released a whoosh of air. For a moment, he rested his head on his forearm and breathed, smelling the musty dirt of the crawl space, thanking God nothing had been overly sophisticated.

"Sam?" Smiley called from the opening. Worry tinged his voice.

"I'm coming out."

CHAPTER 23

JODIE FOUGHT HER FEAR, hating the shaking snaking through her every other minute.

Don't shift your weight.

Sam was gone and she'd heard him and Smiley talking. The shock of seeing him in the doorway almost sent her over the edge. But then she remembered what Mike had said about Sam and Smiley coming to talk to Collins. She'd ignored him, so focused was she on confronting Collins herself.

She looked at the small booklet he'd given her. A pocketbook of Psalms. It was well-worn and frayed; he'd obviously had it a while and opened it a lot. Inside the cover, she saw an inscription.

To a friend who sticks closer than a brother. Iron sharpens iron, buddy. Stay sharp.

Rick

His partner had given him the book. At one time it would have been a gift Jodie would have devoured happily. But now when she read the Psalms, nothing connected. There was a barrier between her and heaven. Any connection she'd felt before blew up in the mountains with her team. She fought the tears that threatened. The wall between her and God was impenetrable.

Was the wall on God's end or hers?

Sam obviously believed, despite what happened to him. More for Sam than for herself, Jodie opened the book to Psalm 46, not expecting the words to touch her as they had in the past.

Tears blurred her eyes. She squeezed them out, slowly focusing on the first line, then the second. As she read, the words seemed to kindle a fire in her chest. The last three verses battered the wall, letting light shine through in places.

"He makes wars cease to the end of the earth; he breaks the bow and shatters the spear; he burns the chariots with fire. 'Be still, and know that I am God. I will be exalted among the nations, I will be exalted in the earth!' The Lord of hosts is with us; the God of Jacob is our fortress."

Jodie closed the book, wishing she felt some revival in her soul. Tears fell, but not tears of illumination. She couldn't stop the tears, but while she cried, she prayed, imagining her prayers as rocks she flung at the wall. They hit and bounced off, but she just kept praying. She hated the idea that it was foxhole prayer, but it was all she had.

All the guilt over the loss of her team came roaring back. In her mind she again saw the image stalking her: Tiny, bloody, looking at her accusingly. *"You let us all down, Chief."*

Ian's glare. *"Why didn't you just wait?"*

The weight of grief and guilt made her knees waver.

When she heard the door open, she held her breath. Sam strode into the kitchen, covered in dirt and cobwebs.

He held up both thumbs. "We're good."

Relief rolled over Jodie like a tsunami. It was as if a two-ton weight of guilt pressing her down disappeared. Sam was safe. Maybe one stone had penetrated the wall and created a small crack. Jodie would take what she could get. She stepped forward and threw her arms around him, encircling his waist, burying her face in his shoulder, tears flowing. She felt Sam's arms slide around her, felt him pat her back, and heard him whisper, "You're safe. We're all safe. It will be okay."

For the first time in months, Jodie thought she could finally believe those words.

CHAPTER 24

WHEN SAM, JODIE, AND SMILEY walked around to the front of the house, police cars were everywhere, projecting a strong presence on the block. Gone was the tranquil neighborhood Sam and Smiley had driven into. The houses on either side of Collins's house and the ones directly in front and behind were either evacuated or in the process of being evacuated. Police tape was strung around the perimeter; black-and-white police cars blocking the street served as anchors for some of the tape. Crowds gathered on the boundaries.

Sam wondered when the press would arrive. As if reading his mind, a news chopper flew overhead.

Down the street he saw a large black motor home with flashing lights on top and guessed it was the command post vehicle.

"Bomb squad isn't here yet," Jodie said.

From the perimeter near the big motor home, a man yelled, "Jodie!"

Everyone turned.

"That's Uncle Mike," Jodie said.

"Well, let's go talk to him," Smiley said.

Sam followed, adrenaline rush dissipating fast. He was tired, hungry, and for the first time in months he felt whole again. He'd faced a demon and conquered it. Somewhere in the battle to force himself to defuse the IED, it pinged in his brain: he had done all he could for Rick. The accident was not his fault. Rick's death wasn't his fault. A healing had started—he felt it.

The world looked new and different now. Sam was certain he could face anything.

Jodie slipped under the tape and her uncle grabbed her in a hug. Sam and Smiley slipped under as well.

When Mike let Jodie go, he faced Sam with fury in his eyes. "Just what do you think you were doing?"

"Excuse me?" Sam had to take a step back.

"You put this entire neighborhood at risk. Why didn't you wait for the bomb squad?"

"I made a judgment call—"

"You made a reckless, stupid, against-orders call."

"Hey, hey, enough," Smiley intervened. "You need to calm down."

"Don't tell me to calm down. He needlessly risked my niece's life. Your life. I'll file a formal complaint. You were told to stand down and wait."

"Stop it." Jodie stepped between Sam and her uncle. "He saved my life—again—and risked his own."

Mike put his hands on his hips and stared at Jodie. "You and

I have our own situation. You need to explain to me what you were doing here. You're not on the job anymore. You had no business being in Collins's house. As for him—" Mike directed his ire back to Sam—"I'll wait for the professionals to give me the situation report. But he clearly violated a direct order."

"Mike, please, calm down. Jodie is okay." An older woman had entered the fray.

Sam watched as she grasped Jodie around the waist with one arm while holding a small dog in the other.

"Estella, glad you're here," Jodie said. "I want you to meet someone." She turned to Sam. "This is Sam Gresham, San Bernardino County deputy." She pointedly glared at her uncle. "He's like a guardian angel for me."

"Nice to meet you, Sam." The woman released Jodie and shook Sam's hand. "I'm Estella Perkins."

Sam recognized the name and realized this must be Gus Perkins's widow. He started to say something when a large black vehicle with *LBPD Bomb Squad* emblazoned on the side pulled up. Right behind it was a news van, and with its arrival, chaos broke out.

■ ■ ■

Jodie let Estella drag her away from the activity and into her house. She didn't relish facing the press, not because she was afraid, but because she never liked dealing with the press. She also knew she'd eventually be held accountable for the lies she'd told this day.

A certain clarity returned to Jodie's mind after Sam saved her life for a second time. While she was glad to get away from her uncle's anger, it was justified. She had no business coming here, no business being in the house, and she felt shame for all the deception she'd used along the way.

Would her search for the bad guy and closure ever end? She realized Bass and Mike and Estella were telling her the truth when they insisted the IED was not her fault. Yet she still felt hollow, empty, and even more angry.

She'd done nothing wrong to provoke him—the bomb setter. No unknown sin of hers had led to the blast. There was no way she could have known or prepared for such an event. He'd set an IED at his own house to kill *anyone* who happened into the house.

All the clarity simply increased her anger.

Collins had taken her team, her friend Jukebox, her career, and very nearly her life. He was not going to take anything else.

"What is going on out there?" Levi asked.

Jodie sat on the couch with Macnut's head in her lap and told them what had happened in Collins's house.

"Who was the dead guy?" Levi asked.

"The coroner will have to tell us."

Levi looked at her with pain in his eyes. "Kent used my dad?"

"Appears so," Jodie said. "Your dad had a big heart."

"It got him killed."

Jodie sighed, feeling Levi's pain but not knowing how to alleviate it. "Maybe, Levi. But I knew your dad well, and I wouldn't change a thing about him. He was a good man."

Levi shook his head and left the room. Estella did what she always did when she was stressed and felt like people needed to be taken care of. She started to cook. Jodie tried to relax. Stroking the dog comforted her, but the events of the day swirled in her thoughts. She wanted to talk to Sam. But she wasn't ready to face her uncle. He'd be furious about what she'd done to get into Collins's house.

Someone knocked at the door, and she hoped it was Sam. Levi

answered the door. Tara. Jodie held her breath for the dressing-down to come.

"Hey, girlfriend—" Tara stopped, frowned. "What's wrong?"

"I'm fine. Are you here to tell me what trouble I'm in for breaking into Collins's house?"

Tara smiled. "Above my pay grade. To be honest, I might have done the same thing. Nope, I came to ask what in the world is going on?"

"I wish I knew."

Tara sat next to her, and Jodie told her what had happened.

"I can't believe it. So now we know this guy had a vendetta because he wasn't hired, huh?" Tara shook her head and leaned back against the couch. "To go through all this . . . Good thing he wasn't hired. What a nightmare he would've been in uniform."

Jodie said nothing. Something about Tara's explanation still made no sense to her. Even when she repeated the scenario in her mind—*Collins is rejected, so he sells his house, moves down the street from Gus, gets close to Gus, spends most of a year finding out all there is to know about what Jodie's team is doing, then blows them up*—it made no sense to her. Being dropped from the academy affected him, true, but it wouldn't affect anyone else the same way. He couldn't have done this all on his own. And she was bothered by a thought she couldn't shake: there had to be a cop helping him. Could he have gotten all the intel he had simply watching and talking to Gus?

"How are you holding up?" Tara asked, interrupting the horrible thought Jodie did not want to have and was not about to voice.

"I'm okay. Glad Sam Gresham was here."

Tara sat up. "Me too. I have to go meet this superhero." She stood. "You sure you're okay?"

Jodie nodded, wanting to say she was better than she had been in three months.

Estella poked her head out of the kitchen. "Tell him there's food here if he's hungry. I had a batch of lasagna in the fridge I'm heating up. It will be ready in a few minutes."

"I'll let him know," Tara said as she walked to the front door. "But he'll probably smell it as soon as I open the door. What a great aroma." She opened the door and was gone.

"I have to agree," Jodie said. "It smells awesome, and I'm starved."

CHAPTER 25

AFTER ESTELLA USHERED JODIE AWAY, Sam watched as the bomb squad sergeant took firm control of the situation, tasking Mike King with setting up a safe place for the arriving news crews. Darkness had fallen but you wouldn't know it in this section of the block. Police lighting had everything bright. Once the sergeant finished setting up a perimeter, he walked to where Sam and Smiley stood. The name on his utility jumpsuit read TJ Barstow.

After introductions were made, he said, "I run the bomb squad for Long Beach. And I worked hand in hand with the Feds on the IED investigation, so I'm up to speed on the situation. Right now, the two of you need to tell me what happened in that house." He faced Sam and Smiley.

Smiley deferred to Sam. He explained everything he'd seen and done.

"C-4? You're sure?"

"I was an explosives disposal technician in the Army—I'm sure."

"And it was wired?"

"I defused it."

Barstow raised an eyebrow and stared at Sam. The sound of a large diesel engine broke his concentration.

"That'll be the explosive disposal truck. I've got to get a team in there. Don't go far." He left Sam and Smiley to mobilize his team.

C-4 was generally very stable, so its removal shouldn't be a problem. The disposal team would still take extra precautions. The last thing anyone wanted was an explosion in a residential neighborhood because someone made a mistake.

"Looks like we'll be here for a while," Smiley said. "I'm calling our boss." He stepped away to phone headquarters.

Sam brushed off as much dirt and dust as he could from his clothes, noting a tear in the knee of his pants. Fatigue had now set in. It had been a long day, physically and emotionally. The last thing he wanted to do was fall asleep on the job. He leaned against the emergency response motor home and watched everyone go about their jobs. He prayed for everyone's safety.

He reviewed the investigation so far in his thoughts, concentrating on what was similar and what was different about the two IEDs. The one in the mountains had been incredibly complex, while the one here, incredibly simple. It was almost as if this one had been set up by another person.

Sam went still with the thought. Two killers instead of one would turn the investigation on its head. Especially if the second killer were a cop. He hated even thinking the thought, but everything pointed to someone with inside knowledge of law enforcement.

He decided to keep his thoughts to himself until Barstow made his observations. Barstow had studied what was left of the first device; he was the current expert.

Sam watched as Barstow and his team walked to Collins's house and went inside. Sam expected they would survey the crawl space and then decide upon the safest way to remove the explosive.

After about twenty minutes, Barstow emerged from the house and directed the explosive disposal van to enter the perimeter and park in Collins's driveway. He then strode over to where Sam was standing with Smiley. At the same time, Mike King walked over. Sam expected another dressing-down from Jodie's uncle, but it didn't come. The man still glared at Sam, but it appeared as if he just wanted to listen to what Barstow had to say.

"You took quite a chance, Gresham." The sergeant held Sam's gaze with his hardened cop stare. It bordered on respect, tinged with a touch of disbelief.

"Yes, sir. I figured it was the only chance we had at the time."

"Yeah, you figured right. Never thought I'd say I was happy to have someone disobey my order, but you certainly made the right call. If you would've waited, we wouldn't be having this conversation right now."

"Yes, sir."

"It appears as though we can remove all the explosive material without too much effort. It will take some time. You and Detective Smiley can wait in the response van if you want to hang around."

"Yeah, we want to see this through," Smiley said.

Sam just wanted to make sure Jodie was okay.

Barstow turned to King. "No one is allowed inside the

perimeter until we've cleared the house. As for the contents of the freezer, call the coroner and apprise him of the situation." Barstow left them, heading back to Collins's home.

Sam felt King watching him. When Sam turned to face him, the older cop said, "There's coffee in the response van." Then he walked toward the house Jodie had gone into.

Since he was ready for some coffee, and he wanted to sit down, Sam took King's advice and entered the response van. He saw a small bathroom off to the left and went in. In the mirror he noted his filthy appearance. He tried to wash off as much dirt as he could. His shirt was probably history, like the torn pants. At least the tie and coat survived. After cleaning up as best he could in the tight space, he went back to the conference room and inhaled one doughnut and contemplated a second. For the moment though, he sat in a comfortable chair and sipped his coffee. Coffee and doughnuts, fortifying cop food.

Smiley had followed him in. He ate two doughnuts and then sat, put his feet up, and closed his eyes. So much of police work was waiting.

Footsteps sounded and when Sam turned, he saw a woman approaching. A badge hung around her neck, so she must be one of the investigators.

"Sam Gresham, I presume?" the woman asked. She was short and stocky, with close-cropped dark hair and a serious expression.

Sam stood. "Yep."

"Tara Corson." She extended her hand.

Sam shook it. He recognized the name from the reports he'd read. She'd been part of the original task force. "Nice to meet you."

"I'm honored to meet you. You've saved my friend's life twice."

"How is Jodie?"

Corson cocked her head. "Jury is out. Are you hungry? Estella has invited everyone in for a meal—unless, of course, you'd like to continue to stuff your face with doughnuts."

"I am hungry . . ." He looked at Smiley.

"I am propelled by the doughnuts—for now," Smiley said with a smile. "You can go. We'll know where to find you if we need you."

"Can I ask you a question?" Sam said to Corson.

"Shoot."

"Is there any fallout from this? Is Jodie in trouble for breaking into the house?"

Corson shrugged. "Mike is irritated, sure, but who is the victim? Collins? I guess if we find him, and he wants to press charges for trespassing. There's little anyone else could do."

"I'm sure she knows she shouldn't have done it," Sam said. "But it's an odd conundrum. If she hadn't broken in, a lot more people could have died."

"The situation wasn't lost on me, so I'm sure it's not lost on Mike."

"Thanks."

"Go eat."

"You're not eating?"

"I just had lunch. I have to get to work."

Sam nodded and left her there. The desire to see Jodie and his own hunger—he didn't know which was stronger—had Sam hurrying up the street. A minute later he was at Estella's door.

A young man answered his knock.

"Hi, I'm looking for Jodie King."

"Are you Sam?"

"Yep."

"Come on in."

"Thanks." Sam walked through the door, his mouth watering as the smell of something wonderful coming from the kitchen assaulted his nose.

Sam saw Jodie first. She was seated at the table sipping a soda. He thought her eyes brightened a bit when she saw him—was he imagining things?

"Here comes my guardian angel." Jodie toasted Sam with the glass in her hand.

Sam felt his face burn. "Just doing what I was trained to do," he said.

"Well, thank you."

He smiled at Estella Perkins.

"Can I get you something to eat?" she asked.

"For sure."

Jodie pushed a bottle of water toward him. He opened the bottle and drank half of it down.

"Wow, you were a quart low."

Sam nodded. "Starved too. One doughnut didn't do it."

Estella put a plate in front of him heaped with a slice of delicious-smelling lasagna.

"Wow, this looks way better than the hamburger I was thinking of."

"Plenty more where this came from."

Sam dug into the food. Estella's son, Levi, joined them at the table but didn't seem to have much appetite.

"Can you tell me what's going on down there?" Levi asked.

Sam swallowed. "I'll tell you what I can. Will you tell me how well you knew Collins?"

"He ingratiated himself to Gus," Jodie said. "He said his name was Kent."

"Kent was his brother's name," Sam said. "He was a Marine who died overseas."

"He was a gadget guy—my dad's nickname for him," Levi said, voice bitter. "He was always telling my dad he had an upgrade for him. I betcha he hacked everything. What a user."

Sam considered this as he drank some more water. "You're right. It seems as if he moved here with the intent of pumping your dad for information." He didn't want to comment on his idea of a cop accomplice at the moment.

"They won't let anyone into the house until they remove all the explosives."

"Are we in any danger?" Levi asked.

Sam shook his head. "The bomb squad has things under control." He felt so much better now with solid food in his belly. He also noticed Jodie looked different. He saw a spark of life in her eyes and was glad.

There was a knock at the door and Levi got up to answer it. Smiley and Mike King walked into the kitchen.

"It certainly smells wonderful in here," Smiley said, casting a raised eyebrow at Sam.

"There is plenty for everyone," Estella said. "Have a seat. I'm used to feeding cops."

Introductions were made. Mike King nodded at Sam, contrite, Sam thought.

Smiley took a seat next to Sam, thanking Estella. Mike sat on the other side of Jodie.

"What about you, Mike?" Estella asked.

"I'm not hungry." He looked at Sam. "I guess I owe you an apology."

"Don't worry about it. This situation would stress anyone out."

He nodded and seemed to be ready to say something else, but then a commotion sounded at the front door. Conversation stopped and everyone's attention turned to the front door when Levi began protesting with a male visitor. Sam feared a reporter had made it inside the police tape.

"I just want to see Jodie," a male voice said.

Sam saw Jodie stiffen. A tall, bearded man strode into the kitchen. He had all the markings of a drug cop in Sam's estimation.

"Ian, what are you doing here?"

The name clicked with Sam. Ian Hunter was the team member who had not been present at the raid. He looked gaunt and haunted and he was fixated on Jodie.

"What is going on? You've been chasing a suspect and you didn't tell me?"

"Ian, it's more complicated than that."

"I'm not stupid—"

"Ian, it's good to see you again." Estella stood. "We're decompressing here, not fighting. Can I get you something to eat?"

Her motherly manner took all the starch out of Ian.

"Uh, what? No thank you. I'm not hungry."

"Then have a seat." Mike pointed to an empty chair on the other side of the table. "We're waiting for the bomb squad to clear the house."

Ian's eyes roamed the table. There was no seat next to Jodie, and Sam wasn't going to move. His eyes came to rest on Sam.

"Are you Gresham?"

"I am." Sam stood and extended his hand. Ian extended his as well and they shook while he cast an appraising glance over Sam.

"Ian Hunter. You defused an IED?"

"I was in the right place at the right time."

He studied Sam for a moment, then looked at Jodie. "Can I have a minute?"

Sam saw irritation crease Jodie's forehead.

"I'm tired, Ian. Can this wait for another day?"

It was Ian's turn to be irritated—Sam saw it in his face, the jaw muscle twitching. Ian looked ready to say something, but Mike spoke up first.

"We're waiting on the coroner, Ian. You can do us a favor, if you have the time."

Ian turned his attention to Mike. "What?"

"This kid, Dennis Collins—we're going to be tearing his life apart. Can you look at him through narcotics, maybe get gangs involved? There must be more to him than we've found so far."

As far as Sam could tell, Ian had himself under control now. "He was backgrounded here, I understand."

"He was," Mike said. "Get a copy, start digging. Tara and I will be tied up with this for a while. I'll try to get you a spot on the task force."

"I'll get right on it." Ian's energy was focused in a different direction now. "I just want to be kept in the loop." He left.

"What if Collins is one of the dead?" Jodie asked her uncle when Ian was gone.

"I saw him leave," Estella said. "I distinctly remember him climbing into an Uber."

"He didn't have a car? He has a license."

"He never had a car. He took an Uber or rode the bus. Sometimes he borrowed a car from his friend, I think."

"What kind of car?"

Estella waved a hand. "I don't know cars. It was blue."

"It was a Jeep Cherokee, old style, big tires, raised up for off road. In real good shape," Levi called out.

There was silence for a moment as everyone looked toward Levi.

"What?" he asked. "I like cars."

"Thanks, Levi," Mike said. "Do you know what friend?"

Levi shook his head.

"How long ago did he leave?" Smiley asked.

"Last Thursday or Friday."

Sam considered this. "The body was thawing and decaying for a couple of days at most," he said. "The neighbor would have noticed sooner and called police about the odor if Jodie hadn't shown up."

He wasn't sure he wanted to comment about the device. Collins obviously wanted to kill someone. Was his target whoever did find the body? A dead body in the freezer in his house shed a whole new light on Collins. Sam hadn't seen anything in his background suggesting he could pull off what he apparently had pulled off.

"What about the IED under the house?"

Sam swallowed and looked up, realizing someone was talking to him. Mike King held his gaze.

"What about it?"

"Was it like the one in the mountains?"

Sam took a sip of water before answering. "It was different in a lot of ways. Simpler because he had C-4 as his explosive source. In the mountains he used natural gas as his explosive. It took a lot more time to set up the IED in the mountains, from what I've read. The trigger was different. With this one, Jodie stepped on an activation switch connected to a detonator. Overall, at least to me, it looked hastily set up."

"A time delay?"

"Yeah, I don't think it would have gone off if Jodie had lifted her foot. I think she simply triggered the timer."

Jodie looked surprised, but she said nothing.

"Why?" Estella asked.

Sam shrugged and scratched the stubble on his chin. "I think I'll wait to make any more assumptions until the LBPD bomb squad has studied the device. But there was an awful lot of C-4 under Collins's house."

Mike turned to Estella. "What about it, Estella? Did this kid ever give you any indication he was a homicidal maniac?"

"I barely said two words to the boy. Gus just thought he was a sad misfit."

Misfit for sure, Sam thought. He turned toward Jodie and caught her watching him. He smiled and she looked away.

He couldn't deny that he felt a connection with Jodie, a connection he hoped she shared. Sam remembered how tightly she'd hugged him after he'd defused the IED. Even though their relationship started unconventionally, with bombs and the threat of death, he prayed they would have a future with a lot more promise.

CHAPTER 26

JODIE ABSENTMINDEDLY PETTED MACNUT while she listened to the conversations going on around her. She didn't like the idea of Ian on the task force, but she was glad Mike had spoken up and gotten rid of him. After everything she'd been through today, the last thing she wanted to do was talk to Ian. His showing up like he had really bothered her. She'd been very clear they were over.

Her gaze fell on Sam Gresham, her hero for a second day. He was a believer, she thought. At least he'd handed her a book of Psalms. How did he reconcile God's plan with the death of his partner? Did he still believe God heard his prayers?

Her thoughts drifted back to the days and months after her parents' deaths. It had been hard to lose them, but in an odd way it was simple as well. Her family became the church family and the emphasis in her life was on a good God who heard prayers. Talking to God and believing he heard helped her feel safe. She didn't understand—she simply believed. And often she felt God's presence, knew he answered her every cry.

Why was simple belief so hard now?

Jodie had no answer.

Thinking back to that time made her realize again how much she'd missed the family of faith. Being around Estella reminded her how warm her family had been. At one time, Estella, Shannon, and Tracy were all people she'd loved being around. But she wasn't the same person anymore. She was broken, with pieces missing. How could anything ever be like it was before? Even as she asked herself the question, she knew nothing would ever be the same— not ever.

Eyes open, she studied Sam. The old cop, George Upton, made her angry when he told her God could turn evil into good. But . . . *God works all things out for good.* The verse from Romans still didn't give her the peace it used to. Yet, here today, she didn't know how she ever would have met Sam under any other circumstances.

He turned toward her, catching her watching him, and she felt her face redden. Levi got up to answer another knock on the door, and Sergeant Barstow entered.

"We've cleared the house of all explosive material," he announced. "The coroner is en route for the bodies, but before they're removed, Detectives—" he looked at Mike and Smiley—"there's something you all need to see."

"You said *bodies*," Jodie interrupted. "There was more than one?"

He nodded. "We think there are two. We didn't move anything, but there are clearly two more legs underneath the first body."

Jodie stood. "I'm coming with Mike."

Mike looked at her and held up a hand. "Jodie, I'd love to have you come in an official capacity, but you quit. And you've spent today poking your nose where it doesn't belong. You'll be in a bad place if someone wants to make trouble for you. You should stay put."

Barstow jumped in before Jodie could speak. "Sorry, Mike, I will overrule you here. She needs to come."

Mike frowned and then gave a wave of his hand. "Fine."

Jodie kept her mouth shut and fell into step with Sam as they all followed Barstow out of the house. The neighborhood was awash in emergency vehicles and news vans. Residents were out in force, watching, as was the news media. There were even news choppers circling in the sky above. Jodie heard an occasional hollered question.

"Is it true there was a terrorist in our midst?"

"How many dead bodies are in the house?"

"Is this a house of horrors?"

"You doing okay, Jodie?" Gresham asked.

"I . . ." She paused, organizing her thoughts. "I've come to grips with reality. Collins is crazy, but . . ." Her voice trailed off. She wasn't certain where to go next.

"But what?"

"I don't know. . . . The only thing I am sure of is I'm glad you came by when you did."

"I'm glad I was there as well. It's hard not to see God's hand in things when everything goes well. You have to look harder when they go sideways. Remember, God works all things out."

She jerked toward him. Romans 8:28 had just popped into her mind a minute ago, though she'd not read her Bible in months.

Her prayer, the unanswered one, had the same verse at its core. How would the death of her team ever work out for good?

"All things work together?"

"Yeah, they do, eventually. I believe it."

"Your partner, my team . . ." Jodie felt her jaw tighten.

"I'd be lying if I told you I understood the how and the why of it. George also said, 'Trust what you do know, not what you can't see.' What do you know about God, Jodie?"

The question gave her pause and Jodie stammered, "I, uh, well, I know he's in control, but I will never understand the why of it."

"Maybe not here in this life." He smiled and Jodie felt some tension leave her. There was a sure confidence about him. "I hate to sound so philosophical, but honestly, from personal experience, you need to find one thing to hang on to, one true north, or you'll spend your life flapping in the breeze."

"What do you hang on to? What's your true north?"

A half smile played on his lips.

"Too strange a question?"

"No, it's not. I'd just forgotten what I need to hang on to. What happened here today took a burden from my shoulders. I can see things clearer now than I have been able to since the accident. My true north? I guess it would be this: God is good, Jodie, even when life isn't."

Jodie held his gaze, the cool assurance in his eyes a comfort. She had heard the same expression her whole life. She believed it, didn't she? Why couldn't she hang on to it now and stop the madness in her soul?

They'd reached Collins's driveway, and Barstow was talking about the bodies.

"We don't know how long the bodies have been in the freezer.

There are some indications they've been dead longer than it appears, and they were frozen for some time. The coroner will have to make the final estimation. The suspect had the freezer on a timer. The unit only recently turned off, so the process of thawing and decay began a few days ago. I don't need to tell you people to glove up and refrain from touching anything."

"Have you identified the corpses?" Smiley asked as gloves were handed out.

"I'll leave identification to the coroner. What is going to be of interest to you right now is what we found in the guy's office."

Barstow entered the house by the front door, and everyone followed. They walked by a large bedroom, the master, Jodie thought. From what she could see, it was neat as a pin. The bed was made; there were no obvious personal objects.

They crossed the living room to the third bedroom, which Jodie pegged as Collins's office. The smell of decay permeated this side of the house. The odor would linger long after the coroner removed the bodies.

The office was lit up bright, much brighter than what would have been standard. Collins liked to see what he was doing. She followed everyone into the small office and froze, feeling as if she'd been struck by lightning. Even her toes tingled when she saw what the lights illuminated.

The room was covered in photos of all sizes, of various law enforcement agencies and personnel, overlapping like the scales on a fish. There were even boards over the windows so every space was covered by a photo of something. But as her eyes focused and she realized what she was looking at, she grew numb. It was like looking at a photo album of RAT's work assignments for a year.

"Besides the photos," Barstow said, "there's a bag of burner phones, a package of tracking devices, and a closet full of technology. It will be a while before we catalog everything in this room."

Jodie barely heard him. She couldn't believe what she was seeing. There were photos of her and her team at crime scenes all over Southern California, for the year preceding the IED. There were photos of Gus and his family. There were aerial photos of the cabin in the mountains, arrows marking escape routes. Her whole body stiffened as the realization sank in. This guy had been following their lives. But mostly *her* life.

There were photos of Jodie at her home in Seal Beach, of her surfing, jogging, playing volleyball, coming out of church, going to the market. This creep had photos of just about every moment of her life for the past year, before the IED.

"He really had an obsession with you," Gresham commented.

"No kidding." Jodie walked closer to one of the walls where it looked as if Collins had a timeline of her team's activities. He did. There was a detailed timeline leading up to the IED explosion in the mountains. Some of the notes he'd written on Post-its were comments and orders Jodie herself had issued.

Hayes is cagey and slippery. Be careful.

Know the floor plan. We need to be quick and decisive.

Don't be complacent. Every warrant is not the same.

She put a hand over her mouth, suddenly feeling sick to her stomach. "He knew everything."

"Is it possible Gus was—?" Sam was cut off.

"No," Mike said with not a little force.

His reaction had Jodie turning toward him. Gus and Mike went through the same academy and had been friends for years. He felt the loss of Gus as much as she did.

Right now her uncle's face was dark with anger. "Gus was not a corrupt cop. I don't know how this kid got all this information, but Gus didn't give it to him."

"Of course he didn't," Smiley chimed in. "This kid is a tech whiz. I'm betting he cloned phones, listened in on conversations. Unfortunately, spying on people isn't hard to do today. Maybe he got close to Gus, took advantage of the man's benevolence."

"There's a lot of evidence to sift through, Mike. Technology crimes will be busy," Barstow said. "The chief is on the way. This investigation is high priority."

"Why did he leave all of this for us to find?" Jodie asked.

"I'll bet he expected it to be destroyed in the explosion," Gresham said.

"We worked out a possible scenario," Barstow said. "He had the freezer on a timer with the lid open, so when the flow of electricity stopped, thawing and decay would start. It's been warm. Someone would have been in here sooner or later to investigate the smell. What do cops do when they have an abandoned structure with decaying bodies inside?"

"They lock it down and then go wait in their cars, away from the odor, until the coroner arrives," Jodie said, mind churning with the ramifications of this guy's evil.

"Right," Barstow confirmed. "But any cop who saw this—" he waved his hand around the photo walls—"would be forced to slow down, call out detectives, bringing more people into the mix. They'd search the house. The pressure switch you stepped on activated a timer on the bomb. You heard the click and thought it was the same thing Gus stepped on, so you didn't move. I doubt anyone else would have thought it was anything but a creaky floorboard. The C-4 would have detonated after forty minutes, about the time it would have taken to have a house full of cops and techs."

The room went silent as everyone digested this information.

"He wanted another big kill," Sam said.

"Yep, our guess is he wanted as many people as possible in the house—then boom, more death and all the evidence destroyed. There also would have been collateral damage on either side, and behind." Barstow looked at Sam. "Thankfully you were able to defuse it."

"So it wasn't the same as in the mountains," Smiley said.

"No, it wasn't. In fact—" Barstow paused and looked around at everyone there—"this device looked as if it were set up by a different person."

"What?" Mike asked.

"You'll have my full report shortly."

Smiley cursed. Mike whistled low and Jodie stiffened. He'd voiced what she'd been thinking. Though he didn't suggest the suspect was a cop, hearing him voice her thoughts . . . well, it was nonetheless distressing.

Mike turned to her. "Two killers? Jodie, you're going to need protection. I'll get a black-and-white to escort you home."

"I don't need babysitters."

Barstow interrupted. "Your uncle is right, Jodie. You all need to discuss this in the command post van. I'm told they've set up a conference table. Lab people are here waiting to go over this place with a fine-tooth comb."

Jodie, stung over the idea of having a babysitter, turned and left, more than happy to get out of the house. She felt someone behind her and hoped it was Sam. The command post van was parked in front of Collins's house now. It had been moved there as soon as the explosive threat had been mitigated. Now it was further inside the perimeter and further away from the press.

As soon as Jodie stepped inside the modified motor home, she saw the conference table. A pot of coffee brewed next to a box of doughnuts. She filled a coffee cup.

"Can I have one of those?"

Sam had followed her in. He looked as tired as she felt. The stubble on his chin was lighter red than the hair on his head.

"Sure." She gave him the cup she'd poured as everyone else filed into the room. She poured herself another cup and then found a seat at the table. Sam took the one next to her.

"You shouldn't dismiss what your uncle said, Jodie. You might need some watching just for a bit," Gresham said.

She turned on him in surprise. "What?"

"This guy has too much intel—the warrant service, your visit to the mountains, your whole operation. Sergeant Barstow just said he probably had trackers. It makes sense that every part of your life needs to be swept for listening or tracking devices."

"He's right," Mike agreed. He took the seat across from Jodie.

She folded her arms, creeped out and angry about what this guy had done to her life. Hating being ganged up on. Especially because even in her anger, she could see the logic. "All this because he wasn't hired to be a cop?"

"Maybe," Mike said.

"Him and his partner," Sam said. "There are two people working on this, like Barstow suggested. It's the only thing making any sense."

"Agreed," Mike said. "For some reason they are after you, Jodie. And until now they've been very efficient killers."

Jodie rubbed her arms, suddenly feeling cold, almost as cold as she'd felt in the mountains when she watched fire consume her team.

CHAPTER 27

JODIE'S ADRENALINE RUSH quickly dissipated. The anger still smoldered, but she was tired. It had been a long, disturbing day. The photos had gotten under her skin like an army of red ants.

Mike and Smiley were speaking in low tones, but she'd tuned them out. She'd just finished her cup of coffee and prepared to pour a second when the chief appeared in the doorway. Janet Masters had been chief for a year and a half. She was the first woman to lead the LBPD. Jodie had always liked and respected her. Before Jodie quit, Masters had pleaded with her not to. She didn't understand how hard it was for Jodie to stay—no one really did.

"Jodie, Mike. The coroner arrived with me. He's already in the house and from what he just told me in a text, the bodies are not completely thawed or badly decomposed. He'll have to take the entire freezer back to the morgue before examining them." She sighed as if she had something disturbing to say.

Smiley picked up on it. "Was there more?" he asked.

"There was a backpack in the freezer," Masters said. "The coroner was able to remove it without disturbing the bodies. It contained two wallets. One had an ID belonging to Norman Hayes—"

"Hayes?" Jodie stared.

"Not certain he's in there, can't see the bottom body."

"It could be planted?" Sam asked.

"Anything is possible at this point." Masters held Jodie's gaze. "The second ID is a passport belonging to Archie Radio. It's not positive of course, Jodie, but the top body resembles Archie."

Jodie felt her heart drop. She'd thought Jukebox was likely dead, but as long as there had been a question mark, she could still hope. Hope disappeared like a puff of smoke.

"I'm sorry, Jodie."

"Does he know how they died?" Sam asked.

"Preliminary, the body on top has a GSW to the head. Any detailed information will have to wait until the coroner has the bodies in the morgue."

"We're working the shooting of our deputy as well. Have you come across anything to tie Collins to that?" Smiley asked. "Weapons, ammo, anything?"

"Not so far. But I did get a call from Detective Fenton, your shop. He's going to meet with Sergeant Barstow's team. He came across a report of stolen C-4 from a National Guard facility. The material recovered from the house might be that loss."

"You're kidding." Smiley shook his head. "This kid is shaping up to be a supervillain."

"If he took it," Mike said. "He might have bought it from the thief. In any event, it's a good lead."

"It's one mystery solved," Sam said. "I wondered where he got such high-quality explosive."

Masters looked at Jodie. "Are you okay? I'm sure what you saw inside the house was unsettling."

"It was, but I'm fine." Jodie said it with feeling to try to make herself believe it. "It's all important to the investigation. And if it's okay with you, I'd like to go back in the house and take another look before it's all torn down." As creeped out as she was by the room full of pictures, she wanted a second look at them. Maybe there was a clue somewhere on the walls, something to blow things wide-open.

"Certainly. Sergeant Barstow and his team are helping the coroner remove the freezer. There are technicians in the house photographing everything. So the house is busy. But I'm sure you'll be unobtrusive."

"I will."

Jodie made to leave, but Masters stopped her with a hand on her shoulder. "And, Jodie—" her face was cop hard and set—"I expect any and all of your extracurricular investigation to stop here and now, clear?"

She felt her face flush. "Yes, sir."

"Mind if I go with her?" Sam asked.

Jodie was glad he'd spoken up. She would be happy to have him with her in that room.

Sam got an affirmative nod, and he and Jodie went back into the house. Sergeant Barstow was speaking to the coroner when they stepped in.

"My men entered," Barstow said. "We had to clear the room,

make certain there weren't any more explosives. We tried to ascertain how many bodies were in the freezer. We saw the timer attached to the unit. Unsure how long it had been on, but the timer shut it off four days ago."

Sam touched Jodie lightly on the arm and she turned to face him. "He set it to shut it off on Saturday, when he went up to the mountains to shoot you."

She held the gaze of those clear green eyes. "But how did he know?"

Sam shrugged. "We'll find out."

Jodie sighed, satisfied for the moment with the hopeful sentiment. Like a good partner, Sam's steady presence calmed her. She was glad Sam had come. Her trust in him had grown exponentially.

"I wonder if he expected to kill me and then flee the country," Jodie said.

"Anything is a possibility."

She turned her attention to the removal of the freezer. As she watched Barstow's people follow the coroner back into the room with a dolly to move the freezer out of the house and into the coroner's van, she thought of poor Jukebox, stuffed inside. Pain vibrated through her. When would the hits stop? *Lord, why can't anything ever be easy?*

"Did you want to wait?" Sam asked.

"What? Oh . . ." Jodie understood he meant wait for the bodies to be removed. "I think so. Once they get the freezer out of the house, the smell should dissipate a little."

It took about fifteen minutes for the men to load the freezer onto the dolly and carefully move it out of the house and toward the waiting van. The buzz of news copters overhead reminded her of a swarm of angry bees.

An image of the little guy she'd interviewed bringing the freezer into the house and then having the wherewithal to kill Hayes and Juke and stuff them in the freezer flashed in her thoughts.

Who on earth is this guy?

Hayes was a handful for police. How could he possibly be any less hard to handle for Collins?

There was no way Collins was working alone.

CHAPTER 28

"I GUESS IF HAYES IS IN THAT FREEZER, he had nothing to do with the IED," Jodie said as she watched the men loading the evidence into the van. She could only shake her head over all the time wasted chasing Hayes.

Jodie stopped just inside the doorway to the creepy office with its walls of photos. Two lab techs were in the room photographing and cataloging evidence from the closet and the drawers in the small desk. Soon they would remove all the photos, empty the room. In Jodie's mind's eye, she would always see the walls like this, covered in photos of her life.

"I can't imagine what you're feeling right now," Sam said. He stood just behind her, in the doorway. She didn't turn, just kept looking from photo to photo.

"Seeing your life on display like this must be disturbing."

"What an understatement. I've never felt so exposed. I'm trying to remember the moments pictured, put myself back there." She paused as memories bit. Her team was alive and whole in these pictures. She could hear their voices, the laughter, the serious investigative discussions. For a second, she almost lost her balance, the pain was so sharp and real.

"It's okay, Jodie," Sam said softly. The gentle touch of his hand on her back fortified Jodie. He continued to speak in low tones. "It hurts. The first time I was back in the station without Rick, it was like watching him die all over again. Don't even ask me what happened when I saw someone at his locker."

His understanding tone made her want to lean back into him. She stood still, a little sad when he let his hand drop away.

She didn't turn to face him but knowing he understood so completely steadied her. Jodie closed her eyes for a moment. Then, when she was ready, she opened them, cleared her throat, and said, "I can't help but wonder . . . Did I notice anything off at the time?"

"Did you?"

She shook her head. "I can't remember. Some of these were shot with a drone, I think. Those things are noisy. Why didn't I notice anything?"

"You were focused on the job at hand."

She folded her arms, angry and curious at the same time. "This guy was focused as well. Yet . . ."

"What?"

"All of these photos were taken before the IED explosion. I don't see any taken in the last three months. He tried to kill me three days ago, but he was no longer tracking me?"

"Maybe there's an explanation for why he stopped. Think:

there wasn't much to track. You quit; you aren't high-profile anymore. He was probably biding his time, waiting for an opportunity
to get at you. If his office shows us anything, this guy is patient.
Him not being here tells me he has a plan B."

Jodie turned and met Sam's eyes. They were cop eyes, used to
looking at things differently, used to trying to uncover what others
were hiding. More than anyone in her life in the last three months,
he gave her strength, hope for an ending to this nightmare. Feeling
hope fueled her next statement.

"Is he the one with the plan?"

"What do you mean?"

"All of these pictures, the explosive, the evidence, indicates a
partner somewhere, yet . . ."

"You don't see him being the boss, the one with all the hate."

"Right." Jodie nodded. "Besides, there's no way he manhandled
the freezer on his own. And killing Hayes and Juke—I don't think
he could have accomplished everything by himself. He's the puppet. I want to find the puppet master."

CHAPTER 29

THE PUPPET MASTER.

Jodie's observation was a good one, Sam thought. The obvious reaction to all this evidence being found above an explosive device was that Collins meant for the house to explode, to destroy everything. But what if Collins didn't want everything destroyed? What if they were meant to find all of this, meant to be distracted by the search for Collins? Hayes had apparently been a distraction. What if there was a puppet master in the shadows playing everyone, including Collins?

"I've had enough," Jodie said. "I'm going back to the van."

Sam nodded. "I'll head back in a moment."

He stifled a yawn, admitting to himself he was so tired he was having difficulty concentrating. Yet there were a lot of pluses to this long day. He'd surprised himself when he told her confidently that he believed God was good even when life wasn't. That truth hadn't been clear to him even this morning. Something good had come out of this IED, at least for him. He'd faced his fears and was no longer untethered, flapping in the breeze. Jodie wasn't there yet, but he knew she'd get there. He'd seen a new light in her eyes, something missing the Saturday they met. She was engaged in the investigation. Engagement would help drag her focus away from the guilt and pain.

Sam took one last look at the walls covered in photos and then left for the van.

Smiley stood outside the door of the command post. "I'm about ready to head home," he said. "How about you?"

"Yes and no," Sam said. "I'm tired, but there is so much here, so much investigation still left, I'd hate to leave right this minute."

"Well, the legwork here is going to be done by LBPD personnel. Our part is what happened in San Bernardino. It would really help if we found either the weapon used to shoot at King or the one used on Chad. Other than explosives, no weapons have been found in the house."

Smiley was right. Sam hated to admit it. With what the background paperwork said, none of this made sense in relation to Collins—not the IED, not the two bodies in his house. The crime here was out of his jurisdiction. Long Beach personnel were interviewing all the neighbors. A big question now was whether anyone else had been seen with Collins. Sam and Smiley would be kept in the loop, but Sam wished they were leading the charge.

He wanted to stay in Long Beach for as long as it took to get a clearer picture of who might be working with Dennis Collins. He had his list. Jonah Bennett and Ian Hunter were the two names on it. He feared they were both dead ends. Nothing he'd seen indicated either man hated Jodie enough to want to kill her. There was so much more to investigate.

What he'd seen in Dennis Collins's office was disturbing and frightening. It all led to the deaths of four cops and Jodie's unfortunate CI. He was amazed at how well Jodie was handling the whole thing. He couldn't imagine being on the receiving end of this.

Smiley climbed into the van to grab another cup of coffee and join the LBPD group for any final details before hitting the road. Sam followed. Jodie was already inside, seated next to Mike, who was talking on his phone.

Watching Jodie process everything, Sam wondered how much her life was going to change. This guy had too much information and she was a target. They'd need to find a safe place for her, a very safe place.

His phone buzzed with a text. Looking down, he saw it was from George.

What's happening? Long Beach and Jodie King are all over the news. On TV I'm watching the chopper circle a neighborhood where you defused a bomb?

Sam quickly typed back, **Long story.** In the middle of the text, Sam had an idea, but he didn't have the patience to articulate it in a text. As a stopgap, he wrote, **I may need your help soon. Can't talk right now.**

Whatever you need.

It was time to text his mother, Sam decided. If George had heard what was happening here, so had Mom. His text was brief.

I'm good, will call you when able. Don't worry.

"Anything important?" Jodie asked, looking at his phone.

Sam shook his head. "Just giving my mom a heads-up."

"The nurse?"

"Yeah, we're all over the news. Don't want her to worry."

She looked as if she was about to say something when a noise indicated someone else had entered the van. A stocky bald guy appeared in the doorway. Sam doubted he was a cop, but there was something about him. He and Jodie knew each other.

"Dr. Bass, what are you doing here?"

Sam heard it in her tone, saw it in her posture, and felt it in the atmosphere of the room: Jodie wasn't happy to see him. Sam thought of Doc Roe. Psychologists were big on people spilling their guts about stuff. Talking, talking, talking. Sometimes it helped; sometimes it didn't. As far as Sam was concerned, only prayer helped all the time.

He'd been avoiding Doc Roe, and it looked like Jodie was avoiding Bass.

■ ■ ■

Bass smiled at Jodie as she tried to hide her shock at his presence. While it was no secret she'd talked to him, somehow his being here at this scene made her feel exposed, guilty, and very weak.

"I called him," Chief Masters said. "He did the psych exam on Collins. His observations may be helpful."

Jodie relaxed, a little embarrassed she'd overreacted and gotten defensive.

"How are you feeling, Jodie?" Bass asked.

"Feeling?" She shrugged. "We finally have a name, a face to pin the carnage on. This is what I've wanted for months. I know who killed my team. It's just a matter of catching the dirtbag. I'm fine."

She stated the last two words emphatically.

"I'm glad you now know where to direct your anger," Bass

said. "I truly hope this leads to the closure you need. I understand there's a room full of photos?"

"Yes, there is. I'm creeped out by what I saw. But I've been proved right on a lot of things, so I feel a lot better than the last time I talked to you."

He held her gaze for a moment. "Good to know. Just remember I'm here if you do need me."

Jodie caught Sam's eye as he squeezed around Bass and sat next to her. He leaned in and whispered, "I totally understand. If Dr. Roe had shown up at one of my scenes, even invited, I wouldn't like it either."

Her irritation fled. "Thanks."

"What do you remember about your interview with Dennis Collins?" Masters asked the doctor.

"Nothing in his demeanor would have alerted me to this type of behavior. He was shy, introverted, but nothing he said or did indicated he was dangerous."

Masters nodded and took the seat at the head of the table. "Detective Smiley," she began, "I've reactivated the original task force, including you in it. I'm thankful Detective Gresham was able to defuse the device today." She turned her gaze toward Sam. "Sergeant Barstow tells me this neighborhood would have been severely impacted had there been a detonation."

Jodie saw Sam redden. He probably found it easier to take rebuke than praise. Tiny was the same way.

"I did what I was trained to do. Right place, right time."

Masters nodded and her attention fell on Jodie. "Jodie, we're going to take your car and sweep your home. This guy has been watching you. From what I saw, it looks as if he's crawled under your skin, and we don't want any nastier surprises."

If there was a tracking device on her vehicle, Jodie wanted to know, and she wanted it off. Hopefully there would also be evidence to help lead them to Collins. What was harder to accept was having to be out of her apartment for a bit.

"Where will I go?"

"You can stay with me," Mike said.

"And put you in danger?"

"You know I'm prepared."

"Collins was ready to take out half of this neighborhood. How can you prepare for such devastation?"

"We would provide uniformed resources, as much as possible for protection," Masters said.

"And put more cop lives at risk?" Jodie didn't like where any of this was going, and she did not want to be responsible for another officer's death.

"We're ready now," Mike said. "No one would be a sitting duck."

"I hope you're right. I still want to err on the side of caution."

Sam spoke up. "I know a possibility. A retired cop in the mountains. He has a spare room. It would be the perfect place to stay low for a bit."

Everyone turned toward him.

Surprise snapped Jodie out of her anger. "Where in the mountains?"

"Arrowbear. On the other side of town from where the IED exploded. He's got an attached apartment; you'd have your privacy and you'd be safe."

"You want to send Jodie back to the mountains?" Mike asked.

"If Collins is the guy, he went to considerable lengths to get to the mountains. But he's based here. There is no evidence he has a permanent presence in the mountains."

Jodie watched her uncle and could tell he considered this viable. She didn't like the idea at all. She wanted to stay in Long Beach.

"Who is this guy?"

"You met him the other day—"

"George Upton?" Jodie stared at Sam, aghast.

Sam nodded. "I know you didn't hit it off, but George can be trusted. His house is safe."

Smiley stepped in. "I know George Upton. He was a solid cop. His place would be better than any safe house. And returning to Arrowbear would be the last thing this guy would expect."

Jodie couldn't believe this was a real suggestion. Her, stay with the retired cop?

"George Upton? Does he own a security company?" Masters asked.

"He does."

"I know of him. We don't have another safe house to send her to, now, do we, Detective King?" Masters asked.

"Tara is waiting for a callback. The local FBI office has a place we can use. We're simply waiting for confirmation." Mike turned to Smiley. "You say this Upton is a retired cop?"

Smiley nodded. "Did thirty-five years in harness. Exemplary record. I've been to his house. It's hard to get to. Like Sam said, it's on the other side of Arrowbear from where the IED was. George set the house up to be protected and safe." He gave a half smile. "He's a paranoid ex-cop—you know the type."

Mike smiled at the inside joke. After a long career in law enforcement, it could be difficult not to be paranoid about crime and the threat of crime.

Masters turned to Sam. "Upton is very squared away. I'd say

your plan, Detective Gresham, could be a good backup. Are you certain Mr. Upton would be willing to take on this responsibility?"

"I can call him right now."

"Wait." Jodie spoke up, a little angry this conversation was taking place as if she were not there. "Can we slow down? What about a hotel somewhere in Long Beach? I hate to go so far away."

"I'd rather have you with me," Mike said. "But I see the logic here. This Collins is crazy about explosives. If he were to attempt to take you out in a crowded hotel, many people could be injured." He looked at Sam. "Hopefully the Feds will come through. I don't like the idea of the mountains either. But I'd trust you in the hands of a retired cop who is justifiably paranoid."

Like I'm a child.

CHAPTER 30

"I NEED SOME AIR." Jodie pushed away from the table and left the room. She intended to simply step outside, but it was still a circus with crowds and press. The public information officer had yet to give a statement, so everyone was still waiting for information.

"Jodie, do you need to talk?" Bass had followed her out.

"No, I do not," she said without looking at him. She hoofed it back to Gus's house, dodging the reporters who mobbed her once she was out of the perimeter and ignoring questions hollered her way. At Gus's, Levi was standing in the doorway watching the circus.

"Who was dead in the house?" he asked.

Jodie told him she couldn't say for sure. "How well did you know Collins? Did you ever see him with anyone?"

Levi shook his head. "I only saw the guy a few times. Barely spoke to him. I handle my own computer problems. He was my dad's friend. I—" His voice broke and he brought a hand up to wipe his eyes. "I was kind of happy my dad found someone to help him with the computer, the phone. So he wouldn't bug me. I had no idea . . ."

"No one did, Levi. Don't start blaming yourself."

Levi looked at her with pain in his eyes. "Just find the little cretin, please. Find him."

"It's my mission."

Macnut pushed the door open and rushed at Jodie. Right behind the dog was Estella. Levi turned away and walked to the back of the house. Jodie could tell he was hurt and angry, but she didn't know how to help him. She couldn't even help herself.

"Oh, Jodie, it's you. Can you tell me what is going on over there now?"

"Yeah, I'll tell you." She followed Estella to the kitchen and told her about what they'd found in the house. Estella offered her tea as they sat at the kitchen table.

"No thanks. I'm fine, just tired," she said. "I only want to go home and go to bed."

"Would you be safe? I mean Kent, or whatever his name is, is after you." She sat kitty-corner to Jodie, bent elbow, chin resting in her palm. "To say he's obsessed with you is an understatement." She tsked.

"Yeah, I know," Jodie said, not wanting to share that there were pictures of Gus as well. "Mike wants me to go to a safe house."

"You don't want to."

"No. I don't want this guy disrupting my whole life anymore."

"But?" Estella met her eyes, gaze penetrating. "I hear a *but*."

"I don't want anyone else to get hurt because of me." She almost wanted to take the words back. Collins was simply a killer.

"Jodie, Gus and your team died because of this Kent-Dennis person, this evil man, not because of you."

"Yeah." Jodie frowned. "Still, he's after me. I'd rather deal with him than have someone else become his victim."

"I can understand. But, Jodie, you quit. Shouldn't you leave the search for the people who are still in uniform?"

Jodie sighed and stared at Estella. "I quit because the memories were too much. I quit because the sense of loss was so overwhelming at times I couldn't breathe. I quit because sometimes I can't forgive myself for s-s-s-urviving," she stuttered and stopped to breathe, surprised she'd admitted this truth so freely.

Estella put her hand over Jodie's. "I know the feeling of loss."

"I know you do," Jodie said, putting her other hand over Estella's. "Right now what I want more than anything is the evil man who took so much from us stopped."

"At what cost?"

"What do you mean?"

"His capture can't be the be-all, end-all. It's not all about him. It's about you, too, Jodie. If you choose to live in the past, regretting things you can't change, it will destroy you. God is sovereign. Lamenting the past is denying his control, saying you know better than God. That's not possible. God can fix what is ugly; you need to let him. In one breath you say you realized the carnage wasn't your fault, and in the next you say you can't forgive yourself. Which is it?"

Jodie sat back, pulling her hands away and letting them hang by her sides. "Are you saying I need to forgive *a cold-blooded killer*?"

"I'm saying you can't let bitterness take root. I don't want you stuck in the past. I don't want this evil person to have such a hold on you that you can't move on and live your life. You have so much more life to live."

"I can't move on until he's caught. Don't you want this guy brought to justice? He killed Gus, after all."

"I do want him brought to justice; I just don't want revenge."

"You think I want revenge?"

"Why did you come to his house today? All by yourself?"

Caught, Jodie looked away. What Estella said stung. She did want Collins dead. As dead as those two men in the freezer. As dead as her team.

"How do I not want revenge?"

"You have to let go. You must trust those still in uniform to do their jobs, and you should trust God's control over it all."

"You're right, Estella. I understood as much when I was eight and I lost my parents. I'm struggling with so much more now." Jodie's insides twisted with an onslaught of negative emotions. She was used to the roller coaster by now, but sitting here with Estella, what hit her the hardest was self-pity.

Estella made a face, cocked her head. "What is it, my friend?"

Jodie had to compose herself as the emotions hit like a freight train. Just when she thought she was through it all. When would this all be over?

"I thought I was doing everything right. I was in church every Sunday. I helped out whenever possible—" Jodie fought to keep her voice steady. "We were after a bad guy, for heaven's sake. I need to know why, Estella. Why did those four good people have to die the way they did?" Tears fell and she ran her palms across her cheeks.

"It's not a matter of what you do or don't do. You can't live second-guessing every move. No one in this life is immune from bad things. Trusting God doesn't mean no trials. Trusting God means an ever-present help when trials come. God numbers our days, Jodie. Gus knew that. I'm certain he would never blame you for what happened. His faith was strong."

Jodie sagged into the chair and held her head in her hands. "And mine is so weak. I've felt a barrier between me and God for months."

Estella placed a hand on her shoulder. "Guess who built the barrier," she said gently.

"I didn't feel this lost after my parents' deaths. Back then I could pray and believe. Now I feel as if my prayers go nowhere." She looked up. "Just now, waiting on the switch, I didn't move. All I could think was how more people would die if the IED detonated. When Sam came in . . . I was so afraid he'd die . . ." Her voice trailed off and Estella waited.

"He gave me a book of Psalms. I read Psalm 46 and prayed for his safety. I didn't want anyone else to die. Here we are, safe. Why did God save me this time? Save Sam? And take Gus, Tiny, Gail, and Tim? I'm struggling. Just when I think I see light, it all goes dark again."

"Honey, those questions may never be answered in this life." Estella wiped her own eyes. "I wish I could give you satisfying answers, but I can't. This is where faith and trust come in. One thing I've learned throughout my life is faith doesn't always take away the pain, but it does give you the ability to handle the pain."

"God is good . . . even when life isn't."

Jodie remembered Sam's words as she considered Estella's. Estella felt her pain and understood it. So did Sam. And part of her believed they both were right. She just didn't know how to move forward. "Why is my faith so weak?"

"What have you put your faith in? You or God? I know you like to be in control, Jodie; it's what made you a great sergeant. But at some point, you must let go. It's trite, but let go and let God."

"I'm trying but I don't know how to let go." Jodie swallowed; tears she couldn't stop rolled down her cheeks.

"There is no quick fix, no magic words." Estella shook her head. "Keep putting one foot in front of the other and trust." Estella moved close and put her arm around Jodie's shoulder. "Feelings change. God is the same now and forever. Keep praying, my friend. He is listening."

Jodie fidgeted but stayed close to Estella. Her friend made it sound so easy. What she was saying sounded similar to what Shannon and Tracy said. Jodie could not let go. But she resolved to try. If for no other reason than people she cared about wanted her to.

"I'll try, Estella. I really will."

Estella turned at a noise coming from the front door. "Someone is here, maybe good news."

Jodie recognized the voice as Sam's. "I think they're going to try to convince me to leave, to go to a safe house."

"Do you have to decide right this minute?"

"They want me to."

"Why don't you stay here for the night, then, after you've slept, decide in the morning."

Jodie leaned back. "I don't want you in danger."

"What? With all those cops out there I'd be in danger?"

Jodie considered Estella's words and had no argument.

CHAPTER 31

AS HE STOOD ON ESTELLA PERKINS'S DOORSTEP, Sam worried they were rushing things by whisking Jodie off to a safe house—especially one where she and the host had started off on the wrong foot. He cringed as he remembered the look on Jodie's face when he'd mentioned George Upton.

With Mike King's blessing, Sam had called George and arranged to have Jodie stay with him for the next few days. George agreed immediately.

"She'll be very safe here," he said. "When will you bring her?"

"As soon as possible." Sam had ended the call and told Detective King and Smiley that the plan was a go. "I'm thinking we should probably get her out of here tonight," he said. "Hopefully we won't be dragging her kicking and screaming. She does seem to be a little stubborn."

"You have no idea," King said.

Smiley grinned ruefully. "We can take her with us back to the station, arrange for her transport to George's house, and set up something with him. Security needs to be tight."

Mike handed him a backpack. "This is Jodie's. I removed it from her car. She'll probably need it."

Waiting for someone to answer the door, Sam switched the backpack to his other hand, glad to have a peace offering of sorts.

Calls from the media and onlookers had bombarded him as he made his way from the command post to the Perkins residence.

"Can you tell us what's going on?"

"Who are you? Who do you work for?"

"Was there really a bomb?"

All Sam could say was "No comment." He turned to face the crowd. "Please, these people have nothing to do with the news story down the street. Leave them alone." Relief swept through him when Levi let him inside.

"This is a circus," Levi said. "Will it be over soon?"

"I'm afraid not. There's still a lot of evidence to sift through. The chief is going to issue a statement soon—that might at least get rid of the press. Your neighbors are likely to be unsettled for a while."

"My mom and Jodie are in the kitchen. I'm going to bed."

"Hang in there, guy."

Sam found Jodie drinking tea with Estella in the kitchen.

"Sam, can I get you some tea?" Estella asked.

"Thank you, no, I'm fine. I came to talk to Jodie."

"I've invited her to stay with me for the night. With all those cops out there, we're safer than Fort Knox. I don't think she should make any big moves now. She needs sleep—we all need sleep."

"You're right," Sam said. He saw the surprise bloom on Jodie's face.

"I thought you wanted me to stay with your friend."

"I do, but I don't want you to be forced. We're all tired. Decisions will be easier to make after at least a little sleep. Estella is right. There's going to be a strong police presence here for a while. You'll be safe for the night."

■ ■ ■

"Thank you so much." Jodie wanted to jump up and hug Sam. His words relieved the pressure she'd been feeling, and relief swept through her like a cool wave. "My uncle won't be happy."

Sam shrugged. "I'll talk to him. We can't let the bad guy force us to move too quickly and maybe make a mistake. He'll see the wisdom there." He held out her backpack. "By the way, he took this out of your car, thought you'd need it."

"Oh, thanks." She took the backpack and set it on Estella's couch. "And I promise I will give staying with George serious consideration." Even as she said the words, Jodie tried to think of a way she could turn being sent to a safe house to her advantage. She needed to be in on the capture of the IED lunatic, and she would find a way to make it happen.

Estella stood. "I'll go make up the guest room." She left the kitchen, and Sam sat across from Jodie.

"I'm sorry if my suggestion about George upset you. I—"

"I'm not upset," Jodie cut him off. "Well, maybe a little bit," she conceded. "I didn't like the guy, but he's not the problem. I hate the idea of running and hiding. *I* want to catch this guy. It was my team he blew up."

"Sometimes discretion is the better part of valor. There are a lot of good cops working on this, Jodie. You need to trust them."

"I do." Jodie almost smiled at how Sam echoed Estella. They both handled their pain and loss much better than she had so far. Any trace of a smile faded. Maybe their advice should be heeded, yet Jodie could not see herself where they were at any time in the near future. "I do have one concern though."

"What?"

"We talked about a puppet master, and . . . well, looking at all those pictures and seeing a tough guy like Hayes dead, apparently without a fight . . . Sam, what if the puppet master is a cop?"

CHAPTER 32

SAM YAWNED AS HE LEFT ESTELLA'S. Mind bleary with fatigue, he considered the case. He and Jodie were on the same page. There was a cop in on this. Nothing in the original investigation pointed to law enforcement involvement. Based on the theory Hayes had been living in the cabin and escaped through the tunnel, the FBI concluded Hayes didn't know the exact time of the raid.

But now they had reason to believe Hayes was dead, and with the information at hand, he might have been dead before the raid. Collins could have fled the cabin after baiting the trap. The house here in Long Beach with its creepy photo room proved that Collins had way too much inside information, and Sam doubted he'd gathered it all himself.

He wanted to share theories with Jodie, but right now they

all needed rest. It was time to find Smiley and let him know he believed they'd done all they could here for the night and should head home. He could leave knowing Jodie was in good hands for now.

Sam was so deep in thought, he almost didn't see the man.

"Hey."

Sam stopped, fully recognizing he was going to be intercepted. Most of the crowd was gone; a couple press teams remained, but they weren't pushing against the boundaries of the police tape anymore. It looked as if they were taping reports. The chief must have given them a satisfying sound bite.

"Gresham." The man made it sound like a command.

"Hunter. What can I do for you?"

"Are you certain Dennis Collins is behind the IED?" Ian Hunter faced Sam, hands on hips.

"Reasonably."

"He needs to die." He dropped his hands and moved toe-to-toe with Sam.

To Sam, it appeared as though Ian wanted agreement from him. They were roughly the same height, and Sam could see the anger in Ian's eyes.

"Not my call—you know that," he said.

"Four good cops—all dead. How can you not make that call?"

"I'm not judge and jury."

Ian threw his hands up, body vibrating with frustration. "I should have been there that day. I . . ." He swallowed. "I would have been at Jodie's side, I would have . . ." His voice trailed off.

Sam said nothing, simply waited.

"I can't deal with not being there, not doing something. I don't see how Jodie deals with being there and surviving."

"I think she recognizes it wasn't her fault. It wasn't your fault either."

"Fault?" He chuckled mirthlessly. "You won't be judge and jury, huh? Call me—I will be." His glare was so intense, Sam stepped back a bit.

"Is there a problem here?"

Both men turned at the sound of Detective King's voice.

"No problem," Sam said.

"What are you doing here, Ian?" Mike asked.

"I did what you asked, checked into Collins and gangs. Kid is clean, not so much as a parking ticket. I did find something off."

"What?" Mike asked before Sam could.

"The kid doesn't have any vehicles registered to him." Ian threw his hands up. "How does a guy get around town, much less get up to San Bernardino, without a car?"

"He uses Uber, and he has a license," Sam said. "Estella says he didn't have a car. Sometimes he would borrow a friend's Jeep, but he left his house in an Uber, and from all appearances, he never meant to come back."

Mike arched an eyebrow. "He's got to be connected to someone. I'm going to have uniforms canvass and recanvass. Someone has to have seen Collins with someone at some time."

"I can be in on the canvassing," Ian said. He reminded Sam of a puppy begging.

"We'll see," Mike said. "Thanks for the information about the vehicles, Ian."

"Sure. Where's Jodie?"

"Asleep. No one needs to wake her up either," Sam said, earning him a glare from Ian.

Mike looked at him sideways, then turned back to Ian. "She needs rest, Ian. Leave her be for the night."

"I want this guy caught."

"We'll catch him. Go home now, Ian."

Ian stomped away. Sam could practically see steam rising from his head.

"It's eating him up that he wasn't there that day," Mike said, turning to Sam. "He really is a good cop, but completely out of sorts right now. I thought you wanted to take Jodie to the mountains tonight."

"I thought so too. But everyone is tired, tense. Jodie will be safe at Estella's for the night. I'm hoping she'll come around to the logic of a safe house when she's got a more balanced outlook on things."

Mike regarded him closely. "You understand her, don't you?"

Sam shoved his hands in his pockets. "I hope so."

"I wish I did. Looking for Collins like she did, coming here—" he waved his hand toward the house—"all by herself. She was never this reckless in uniform."

"Trauma changes you. She's lost her balance."

"How long before she gets it back?"

Sam hiked a shoulder, then looked down at the ground, not completely comfortable talking about Jodie like this.

Mike sighed. "I get it. You're not a shrink. But you do know what it's like to lose a partner in the wrong way. Listen, I'd like you to work closer with us. Would it be okay if I mention to Smiley and Masters I'd like you assigned to us?"

Sam worked to contain his enthusiasm. What Mike was suggesting was exactly what he wanted. He'd be closer. He could actively hunt for Dennis Collins.

"If Smiley signs off on it, I'm good with it."

Mike nodded and extended his hand. "I'll see what I can do."

He and Sam shook.

Of course, Sam realized, if they sent Jodie to the mountains and he stayed here and worked, he would still be far away from her.

It'd be worth it if they ended the threat. The sooner the better.

CHAPTER 33

SAM PUSHED HIS FRONT DOOR OPEN around 1:30 a.m. The last time he'd felt this tired was after some tough Army training.

A nice hot shower relaxed him and made him more tired. After a quick wash and dry, he fell into bed, only to have the alarm wake him at 5 a.m. He'd survive. The short sleep refreshed him. He filled a thermos with coffee, ate a protein bar, and headed back to Long Beach. Everyone agreed to his temporary assignment to Long Beach. He would help tear apart Dennis Collins's life and times, looking for any clues about where he might be hiding, where he had his resources squirreled away, and most importantly, who he might be working with.

Today they were serving warrants at his place of employment,

Though Collins mostly worked from home for the tech support company, his background investigation said he did have to show up in person once a month.

Enjoying a light traffic morning, Sam made it to Long Beach in ninety minutes. He'd left early enough to stop off at Estella's house to check up on Jodie.

The incident command RV was still parked in front of Collins's house. The street itself was dotted with black-and-white patrol cars. Sam saw uniforms going house to house. He guessed the uniformed officers would be spending a lot of time today interviewing any neighbors they missed the night before. Someone had to have seen Collins coming and going even after he left the neighborhood in the Uber.

By force of habit, Sam made note of the vehicles in the area. A large black Cadillac SUV was out of place, parked in front of Estella's. Everything else looked much as it had the night before, absent the press and large crowd. He walked up to the front door expecting Levi, but Estella greeted him.

"Good morning, Sam." She looked rested and happy.

"Good morning. How is everything today?"

"Better than yesterday but still not normal."

"I have a feeling normal will take a while."

She laughed. "Come on in. The coffee is ready."

Sam walked into the kitchen and struggled to hide his surprise. Jonah Bennett sat next to Jodie. He wasn't sure why the surprise hit him so hard—Jodie had said Jonah was a family friend.

"Sam." Jodie looked up and smiled when she saw him.

"Hey, you look refreshed," he said, feeling lame. She did look rested, but there were still shadows under her eyes.

Bennett stood and extended his hand. "So this is the famous

bomb killer, Sam Gresham. Nice to finally meet the hero who saved our girl."

Sam nodded and took the hand. Tall and lanky, Bennett had a couple of inches on Sam in height and looked to be in good shape. Muscles taut and wiry were obvious in his tight shirt. His head was shaved smooth, and the mustache and goatee he wore were steel gray. Bennett had to be around the same age as Mike King and Bruce Smiley, but he didn't look it. His grip was like iron.

"Right place, right time, Mr. Bennett."

"It's Jonah. No need to be formal. Or humble. Jodie and I are family, and I'm in your debt for keeping her safe."

"Do you want some coffee?" Estella asked.

"Sure," Sam said. Though he still had a thermos full of coffee in the car, he had time to sit and visit for a moment.

"You're here early. What's up?" Jodie asked.

Besides wanting to check on you? he thought but didn't say. "Didn't your uncle tell you?" He pulled up a chair.

She shook her head.

"They've added me to the task force here. I'm officially on loan. I'm working with Detective Corson. We'll be serving some warrants today."

She smiled, but there was still sadness in her eyes. "Really glad to hear it. Tara's a friend. Good news."

"Yep, I thought so too." To Sam, she seemed uneasy, unbalanced. Grief played around the edges . . . It was different for him. He couldn't put a finger on it, but truly, for the first time since Rick's death, he felt good, almost whole.

"Where are you serving the warrants?" Jonah asked.

Something about the question bothered Sam. If Jodie had

asked, he would have had no problem saying. But he didn't want to tell Jonah.

"I'll find out when I get to the station." He sipped his coffee. "I stopped by to see how you were doing, Jodie. Glad you got some needed rest."

"I did. And Estella makes certain I'm not hungry. I think if I stay here much longer, I'll gain fifty pounds."

"You're not staying here much longer, are you?" Bennett asked.

"Jodie's lodging still needs to be decided," Sam cut Jodie off. As far as he was concerned, too many people already knew about George's house.

"Yeah, we need to talk about that." She gave Bennett a look.

"I get it. I'm a party crasher. All right, I'll say my goodbyes." He bent down and kissed Jodie's cheek. "Take care." He turned to Sam and nodded. "Good to meet you. Everyone, be safe."

■ ■ ■

After Jonah left, Jodie looked at Sam. "You didn't want to tell him about the mountains, did you?"

"No. I think the less people know, the better."

"I trust Jonah." Jodie stared long and hard at Sam. She wasn't angry, but she wondered if there was something behind his mistrust of Jonah, other than generic cop paranoia.

"I don't know him. I'm not inclined to trust him. That's just how I roll."

Jodie laughed, something she didn't do often.

Sam smiled. This close, Jodie noticed the scarring on his right ear, along the right jawline, and down his neck, disappearing under his shirt. A wave of sadness gripped her by the throat. *He will look in the mirror and always be reminded of his loss. Yet he's moving forward; he's not stuck there, at the crash.*

How do I get there? she wondered. *My scars are all inside. I can't see them but they torment me. Maybe following his example can help me.* She remembered Tara's comment about him. *"He's a superhero."* A little over-the-top, maybe, but true in this case. Sam was also very genuine.

Jodie swallowed the sadness and returned Sam's smile.

"Since you're in such a good mood," he said, "what have you decided about going to George's?"

"There's been a change in plans," she said, then bit her bottom lip.

"What?"

"I guess the Feds came through with a safe house. I'm sure Tara will fill you in." She saw something cross his features—she wasn't sure what—but then the cop face was clearly set.

"Oh, well, good. I hope a federal safe house would be just as safe, if not more so than George's."

"I don't want to go," she said, seeing Sam's good humor fade. "But it's probably the best option right now."

She watched Sam relax.

"True," he said. "Barring any catastrophes, I hope I can help you relocate."

"I hope so too. Not sure what the plan is, except we're leaving later tonight."

"I'll pray we find the guy before we have to take you to any safe house. Sound good?"

"Definitely."

CHAPTER 34

SAM MADE IT TO THE LONG BEACH POLICE STATION with barely a minute to spare. He shook off the disappointment of not taking Jodie to the mountains. The most important issue was her safety. He kept telling himself her safety was important to everyone, and some of the disappointment eased.

Tara Corson was waiting for him in the lobby. There was such a contrast between Jodie and Corson. Where Jodie was tall and lithe, Corson was short and stocky. With her close-cropped dark hair, she looked as if she meant business—not in a bad way, but in an intense cop way. Under her arm she held a thick file folder.

"We meet again, Sam Gresham," she said when he arrived. "Good to see you."

"Likewise." They shook and he noticed her gaze lingering on his scars.

"Do you need coffee or are you ready to get going?"

"I'm ready to go," Sam told her.

"Great, follow me." She led him through the station to the back parking lot, talking as they walked. "We're serving the paper on Collins's place of business, Computer Relief. On a tangential note, though it took a lot of time, I contacted the Uber driver who picked Collins up."

"Get anything useful?"

"Some. He made the pickup Thursday night, not Friday. The driver took him to the train station in Fullerton."

"Train?" This truly surprised Sam. "He wants us to believe he fled by train?"

"Yep. Interestingly, Collins hacked someone else's Uber account to book and pay for the ride."

"How about the train ticket?"

"Don't know. Fullerton PD has been all over the station and can't find any proof Collins even got on a train."

"Misdirection. If he left on Thursday but was in San Bernardino on Saturday to steal a car and then try to shoot Jodie, it's certain he found a way to San Bernardino. Is there a BOLO out for Collins?" Sam asked.

Tara nodded. "Yes. If he's in the country, we'll find him."

"Do we know if Collins is still on the books at Computer Relief?"

"According to the owner, yes. However, he hasn't turned in any work for at least a week, and two projects are overdue. The phone number Computer Relief had for him is out of service. Sounds as if he's on his way to being fired with or without police attention."

They reached a plain car and she unlocked the doors, turning to hand him the folder she was holding. "You'll have time to look this over while we're on the way to the business. It's in Signal Hill, the city within our city."

Sam took the folder and walked around to the passenger seat. He read as Corson drove. The file included interviews with all the neighbors and a further interview with Collins's boss.

He sighed and rubbed his creased forehead in frustration. There was a gap here. How did Collins make the connection to move down the street from Gus Perkins? Gus hadn't been involved in the hiring process at all. As far as RAT went, Jodie was always the face of the high-profile team. And Jodie only stepped in for the interview because her uncle was sick at the time.

"I can hear your frustration," Tara said, smile in her voice.

"None of this adds up."

"It sure doesn't."

The deeper Sam got into this investigation, the more questions were raised. His thoughts went back to the IED and the careful planning for the setup in the mountains. It hinged on a knowledge of police work. Fugitive warrants were most often served early, just before dawn. The service had to be announced three times. Whoever was in the cabin on the day Jodie's team knocked might not have known the exact day the team would arrive, but they knew how much time they had after the first knock.

The timing of the freezer shutting off, the delay on the IED under Collins's house—all set with police procedure in mind. Careful planning, yes, but Collins and his partner were also playing the odds. No run-of-the-mill crook planned so well. More certain now than ever about Collins getting inside help, Sam thought about Ian and cast a side glance at Tara. Collins hadn't learned to kill and evade by himself. Ian was already on Sam's list; should Tara be there as well? He didn't know them, so it was hard for him to trust them—even though they were officers.

Sam decided he wasn't going to trust anyone.

"That took a lot of guts, you know?"

"What?" Sam looked up from the folder, frowning.

"Crawling under Collins's house, looking for a bomb."

"Ah, it's what the government trained me for."

"Yeah. Good for Jodie. Things are turning around for her now."

"What do you mean?"

Tara hiked her shoulder. "Until that IED, Jodie led a charmed life at work. Nothing was ever amiss. She pretty much got whatever she wanted. Guess her luck is back now."

Sam considered Tara's statement, which rubbed him wrong. "When people work hard for things, there's no such thing as luck. I don't believe in luck."

"Not everyone who works hard gets what they deserve."

"I—" He cut his response when he realized they had arrived. Tara sounded bitter, and Sam wondered about her attitude.

"We're here." Tara pulled into a strip mall parking lot. One small storefront bore the name Computer Relief.

"No wonder he only had to be in the office once a month. Doesn't look like the place is very big," Sam observed. He also checked out the parking lot. He thought he'd noticed a vehicle following them. Old habits died hard. When Sam worked patrol with Rick, his eyes constantly roved, noting their surroundings, whether or not he was driving. An older blue Jeep Cherokee with off-road tires was a couple of cars behind them. The SUV didn't pull into the lot directly behind them but continued to the next driveway. Sam turned to get a better look and the vehicle made a quick left, toward the other end of the strip mall.

As soon as Tara stopped the car, Sam got out, craning his neck to glimpse the driver.

"What?" Tara asked when she opened her car door.

Sam took three long steps toward the back of their car, giving up on the Jeep driver, trying to get a better look at the license plate of the SUV.

"That blue SUV—doesn't it look like the one Levi said Collins borrowed?"

"Where is it?"

He pointed and heard her come after him.

"Hey!" Alarm sounded in Tara's voice.

A horn blared and Sam jerked to a stop, wrenching his gaze from the blue SUV to the red Tesla that had very nearly hit him.

Holding his hands up, he nodded apologetically to the driver. "Sorry."

He stepped back, looked to where the blue SUV had been, but it was gone.

"Did you see it?" he asked Tara.

"No, I didn't. You want to go after it?" she asked.

Frustrated he'd lost the vehicle, he shook his head. "It's gone. Maybe I was wrong. Let's get to the warrant."

He filed the car away in his memory and saw Tara watching him quizzically.

"You sure?"

"Yes, we have a job to do."

"Okay." Together they walked to the door of Computer Relief. Tara explained what they would see.

"I contacted the owner by phone. He should have everything ready for us—files, phones, computers, etc. The only thing he balked at was giving us the names of his clients."

"You changed his mind, I hope."

"The warrant changed his mind. I included everything I could think of when I wrote out the affidavit. We should get the names and information of any clients Collins worked with, even tangentially."

Inside, Tara spoke to the owner and showed him the warrants while Sam checked out the office. In the background he heard the owner's concerns. If his clients believed he'd hired a hacker, this could destroy his business.

"I'm careful. I watch their work. I can assure you Dennis is not a hacker."

I'm pretty sure he is, Sam thought, eyes moving around the room. A receptionist sat at the main counter to greet people as they entered the store. Behind the reception desk was the main office and then what looked to be a work area. The office space contained four desks with computers on them. There were three techs working—at least Sam assumed they were techs. Two wore headsets and were speaking with people, fingers flying across keyboards. One tech didn't seem busy at all; he appeared to be watching Sam and Tara closely. When he caught Sam looking at him, he turned away, busily clicking computer keys.

"Any other questions?" the owner asked.

"Yeah," Sam said. "Was Dennis particularly close to anyone here? Someone maybe he partied with?"

"Ah, Martin. Dennis didn't party though. A whiz with computers, for sure. He wasn't the friendly sort, but he and Martin seemed to hit it off. They both applied to the police department together."

Sam's antenna went up. "And neither made the grade?"

"Oh no, Martin was hired. That put a chink in their friendship, I think. In any event, he only lasted in the academy for a month and a half. Martin's sitting over there." He pointed to the tech who'd been watching them. "I was glad to take him back. He's almost as good with computers as Dennis."

CHAPTER 35

AFTER SAM LEFT, Jodie's phone rang. It was Mike. She answered right away.

"News about my car?"

"Yep. There were three separate GPS trackers on the under-carriage. One was easy to find; the others were hidden. This guy took his time putting these on your car. He wanted to know where you were at all times."

Jodie grabbed a fistful of hair as anger and indignation roared through her. "How in the world did he have the time to place those on my car?" She released her hair and held her hand up in the air.

"We're playing catch-up here, Jodie. But before long, I plan to be in the lead."

"Thanks." She stood, smoothed her ruffled hair, and started

to pace. *Why did I ask such a stupid question? I don't have a garage. Someone could have put the trackers on the car anytime during the night.* The thought of this guy working on her car when she had no idea, besides making her angry, made her feel doubly exposed.

"We sent what we removed to the FBI. They can trace the purchaser much faster than we can. Chances are good we'll find out who bought them."

"You're thinking it's someone other than Collins?" Jodie asked.

"I don't know what to think. It's just more and more obvious Collins has help." Mike's voice grew muffled for a moment; then he came back. "I just got an email from the coroner. They removed the corpses from the freezer. They both had gunshot wounds to the head. They were executed."

Jodie closed her eyes and rubbed her forehead. "Poor Jukebox."

"I'm sorry, Jodie," Mike said. "This guy Collins is turning out to be a lot more than a computer geek. Nothing I read indicates he's capable of doing all this."

"Yeah, whenever a serial killer is caught, all the neighbors say, 'But he was such a nice guy.'"

"I'm just hoping the trackers will give us a clue as to who his partner is."

Jodie said nothing.

"Are you still okay with the safe house?"

"It's probably wise. Will I get my car back?"

"I'm thinking it's better to leave it parked at your house. Kind of a decoy. You won't need it in hiding anyway."

Jodie bit her tongue. She saw the logic in the ruse but hated it just the same.

"I'd like to have some techs go over your apartment, just to be on the safe side," Mike continued. "I'll grab a couple, then send a black-and-white to pick you up, say after lunch?"

"What do you think he put in my apartment?"

"At this point nothing would surprise me. Your computer needs to be examined, and your phone, again. It may be nothing. I want to be sure. Cloning phones is too easy and this punk is a tech magician."

Jodie wanted to scream. This maniac had taken just about everything from her, including her ability to be independent, to stay in her own home.

"You okay, Jodie?"

"No, not really." She closed and opened her free hand, wishing she could smash a fist into Dennis Collins's face. Not very Christian but certainly very real.

"We'll catch this guy—I promise."

The call ended and Jodie worked to calm down.

"Are you all right?" Estella asked.

"No, but I'm trying."

"Nothing else you can do. While you're trying, can you help me pack up the den? Manual labor always calms me down."

Impatient but realizing there was nothing she could do to speed things up, Jodie busied herself helping Estella pack.

"You're not actually moving for another three months," Jodie asked. "Why pack now?"

"Gus and I lived in this house for thirty years. There's a lot of stuff to go through, a lot of stuff to get rid of. I wanted to take my time."

They were in the den sorting through photos, DVDs, and books.

Jodie couldn't help but notice one particular photo, because her uncle Mike had the same one. She picked up the old photo of an academy graduation. Mike, Gus, and Jonah, young, newly minted police officers, all together in the second row, smiled. Jodie's throat thickened and she sniffled. So much promise in this photo. Now Gus was dead, and Jonah sold real estate. At least Mike still carried on. But it made her sad.

"One of my favorite photos," Estella said. "I see Levi when I look at young Gus." She took the picture from Jodie and dusted it, smiling.

"Did you know Gus then?" Jodie asked.

"No, we met later. He had five years under his belt. I'm kind of glad I didn't know him before then."

"Why?"

"Gus admitted to me that he was a wild child—they all were. *Arrogant* and *badge heavy* was his description. I hate to say it, but Mike was a bad influence. He was the ringleader."

"No way." Jodie couldn't see this. Uncle Mike was so rigid and by the book, she couldn't imagine him being wild.

"Jonah and Gus had their moments," Estella said as if reading Jodie's mind. "But you know what calmed Mike down?"

"What?"

"You."

"Huh?"

"Yep, when his brother died and you became his responsibility, Mike decided to straighten up and fly right. Gus and I were dating at the time. Mike hadn't been going to any church, so when you showed up, we brought the two of you to ours."

"I vaguely remember going to church with you, I guess, but so much of my adjustment to life without my parents is jumbled in my memory."

"Mike wanted to raise you right, and he did." She smiled, handed the picture back to Jodie, then patted her on the cheek.

The doorbell rang. "Ah, I have to get that. Levi is at the market, doing my grocery shopping." Estella left to answer the door.

Jodie stared at the photo for a few seconds, then wrapped it and packed it away, vowing to ask Mike about his wild days.

Estella came back into the room, wringing her hands as she often did when she was nervous or upset.

"Jodie, Ian Hunter's at the door. I wasn't sure you wanted to see him. I tried to get him to leave, but he's insistent, and he's angry. What should I do?"

The last person Jodie wanted to talk to was Ian. But looking at Estella, she knew it wasn't the older woman's job to tell him.

"I'll deal with him." She set down the book in her hand and walked to the front door. Ian was a good cop; he'd proved himself time and time again when they worked together. Yet he couldn't get past that day. Jodie tried hard to be patient with him, but in the shadow of his anger and accusations, she had no idea how to reach him.

Macnut followed her to the door; he'd been her shadow the whole time Jodie had been at Estella's. Jodie opened the door only a crack to keep the dog in. Ian's back was to her, but he turned when he heard the door open, and Jodie saw the anger in his features. Ian never did have a great cop face.

"Ian."

"Jodie, what is going on? What do you have against me?"

"I don't know what you're talking about."

"Can I come in? Or do we have to do this in the doorway?"

"Estella has dogs. I know they're not your favorite. Give me a minute." She opened the door a small bit, and keeping Macnut back with her foot, she stepped out on the porch to speak with Ian.

"What's happened?" she asked, facing him on the porch.

"Funny you ask. I've been blindsided—stabbed in the back more like it. I was supposed to have an assignment on the task force. Yet today I find out that the cripple stole my spot."

"Cripple?" Jodie frowned and then she realized he meant Sam. "Name-calling is so unwarranted." She folded her arms and glared at him. "Sam Gresham has proven himself a good cop."

"He doesn't even work for the PD. This is my case. They were my friends, not his."

"It wasn't my decision." *But I'm glad it was made,* she thought. "To be honest, they probably think you're too close. So do I. You're not acting yourself."

"Myself?" He snorted in disdain. "You owe me something, Jodie. Talk to your uncle."

She leaned back against the door. Jodie had no wish to hurt him, but she couldn't throw him a bone.

"Ian, I can't change what happened. I'm sorry. I miss everyone as much as you do, and I want to see justice done. You're angry— I understand—but I think you need to sit this one out and take care of you."

"Spare me your pity. I get it." His face was red with rage. "You should have waited. Those deaths will always be on your head."

"Yes, I know."

CHAPTER 36

WHILE THE COMPUTER RELIEF OWNER read the warrants, Sam turned to Tara.

"I think I should go chat with Martin."

She frowned. "Now?"

"Here on his home turf he might be more inclined to open up. I don't want to drag him to the station."

She took a beat to consider his suggestion, and he really didn't think she liked the idea. This surprised Sam. Divide and conquer was a successful tactic for him and Rick. Maybe he'd been without a partner too long. Well, if she wanted them to stay together, he'd deal with it.

Finally she nodded. "Yeah, okay, I can handle the records."

Tara stayed with the owner, poring over the accounts Dennis was responsible for, while Sam took Martin to a private room in the store.

"Martin, I'm Detective Sam Gresham. I appreciate you taking the time to talk to me about Dennis."

"I'm not sure what I can tell you. Yeah, we were friends and stuff, but he was never the most open of people." He seemed to want to say something else, and Sam wanted to keep him talking.

"You have a question?"

"I saw the news, the reports about a bomb under his house. Do you really think Dennis planted C-4? And he killed those four officers up in the mountains?"

"The evidence points toward him."

Martin shook his head. "I thought he was a little off, but murdering people is crazy."

"Off how?"

"He could be obsessive."

Sam prompted him to keep going.

"Like being a cop. He got me started. We studied together, worked out together—he was way more into it than I was. He even had a private trainer."

"What, like at a health club?"

"No. He claimed he had a cop buddy helping him train."

Sam stiffened. Would finding the other half be this easy? "You're sure it was a cop?"

"Dennis said so."

"Did you ever meet this guy?"

"No. I wasn't sure he was telling the truth. The guy could have been a security guard for all I knew. Dennis could exaggerate at times. Or maybe he just had a YouTube video with a workout he followed. It didn't seem to help. He barely passed the physical test. Even I did better on it than he did."

"Did he say why he wanted to be a cop?"

Martin shrugged. "He had this war-hero brother, Kent. Denny hated him but idolized him in some way. I think . . ."

"What?"

"I'm not a psychiatrist or anything, but somehow I think Denny wanted to become a cop in order to prove he was as much a man as Kent. His parents treated Denny like a redheaded stepchild—those were his words. Kent was their pride and joy. He told me they died after Kent did because they didn't want to live without him."

Sam made a note to double-check on how the parents died. Given what they were learning about Dennis, anything was possible.

"Did he take it hard when he wasn't hired?"

"I guess. He cut me off because I was hired. Though I didn't last long."

"What happened to you?"

"I had trouble identifying threats from suspects in role-playing. I can identify any virus on a computer, just not in real life." He rolled a pen around in his hands. "I guess I'm more of a machine guy than a people person."

"Was Dennis more friendly after you washed out?"

"Yeah, but it wasn't the same as before. When I was rehired here, I hoped we could go back to the way things were." Martin made a face. "He was different, more secretive. He had no time for me."

"Does Dennis have a knowledge of explosives?"

Martin nodded. "Kent was a bomb tech. After he died, Dennis got all his stuff. From what he said, the stuff sounded classified.

But I just thought Dennis was boasting, making things up. The Army doesn't let classified stuff slip out, does it?"

"Bomb-making information is all over the Internet. Dennis is a hacker, right?"

Martin cast a furtive glance toward the office. "Dennis has skills for sure."

"Is there something you want to tell me? I'm here about Dennis, not you."

Martin swallowed, Adam's apple bouncing, voice a whisper. "He bragged about hacking the bank at the corner. Claimed he had plenty of time to take a lot of money from a dormant account. They never had a clue."

"When was this?"

"He told me about it after I was rehired, so he must have done it before then. When I got back to work, he hated cops, or so he said. He said cyber cops were the easiest to bamboozle. *Bamboozle* was his favorite word. He thinks it makes him look sophisticated."

"Back to the explosives. Did you ever see what he said he had?"

"No, but he and his cop trainer friend did stuff with it. One time he said something about them hiking into the wilderness and blowing up trees, using Kent's equipment. I honestly thought he was fantasizing."

"You never found out who this other friend was?"

"I never met him. From the way Denny talked, he was smart, and he had money. It was a lot for Dennis to say someone was smart. He really thought he was always the smartest guy in the room."

"You sure it was a *him*?"

Martin laughed. "Yeah, Dennis couldn't talk to girls."

"You were close when he sold the family home and moved, weren't you?"

Martin nodded.

"Did he say why he moved? Was the other house a dump? I mean, he barely moved half a mile away."

"All I remember was Dennis said he moved because of the memories." Martin rolled his eyes. "Dennis is not the sentimental type. He owned the house free and clear, so I guess it was his prerogative to sell."

Sam sat back and thought for a moment. According to Estella, Dennis didn't have a car. He wondered if Martin knew anything different.

"Do you know what kind of car Dennis owns?"

"None. He doesn't have a car. Dennis is all about Uber. He wants someone else to worry about the wear and tear of a car."

"Yet sometimes he drove a car, a Jeep?"

"Oh yeah, the Jeep belonged to his buddy. Sometimes he'd loan it to Dennis."

Some buddy, Sam thought.

CHAPTER 37

AFTER LUNCH a black-and-white showed up at Estella's to take Jodie back to her apartment, where Mike was waiting with an FBI lab team. They had the tools to check for surveillance and listening devices. Jodie was surprised the FBI had gotten involved so soon. But then, they were involved with the original IED invest.

"We already had the bomb squad come by. The dog was sent in and hit on nothing." Mike had a key to her place; she'd given it to him a long time ago so he could water her plants when she was on vacation. "But before we started going through your things, I wanted you to be here."

Jodie gritted her teeth and walked through the door when he opened it. Somehow her cozy apartment didn't feel so cozy anymore. Even if they didn't find any trace of the guy here, her personal space had been violated.

Jodie picked up her laptop. "Am I going to lose anything from this?"

"Maybe," the tech said. "It depends on if we find a hack, and if we do, how invasive it is. Is your stuff backed up?"

"Yes, everything is backed up."

"Hopefully if there was a hack, it will lead us right to the hacker. I'll need your phone as well."

"I knew this was coming but I still hate it. How long will you need it?"

"Not long. I'll work on it first. There are a lot of ways he could track you: your phone, your car. I want to be thorough. I'll check it, secure it, and give it back."

She handed him the laptop and phone and he sat down to go to work. The other tech had a sensor and was looking for any unauthorized electronic devices. Jodie walked into her bedroom and began to pack up a few things. Anger vibrated through her. The sense of violation was so strong it made her want to lash out.

But Sam's Psalm 46 calmed her. *"Be still, and know that I am God."*

It was all she could do for the moment: be still. Jodie was powerless.

Eager for a distraction, she turned to Mike. "Why did you promise Ian a spot on the task force?" she asked as they walked into the kitchen.

Mike rolled his eyes. "I guess in a way I kind of did."

"Mike! He's mad Sam got a spot. Why did you lie to him?"

"It was a crazy night, we were busy, and he was crowding. I just wanted to get rid of him. Why?"

"He came by Estella's. In his mind his spot was stolen."

"I think Gresham is a better fit. Don't you?"

Jodie couldn't disagree. "I do. I hope Ian gets over it. Honestly, I don't blame him because you never should have promised."

"You're right. I was wrong. He'll calm down."

"I'm afraid he'll do something stupid."

"If he hasn't learned self-control by now, he needs to turn in his badge."

"I hope you're right."

"What did he say exactly?"

Jodie shook her head.

Just then, the tech walked in. "Your phone is clean, but you were definitely hacked." He handed her the phone.

"How?"

"This guy installed spy software on your laptop. He was tracking your computer activity, reading your emails, checking out the sites you visited. He most likely gained access to your system by installing a virus in an email you trusted, maybe. This is the kind of hacking we see in cyberstalking cases. He simply watched everything you did. He may have even intercepted emails. I'll need more time with the laptop. I'll give you a call when it's cleaned up."

Jodie felt punched in the stomach.

"Can you figure out who did it?"

"I'll do my best. It's quite a challenge. I've seen a lot of hacks, and this is, so far, the best and most difficult to track."

■ ■ ■

Sam finished up with Martin and went to help Tara with all the Computer Relief records she was sifting through.

"Anything?" he asked.

"One or two concerning things." She chewed on her bottom lip.

"You look frustrated."

"I am. I've been looking for anything remotely connected to Jodie. Look at this list." She handed him the legal pad she'd been writing on.

The first name on the list was a fitness center, followed by a medical center and a coffee shop. The fourth name on the list hit him right between the eyes: the real estate offices of Jonah Bennett.

Sam looked up. "Jonah Bennett?"

"Yep, good old Uncle Jonah."

"You sound as if you don't like him."

"The old geezer hit on me. I could be his daughter."

Sam stretched out the fingers on his right hand, pushing them back with his left hand. Jonah was family to Jodie. Was this a coincidence, or did Collins see Jonah as an additional avenue to get information about Jodie? "I doubt the big boss is responsible for hiring tech help. Someone from his office probably called Computer Relief."

"Maybe." Tara was watching him.

He looked back at the list. "These others are important because . . . ?"

"Collins was the tech on all four of their repair tickets. Jodie and I both work out at the gym, or we did before the IED. He worked on their customer billing accounts."

"Okay."

"The medical center is where Dr. Bass works. Collins specifically set up everyone's entire billing and appointment system."

"So the hacker could have gotten her medical records."

"Yes."

"And the coffee shop?"

"Jodie liked this place for team meetings. She and her guys would meet there. If they were on the network there, who knows."

"That's a long shot."

Tara shrugged and shoved files into a folder. "I will pull at every string I can. Was the coworker any help?"

"Not really. He gave me some ideas about why Collins flipped out—nothing earthshaking. From the way he talked, I don't think they were really close friends."

"I don't think this kid was truly friends with anyone. He's a misfit. Let's head back to the station."

As they left Computer Relief, Sam looked for the blue Jeep and didn't find it. He knew he'd feel a lot better about everything the sooner Collins was in custody.

CHAPTER 38

ALONG WITH HER BACKPACK, Jodie packed a small suitcase. Mike drove her back to Estella's.

"I'm glad you decided to go hide," Mike said. "I'll sleep easier. The Feds will send someone here to pick you up a little after dinnertime."

Like I had a choice. "They'll pick me up?"

"Yeah. No one else needs to know where you're going. You agree, right?"

"I was, uh . . . I was hoping Sam could take me."

"It really wouldn't make sense, Jodie. The Feds can handle it and keep you safe. The less people know where you are, the better."

Jodie was quiet for a moment. She'd come to think of Sam like a partner. She wanted him to know where she was. It was unsettling to think of putting her life in the hands of strangers. *I'm just being silly . . . aren't I?*

"I hope it's only for the night," she said. "With everyone working this case, I expect Collins and his partner will be in custody before long."

"You wouldn't think, just looking at this kid's background, he'd be capable of doing everything we think he's done. You know what bothers me the most?" Mike asked.

Jodie looked across the car at her uncle. She did know. "You think his partner may be a cop?"

He met her gaze briefly before returning his focus to the road. "I hate to think it, and I have no one in mind, but this guy . . ."

"I know what you mean. Sam and I talked about this last night."

"You told Gresham?"

"I trust him. He's not going to announce the theory from the housetops."

"It's too obvious. Everyone will come to the same conclusion if they haven't already. We're going to have to figure this out and pounce on the guy before he can cover his tracks. I've shut everyone out of the invest on the computer. It's flagged now. If anyone unauthorized tries to pull up the file on this investigation, warning bells will go off."

"Who is authorized?"

"Me, Tara, Gresham, one or two Feds, and the chief. Period."

Jodie considered this. Officers could generally access ongoing investigations only if they could show a need to know. An unauthorized access would be logged but not necessarily set off warning bells. If Mike set an alert, he'd know immediately if someone accessed information they weren't supposed to. *Unless, of course, Collins knows how to defeat such an alert and his cop buddy gets in.*

Oh, Lord, she prayed, *who have I worked with for fifteen years that hates me so much they'd try to murder me again and again?*

· · ·

Back at the station, Tara gave Sam a thumb drive with some information to review. They'd decided to divide up the list of clients. He reviewed what the clients had requested and what Collins said he actually did. Sam found the work request for the medical practice where Bass worked the most troubling. The request was from two months ago. Collins could have discovered a lot about Jodie from his files. He could have used the information to help set up the trap in Arrowbear.

The timing was about the same, but the gym and the coffee shop did not register as big deals, though Corson was running with them, leaving him to ruminate about Bennett. This request was for further back, more than a year. The warrant the judge had signed off on had asked for eighteen months' history. While Sam didn't think it was as big a red flag as Corson did, he called Bennett's office. When he told the receptionist who he was, he was put through immediately to Jonah.

"Sam Gresham, I'll admit I'm surprised to hear from you. What can I do for you?"

Sam told him about Computer Relief and Dennis Collins.

"Wow, I don't know what to say other than he'd never get any information about Jodie from one of my offices. She's never been a real estate client."

"We're contacting anyone with ties to both Collins and Jodie."

"I get it. I wish I could help. But I have an IT manager who deals with computer issues. Do you want to talk to him?"

"Yes, I would. Can you give me his name and number?"

"Whatever I can do to help."

Sam took the information and called the man. He wasn't much help. It was hard for him to remember so far back. The man had called Computer Relief when their system crashed. He worked with the tech remotely and did not even remember the guy's name. Though the tech had complete access, Bennett was correct: Collins wouldn't have gotten any information about Jodie from this system. One dead end.

Sam hung up and saw he had new emails. The first one was forwarded from Mike King about the preliminary autopsies of the two bodies in Collins's house. They were positively identified as Hayes and Radio, and they were executed. Sam considered the coldness in execution. It was one thing to set up an IED and kill people from afar. Killing someone up close and personal took a lot more guts. Collins or his buddy? Time of death was going to be problematic because the bodies had been frozen for some time.

Sam turned to the medical offices where Dr. Bass worked. He called and asked to talk to their tech department.

"What can I do for you, Detective Gresham?"

He asked about the computer repair they had done.

After a few clicks, the tech said, "Back then we had a system-wide crash. I think the crash happened because of a hack."

"Really? Was anything compromised?"

"I want to say no, but I don't really know. It was way over my head, so we called Computer Relief. I'm good with the system in general, but I'd never seen such a thorough crash."

"So you don't know if there was a specific target?"

"What do you mean?"

"The police psychologist is on your system. Were any of his files broken into?"

"Oh no. I can assure you no client information was compromised. It was a system-wide crash, but patient information is protected from those kinds of incidents."

"Are you positive? I'm not going to tell any of your clients their information might have been comprised. I'm conducting a criminal investigation and I have to know the truth."

The tech went quiet for a moment. "I can't say I'm 100 percent sure. I am 95 percent sure."

Sam asked a few more questions before hanging up. He wondered about the 5 percent. The tech really didn't know what was lost; probably the only person who did was Dennis Collins. He tapped on the table with his pen, then looked up. Tara was standing there. He'd been so engrossed he hadn't heard her walk to his temporary desk.

"Yeah?"

"Are you going to work all night?"

He checked the clock. He had no idea it was so late. The search for connections had him totally involved.

"I've been digging in, hoping something would be uncovered." He stretched.

"You've got a long drive home."

"I'll grab some dinner, then hit the road. Traffic won't be so bad then."

"If you don't want to make the drive, I've got a spare room. You're welcome to crash there."

Sam considered her offer for a moment. It would make his life easier. But it wasn't the right thing to do.

"Thanks. But I wouldn't have taken this assignment if I minded the drive."

Tara raised an eyebrow. "Just trying to be helpful." She turned on her heel and left him curious about why she was so put out. Having no time to try to figure it out, he texted Jodie.

She phoned. "I was just about to call you. There's a federal agent here now, ready to take me to the safe house."

"Oh." Sam didn't know what to say. He'd planned on taking Jodie himself. "Are you leaving right away?"

"Yes. And the location is staying secret. Sorry, I do trust you. The Feds don't seem to trust anyone."

"Okay. It's probably for the best. I'll be praying for you."

CHAPTER 39

JODIE GRABBED HER BACKPACK AND SUITCASE and followed Agent Greto out to the car. He'd been one of the original agents on the IED case, which meant she wasn't riding with a complete stranger. He looked like every other male federal agent she'd ever met: tall, dark hair cut close, wearing a dark suit with a muted blue tie.

"Sorry we wasted so much time on Hayes," he said as they sat in the car.

"Thanks for the apology."

"First thing," he said as he started the engine. "I'll need your phone. You'll be incommunicado for the time being." He held his hand out.

"No, I'm not some silly civilian. My phone was checked. It's free of trackers. I know not to use it."

"Protocol."

Jodie dug in her heels and shook her head. "It's been examined. It's in airplane mode. I've got games on my phone; I need something to occupy me. I know not to call anyone."

They glared at one another for a moment before Greto relented.

"I hope you don't plan on giving me headaches the whole time we're together."

"All depends. I hope you don't plan on asking me the impossible again."

He turned away and concentrated on the driving.

It was dark, and Jodie recognized he was driving to thwart any tails. She paid attention. After about an hour they pulled into the driveway of a small house in Huntington Beach. The house sat up off the street and backed up to an alley. It would have good ingress and egress. The agent opened the garage door with a button, then pulled the car in and shut the door once they were inside. The lights came on and they both got out.

As they entered the kitchen, the agent pointed to the refrigerator. "It should be stocked if you're hungry."

"I could eat. I'll check out the bedroom first."

He nodded. "Certainly." He turned to a keypad on the wall. "I'm setting the alarm. There are sensors on all the doors and window screens. You can open a window, just don't mess with the screen. If you need to go outside for any reason, let me know."

"I can't think of any reason why I would need to go outside, thanks."

He keyed in the code and the alarm clicked on. He then went to the hall and flicked on the light. Jodie followed him to a back bedroom.

He turned the light on there as well, checked out the room. "This is yours."

"Thanks."

He left Jodie in the room, closing the door behind him.

She put her bags down and sat on the bed for a while. Then she went into the kitchen to make herself a snack. She was hungry; she hadn't eaten since Estella's. Greto was watching television. She put together a ham and cheese sandwich, grabbed some chips from the pantry, and went back to her room.

"Sweet dreams," Greto called out.

■ ■ ■

Disappointed not to be taking Jodie to the safe house, Sam began to pack up his stuff. He'd been looking forward to chatting with Jodie for a bit. But the fewer people who knew where she was, the better. Now he could be as certain as possible she'd be safe.

Sam left the station about half an hour after Corson. One of the other detectives told him he'd find an In-N-Out Burger in Belmont Shore. He pulled up the address on his GPS and found it easily. While he was in line, he noticed a blue Jeep in the parking lot, same model as the one he'd seen earlier in the day. There was someone in the driver's seat, but he could only see a shadow though the tint. From where he sat, he could tell the Jeep had no front license plate. He hadn't noticed whether the Jeep he saw earlier had a front plate or not.

Am I being paranoid? Why would anyone be following me? He ate his meal, trying not to continually stare at the Jeep. It was still there when he got up and threw out his trash.

Spotting a tail in the dark would be difficult. He made a mental note of the vehicle's headlight configuration, then started up his rental and headed for the 405 freeway. He entered the flow of traffic, glanced in his rearview mirror, and there was the same car, he was sure.

Luckily, traffic wasn't too heavy. He veered to the right and took the next off-ramp. The vehicle following him didn't take the same exit. He pulled into the parking lot of a strip mall—was he in Cypress or Westminster?—and parked to think.

Am I being paranoid? he asked himself again.

He still wasn't sure, but an idea came to him. He called his friend from the rental agency and asked if he could change rental cars.

"You having mechanical problems?"

"No, the car runs fine. I'd just like a different car. I'm in Orange County right now. Would it be possible to go to an agency nearby and switch the car out?"

"Yeah, it may cost you a little extra money."

"No problem."

According to his friend, the best place to make the switch was the Long Beach Airport. Sam had to backtrack, but he wasn't far away from the airport and in short order he found himself in line at a rental counter.

Once he had a new car and left the airport, Sam was exhausted. It had been a long day. He decided to find a hotel and stay the night. Still wary about a tail, Sam got on the 91 freeway and exited near Disneyland. His thought was to get lost in the crowd. He found a hotel with a vacancy and took a room. In the guest shop he purchased some sweats and a T-shirt, not wanting to sleep in his only other suit.

As midnight closed in, he showered and fell into bed, asleep almost instantly.

CHAPTER 40

JODIE COULDN'T SLEEP. She felt tired, but her mind would not shut down. The neighborhood was quiet. She'd opened a window and heard only crickets. She played a few word games on her phone, then tried reading, but nothing held her concentration. There was a TV in the room, but she had no interest in watching TV. She thought about Macnut. The pup had slept with her last night and she missed him. It made her wonder if maybe it was time to find a different apartment so she could have a dog. Estella would be moving away and taking Macnut with her if Jodie didn't make different arrangements.

Finally she opened the Bible app on her phone. She paced as she read. All of it had been so dead to her for months. She thought things began to change this week when she was standing on an IED. But she was still flapping in the breeze.

"Be real," Sam had said.

"Keep the dialogue open," Shannon had said.

I'm trying.

Every time she got to this point, she felt like screaming. *I lost my parents. Wasn't that enough?*

She thought about giving up, turning her back on God, joining the ranks of those who believed he was a myth. Giving up would not quiet her soul. *"Where would we go? You have the words of eternal life . . ."* The verse echoed in her mind. She forgot where it was but knew Peter had said it.

Jodie put down her phone, fists clenched in frustration. Random conversations replayed in her head.

Sam said he didn't understand his loss any more than I understand mine, yet he seems to have peace moving forward. Is his faith just stronger than mine?

"It's not a matter of what you do or don't do. You can't live second-guessing every move. No one in this life is immune from bad things. Trusting God doesn't mean no trials."

"Faith doesn't always take away the pain, but it does give you the ability to handle the pain. . . . What have you put your faith in?"

"God is good . . . even when life isn't."

Jodie sat on the bed, feeling as though all strength had fled. She'd been trying to mask her feelings. Even when she spoke to Estella, she just wore a mask and refused to look inside, refused to really hear what Estella was saying.

"Let go."

"Move on."

She couldn't do those things as long as she was holding on to the pain of a past she had zero ability to change.

The room was quiet and dark except for the glow of her phone and the red lights of the digital clock.

You always have to be in control.

Was that the reason for the wall between her and God? She didn't want to relinquish control?

I don't know how.

Jodie kept praying, not really knowing what to pray except to ask for clarity, remembering a verse about how the Holy Spirit would translate what she didn't understand herself. She'd felt the barrier between her and God cracking after the incident at Collins's house. Now she was determined to breach it completely.

After a while, she felt as though she'd just been to the chiropractor and every joint in her body had been adjusted. And she was tired, so very tired. Nothing felt different and she fought discouragement.

She stood and picked up the suitcase she'd brought, intending to put on pajamas and go to bed. But then the lights on the clock winked out.

On alert, Jodie stepped to the door and switched on the room light. Nothing happened. Brownouts weren't uncommon in Southern California, but there was no reason for such a thing today. It had been warm, not a heat wave, which usually triggered rolling brownouts.

She went to the window and yanked the screen off.

No alarm. Fear rising, Jodie went back and put her ear to the door. Agent Greto's room was at the other end of the hall, near the front of the house. She thought she heard a soft thump, but it was faint enough to be her imagination. A few more minutes ticked by. Then she heard a door close softly. A creak of a floorboard, footsteps coming her way.

Jodie backed away from the door and grabbed her backpack. She partially dumped it, digging for her weapon. Her heart stopped when a silver disc fell out, twirling on the floor until it lay flat. An Apple AirTag.

Who put it there?

There was no time to ponder the question. She pulled her gun out as the footsteps stopped at the door. She saw the knob turn and was glad she'd locked it. She slid back toward the window.

"Agent Greto?"

The only answer was a sharp bang as if someone put their shoulder to the door. The solid door jolted but held. Jodie jumped. Another good slam might break the lock. She fired two shots from her own weapon at the door—hoping to slow down whoever was out there—before turning and throwing her backpack out the window, then following.

Not knowing how many attackers she faced or if Greto was in fact an attacker, Jodie believed discretion was the better part of valor, as Sam would say. Confirmation she'd made the right decision came when two more shots were fired her way as she launched herself over the fence into the alley behind the house. She thought she heard a man yell, *"We'll get her!"* but she was too intent on fleeing to be sure.

When people ran from the police, the ones who escaped were generally the ones who kept moving and evaded the perimeter. Jodie wanted to evade, so she turned left and sprinted down the alley. Two houses down, there was a narrow walkway between a garage and a fence. She darted into the space, barely fitting, having to turn sideways, soon finding herself on another street. She crossed it. Then jumped into another backyard, praying there were no angry dogs.

Her prayer answered, she crossed the yard as quickly as she could. She opened the back gate and stopped, trying to calm her racing heart, steady her breathing, and listen for any sound of pursuit. After a few minutes, she heard a car motor approaching, driving slowly up the street she'd just crossed.

As quietly as she could, she closed the gate and knelt. Her breathing slowed to normal, and she could think. Gripping her gun in two hands, she waited. The light from the vehicle's head-lights shone in the alley—she could see it through the fence slats.

Jodie pressed her back flat against the side of the garage and held her breath. She'd dumped the tracker, and she prayed it was the only one.

The vehicle slowly rolled past the gate. Unless they'd seen her dart into the yard, she believed she was safe. Still, Jodie didn't budge until she was certain the vehicle kept moving. Surely the gunshots would bring the police. She doubted the shooter would stay in the area for long. And the police wouldn't roll into a *shots fired* call with sirens blazing if there were no reports of a victim.

Glancing at her watch, she saw it was after midnight. Streetlights still shone, so the power outage at the safe house had been deliberate. She wondered about Agent Greto, but she dared not go back.

Who put the AirTag in her backpack? Who had access while she was at Estella's? Mike, Estella, Tara, Smiley, Sam, Levi, even Jonah could have seen her backpack where she'd set it on the couch in Estella's living room.

Her heart hurt. Someone close to her had betrayed her—who?

She stayed kneeling and considered what her next move should be. Her phone had been checked out, so it couldn't have led any-one to her. Besides, if it had, they would have followed her now and discovered her hiding place.

Who should she call? Mike? Tara? Sam?

The AirTag crushed all her trust. Somehow, the cop helping Collins had placed the tag.

Jodie considered her options. She knew several Huntington Beach officers; many of them played volleyball. She should be able to trust them. But they didn't have the whole story, the whole background about what she faced. The scenario sometimes sounded crazy to her, so she decided she wanted some backup when she went to talk to the Huntington Beach cops. There was only one person she believed she could trust: Sam Gresham.

CHAPTER 41

SAM WAS IN THE MIDDLE of a strange dream. It was one of those where he knew he had to move and move quickly, but he couldn't, his legs like lead. As hard as he tried, he couldn't lift his right leg. In the distance he heard a buzzing noise. He struggled to shake the heavy bonds of sleep when he realized his phone was buzzing.

Rubbing his face and blinking eyes still heavy with fatigue, Sam grabbed his phone and sat up on the edge of the bed. "Hello?"

"Sam, it's Jodie." She spoke in a whisper and Sam instantly woke up. Something was wrong.

"What's the matter?"

"He found the safe house."

"Who? Collins?"

"It had to be. I found an Apple AirTag in my backpack. I ran. I don't know what happened to the agent. I'm hiding."

Sam turned the light on and stood, running his hand over his head. "You were tracked."

"Yeah."

"Where are you?"

"In Huntington Beach, trying to stay low. I don't know who to trust. I know you're all the way in San Bernardino—"

"I'm in Anaheim. I didn't go home. Tell me your cross streets and I'll be there as soon as I can."

Sam plugged the information into his phone, pulled on his clothes, and hurried out of the room, taking everything, not expecting to be back. Jodie had given him the address of a church off of Beach Boulevard. He found it easily, and when he pulled into the lot, Jodie stepped out of the shadows. He reached over, opened the passenger door, and she hopped in.

"Oh, Sam, I can't thank you enough."

"Don't worry about it. I'm glad you trust me. What do you want to do now?"

"Go back to the house and see if the police are on scene. If there is a police presence, I believe the threat will be gone."

She directed him back to where the safe house was. It was still dark, but there were two police cruisers, one in the driveway and one parked on the street.

Sam surveyed the street as he drove down it and saw nothing else out of place. The neighbors were out, obviously concerned about the police activity, but he doubted the shooter had hung around.

They parked and got out of the car.

One of the uniforms stepped forward. "Can I help you two?" Then he recognized Jodie. "Jodie?"

"Yeah, hey, Craig. This is Detective Sam Gresham, San

Bernardino Sheriff's office. I just ran out of the house you're all over. There was another guy in there—is Agent Greto okay?"

Sam heard the worry in Jodie's voice.

A paramedic's rig rolled up to the address.

"Hang on," Craig said, holding his hands up, eyebrows scrunched in bewilderment. "I need to catch up. There is a guy in there, alive but unconscious. Maybe drugged. He's an agent? You say you ran out of the house?"

"I'll explain."

Sam listened while Jodie told the officer everything. When she finished, Craig whistled. "I saw the story on the news, about the explosive under the house in Long Beach. I didn't realize someone was after you."

"Did anyone who reported the shots see a car leaving?" Sam asked Craig.

"An officer just texted me that he's talking to a possible witness. All we have at this minute is maybe a dark-colored SUV drove through the alley. They heard one or two possible gunshots."

"Sounds about right."

Craig pointed to the front door. "Let's go see how the agent is doing." Craig's flashlight led the way to the room where Greto was. "There's no power to the house. The electrical panel was destroyed. We made entry because the back door had been forced open."

"How is he doing?" Jodie asked the paramedics making an assessment.

"He's alive, breathing—slow, steady heartbeat. He appears to be under the influence," one of the medics said. "His pupils are constricted. We'll transport and advise you about his condition."

"Thank God he's not dead," Jodie said.

Sam surveyed the house, carefully studying the alarm system, which was wireless and state-of-the-art. The power disruption shouldn't have defeated it. Obviously whoever was responsible must have killed it before he killed the power. Collins was the computer geek with the skills to disable the alarm. And right now, he was their best lead, their target.

This was all too close for comfort. He wanted to get Jodie somewhere safe, right away.

CHAPTER 42

"WHAT DO YOU MEAN he found the safe house? Are you kidding me?"

Jodie had called Mike and told him what had happened. She'd startled him out of a sound sleep, based on the rasp in his voice.

"I wish I was kidding. Someone put a tracker in my backpack."

"What? When?"

"I don't know. All I do know is that they came after me and drugged Agent Greto. He's on the way to a hospital in Huntington Beach."

"Unbelievable."

Jodie pictured her uncle scratching his head.

"How could this happen? Where was your backpack?" he asked.

"On Estella's couch until I packed everything up to leave. This is so messed up."

"Understatement. Where are you now?"

"At the house with a lot of HBPD personnel and Sam."

Detectives had arrived and asked to talk to Jodie. She and Sam were on the porch waiting for them to finish their survey of the house. She couldn't help but notice how all the police activity had destroyed the neighborhood's peace and quiet.

"What is Sam doing there? He didn't go home?"

"He stayed in Anaheim overnight. I called him and he came. I've decided to go with him as soon as HBPD gives the okay. I'm going to stay with the retired cop. It doesn't matter if Collins knows where I'm at. He can try and come get me there."

"Jodie, I'm not sure—"

"I'm positive it's the best place for me. I'll scour my belongings and make certain there are no more trackers." Jodie looked at Sam. He and Craig were chatting. Right now, besides Uncle Mike, he was the only person she trusted.

Jodie ended the call as one of the HBPD detectives came out of the house.

"Jodie, can you go over it one more time?"

"Sure." She went back in the house with the detectives. The tracker was gone, no longer on the floor by the bed where she'd seen it drop. When she got to the part about going through the window, one of them stopped her with a question.

"You never saw either assailant?"

"I never looked back." She stared at him. "Wait, you know there were two?"

He nodded. "The uniformed officer got back to me. He interviewed a neighbor who saw two figures running from the house after your gunshots. They were not close enough to give a good description."

"Ah."

"What is it?"

"I thought I heard someone yell, 'We'll catch her' when I was in the alley. But my pulse was pumping, so I'm not certain. I kept running."

"Interesting." He looked down at his phone. "Just got word the agent at the hospital is awake and alert. He was tased and then drugged, possibly a strong sedative."

"I'm glad he's okay."

"Yep, me too. You as well. It looks as if you have nine lives." He looked from Sam to Jodie. "The two of you are free to go. Be safe."

■ ■ ■

Greto's boss called Jodie as she and Sam were leaving the scene. They'd left before the agent in charge had arrived in Huntington Beach. She explained to him what had transpired at the house, while she and Sam headed for the mountains. He was not a happy camper.

"I have an agent down, Ms. King. This is a whole new ball game."

"There are a lot of cops working to catch the bad guy."

"There are going to be a lot more. We'll be in touch."

CHAPTER 43

"YOU'RE AWFULLY QUIET. If you want to sleep, I'll stay quiet as well."

Jodie looked across at Sam. "I'm not tired. I'm trying to figure out who could have put the tracker in my backpack."

They'd gotten coffee from a convenience store and were now on the freeway. Jodie needed to talk as another close call settled into her consciousness. This attempt hit home even more than the shooting in the mountains because she had felt so safe with Greto.

"Where did you have it?"

"I just threw it on the couch at Estella's."

"So anyone who was in her house had access?"

Jodie's coffee cup stopped halfway to her mouth. "Yeah, and it scares me."

"Well. We knew this was personal. Someone in your department has it in for you. Maybe someone in your life."

"Not everyone would have recognized my backpack . . ."

Sam stayed quiet.

"Wait. You don't think my own uncle is trying to kill me, do you?" Anger flared. Mike was a solid man and a good cop. He'd been her father for all intents and purposes. How could anyone think he might be trying to kill her?

"I don't know what to think." He turned to look her way for a couple of seconds. Jodie held his gaze, seeing concern and care in his eyes, and the anger fled. Sam was not the enemy. And he was making her look in a lot of places she would never consider looking. He returned his full concentration to his driving.

"What I know is," he continued, "I'm glad you called me and I'm glad you're safe."

She considered everything he was saying and realized she had to be open to the most distasteful theory. Though, in complete honesty, she couldn't conceive of Mike being the one after her.

After a few silent miles Jodie cleared her throat. "He didn't kill Greto, which seems out of character. He's been a wrecking ball where law enforcement is concerned. Why do you suppose he showed mercy there?"

"I don't know. Maybe to knock us off-balance. Tasing and drugging the agent took time. If he wanted you so badly, he could have simply gone in guns blazing, killed the agent, and killed you."

"But he didn't. It's almost as if . . ."

"He wanted you alive."

Jodie sighed, then sipped her coffee, knowing it wasn't the caffeine causing her heart to race. "I so want to catch this guy. I remember him boasting in the interview about his computer skills.

It seemed to me like he wanted to go straight from the interview to being a detective in computer crimes." Normalcy returned as she focused on chasing Collins, not him chasing her.

Sam told her about the interview with Martin and the different repair tickets he'd investigated.

"None of those repair tickets bother me, not even Bass."

"Maybe he didn't need to hack so much. We do know he used trackers. I've been wondering about the three scenes: the IED, the shooting in the mountains, and Collins's house. Something came to mind."

"What?"

"With the IED, he might not have known the exact day. Someone, maybe Collins, might have been living there, anticipating your arrival. As I recall, the FBI thought someone was living there as well and never walked it back."

"Yes, they did."

"Well, the same is true of the mountains. He'd been there for a while, maybe anticipating your arrival, but not sure when you'd be there exactly."

"But he stole a car and everything."

"Yeah, but I still think he was guessing. Maybe an educated guess. He knew at some point you'd head up there."

"Because of the help he's getting?"

"I'm not sure. The IED was so well planned, the shooting was haphazard in comparison. And the explosive under Collins's house was simple compared to the first IED. Even the attack on the safe house was half-baked. He certainly got the drop on the agent, which took planning, but you escaped. So much isn't adding up."

Jodie shivered at the thought. "He'll guess we're headed to the mountains."

"I'm counting on it," Sam said.

"What do you mean?"

"We'll be ready." Sam turned and met Jodie's gaze. She saw firm resolve there.

For a moment, there was silence in the car. Then Sam said, "I have a list, you know."

"A list of what?"

"When you told me you believed the IED was directed toward you, I made a list of people close to you who could be suspects."

Jodie didn't like where this was going. "Who did you put on the list?"

"Please understand I'd just met you. I don't know your life. But if this is all personal, it would have to be someone close to you, someone who knows you well." He paused. "Someone you trust."

Jodie blew out a breath. "Okay, so hit me with it. Who did you list?"

"There are four people and a fifth who doesn't make much sense to me, but I felt compelled to add the name. Remember, I didn't make the list to upset you." He cast another glance her way. She motioned for him to continue.

"Jonah Bennett, Ian Hunter, Tara Corson, Mike King."

"What? My uncle Mike? You're crazy." She realized he hadn't said the fifth name. "Who else?"

"Gus Perkins."

"I think you're off base." It was, she thought, but it got her thinking.

"Maybe so, but they are all close to you—they had access—so now we need to think motive. Standing outside yourself, would any of them have a motive? You've told me Bennett is like an uncle. Why?"

"He's known my uncle Mike forever. They went through the academy thirty years ago. Gus, Jonah, Mike, they were all hired at the same time."

"But Bennett sells real estate."

"Now. He made a mistake. I think it was just after my parents were killed and I came to live with Mike. He was fired. But they all stayed friends. I've known Jonah as long as I've been with Mike, so there were no hard feelings."

"Do you know why he was fired?"

"No. I never asked."

"His son died in a drug overdose."

"Yeah." She stared at him. "You've done your research."

"Of course. Keeping you safe is important to me. I want all the information possible."

"Wow, thanks." Jodie smiled, feeling warmth all the way down to her toes. She wondered if she was just giddy from lack of sleep.

"You're welcome. It's nice to see you smile." He cleared his throat and returned his attention to his driving.

"As far as Jason, Jonah's son, goes," Jodie said, getting back on topic, "he was a smart but shy kid. I'm not sure Jonah ever married his mom. Jonah isn't good with women. It broke his heart when Jason died. He had plans for Jason. He'd graduated at the top of his class from Long Beach State and would have been headed to law school if he hadn't gone to that party."

"He was the only one who died. All the others who took the drug just got sick."

"Yeah, I think Jonah knowing his son was the only fatality just compounded the tragedy."

"As far as Jonah goes, what do you mean 'not good with women'?"

"I don't mean abusive. He's a guy. He has trouble making commitments."

"Not all guys are commitment averse."

"Sorry to paint with a broad brush." She glanced at him out of the corner of her eye. "His last girlfriend told me about his inability to commit."

"And Ian Hunter?"

Jodie sighed. "He was an awesome cop. I've known him my whole career. I can't see him killing four cops. You see him now, and he's devastated. Ian is not himself."

"He got in my face. He wants Collins dead."

"He wants revenge. I . . ."

"What? Finish your thought."

"Maybe I want revenge too."

"Justice and revenge are two different things."

"I believed that once as well. Now I'm not so sure."

"Don't get dark on me, Jodie. I'm sure when it comes right down to it, you'll do the right thing."

"Thanks for that."

"The next name is Tara Corson."

She started to speak, then stopped and stayed quiet for a minute.

"Maybe a couple of years ago I wouldn't have called her my friend. We were never close before the IED thing. Yes, we went through the academy together, but we were competitive. We traveled in different circles. I didn't know much about her work. I initially didn't want her on the investigation because she was an unknown. But I think she's proven herself to be a solid investigator. I trust her."

"She seems sharp," Sam conceded. "What happened to your parents?"

Jodie twisted in her seat, wondering at the abrupt change in subject.

"They were killed in a plane crash. They were missionaries on their way back to South America when the plane went down. I happened to be here with another church family because I'd gotten sick and needed to have my tonsils taken out." Jodie got pensive and stared out the window.

"What is it?" Sam asked. "I'm sorry if it's a painful question."

"I was wrestling with this at Estella's. So many people close to me dead. I'm still standing."

"None of it is your fault."

"I hear that, I just don't feel it. Sometimes it's hard, but especially after realizing Collins was ready to blow up the neighborhood—I know it's not my fault. It's just . . ." Her voice faded. In her whole life she'd never experienced such a roller coaster of emotions and she just wanted it to stop.

Sam was quiet.

"Estella said I always must be in control. I guess she's right. I'm beginning to understand how little control over life I really do have."

"So true."

"As I'm trying to let go, some questions just won't leave my head."

"Questions like *why them?*"

"Yes, and *why me*. I know my arm has healed. I just wonder if my soul ever will."

"It will, Jodie. I don't think either one of us will heal all at once. I think it will come in stages. At least that's been true for me."

"Makes sense to me. I have moments of clarity and then . . . well, don't you ever ask why?"

Sam looked at her, understanding in his eyes. "All the time."

"Do you ever get an answer?"

"Not so far."

"How do you deal with no answer?"

"I've come to a place where I have peace not knowing."

Jodie chewed on his response for a moment.

"Estella says I'm stuck in that day. I don't know how to get unstuck."

"George told me I'm carrying Rick on my shoulders. I don't know how to put him down."

"We're quite a pair." She turned to study the side of his face. This close, she could see how ugly the scars were. It didn't matter, she thought. Sam was a solid guy. It should scare her how she was getting so close to him so fast, but it didn't. Intuitively she felt she could trust him with her life, which she was doing now.

Sam glanced toward Jodie. "Can I ask you a question?"

"Sure."

"You're a good cop. Why'd you quit?"

The question caught Jodie off guard more than the question about her parents.

"I tried to go back to work. There were just too many memories. I, uh, you know . . . I just feel like I let everyone down. Tiny, one of my guys, he physically threw me out of the house and ran back in for the others. I . . ." She swallowed. It was hard to talk about this.

"Jodie, you couldn't have saved them. If you'd run back in the house, you'd be dead."

"At one point I wished I was," Jodie almost whispered, surprised to be sharing this dark truth.

"Dead?"

Jodie heard surprise in his voice, but he didn't sound repulsed.

"Yeah. Then my focus changed. I wanted Collins dead."

"Logical transition. And now?"

"Now I want my balance back. Collins is only one piece of the puzzle. I want a clear resolution to this case, and I want what God wants."

"Which is probably the wisest desire."

CHAPTER 44

HEARING THE PAIN AND LOSS in Jodie's voice broke Sam's heart. It made him realize the truth of his own situation for the hundredth time. He couldn't have saved Rick.

"Why did you go back to work?" she asked.

"I wanted to. I needed to," he told her. "I felt like Rick would think I was a loser if I gave up and stayed home and played cripple. We were so competitive, always pushing each other to go higher, faster, farther. If I hadn't come back, I would have felt like a quitter."

"Are you glad you came back?"

"Yes. A couple of things have been difficult. Earlier this week I saw someone using Rick's locker and about had a nervous breakdown."

"But you got through it."

"I did. And I'm especially glad I came back because it meant meeting you."

Jodie smiled but said nothing.

Sam glanced sideways and saw the smile and it warmed his heart. He also noticed she was tired, and he kicked himself for not letting her rest.

"I'll let you relax now, but something just occurred to me. It seems as if we're always running into or from danger. I hope the next time we're together in a car, we're driving toward something normal."

"Normal sounds good," Jodie said. "I'm not sure I'd recognize it."

They rode the rest of the way in silence. The sun was beginning to rise when Sam pulled into Arrowbear.

■ ■ ■

Jodie saw George Upton standing outside his door. She undid her seat belt and rubbed her eyes, then got out of the car to stretch. Sam pulled one of her bags from the back seat while Jodie grabbed the backpack. She had resigned herself to being stuck with Upton in the near term.

She looked around at what was illuminated as the sun rose. His home was a two-story log house, with an attached, single-story room on the side. She wondered if that was the separate apartment. She turned in a slow circle. Upton's was the last house on the street. From what she could see, a fence surrounded the property. Behind was forest.

"Glad you two made it." Upton stepped forward and shook Sam's hand before turning to Jodie. "Your room is all set."

"Looks like you have quite the fortress," Jodie said.

"I believe in security."

They followed Upton into the house. He opened a door off to the left, motioning Jodie inside. She did and found herself in a cozy studio apartment. A bed was against one wall, on the other side was a small kitchen, and in the middle, a love seat and television.

"There's another entrance to the outside over there." Upton pointed. "The yard is secure, and I've activated all the cameras." He walked to a small coffee table in front of the love seat. "This control box is hooked up to the camera system. You can see every camera view on the TV if you desire. I also have motion detectors everywhere. No one is going to get anywhere close to you without me knowing."

Jodie nodded, irritated and relieved all at the same time. It was nice to know she was protected, but to need all of this was very problematic.

"You carrying?" he asked.

"Yes, Sig Sauer 9mm."

"I've got extra ammo if you need it."

"Thank you, but I hope I won't need what's in this clip."

"Understood." Addressing Sam, he said, "Mike King called and gave me the details on what happened last night. There's a rat in the woodpile for sure."

"There must be."

Upton looked at Jodie. "You have any idea who the rat might be?"

Jodie shook her head, yawned. "We talked about this in the car. I really have no idea."

"You're tired." Upton shooed Sam out of the room. "We'll let you get some rest. You can lock the door with a dead bolt after Sam and I leave."

"Don't hesitate to call me about anything," Sam said.

"You'll keep me apprised of everything happening concerning the investigation?"

"You bet."

The two men left and Jodie bolted the door.

Just a couple of hours, Jodie said to herself. *I don't want to sleep the whole day away.*

She realized how good the bed looked. She was exhausted. She washed up, changed her clothes, and fell into bed.

Before she turned out the lights, she looked around at the cozy studio. Cozy, yes, but still a prison.

CHAPTER 45

"YOU LOOK BEAT YOURSELF," George said to Sam after he closed the door. "Not sure you'll ever get the wrinkles out of those pants."

"Yeah, they're my only good pair of suit pants left. I was tired, but I think I'm getting a second wind."

"Still, you should go home and go to bed. You'll need the rest."

"I will. First, a question for you: do you know anything about Jonah Bennett?"

"The Realtor?"

"Yeah."

"He's a pretty ruthless businessman but a canny one. He sells a lot of property on the mountain."

"He was a cop at one time."

George's eyebrows rose. "Really? His son died of a drug overdose as I recall. Where was he a cop?"

"Long Beach. He got fired, but I don't know why. Any way you can check around and find out? I know you have contacts."

"I do. Janet Masters, the chief down there, just had my company install a security system for her parents' home in Rialto. I'll find out right away."

"Thanks."

"You think Bennett has something to do with what's happened to Jodie?"

"He's one of the names on my list. So are Mike King, Ian Hunter, and Tara Corson. Maybe ask about them as well?"

"Casting a broad net."

Sam shrugged. "I like to be thorough."

■ ■ ■

Sam left George's and went home to change. He wasn't lying when he said he felt like he'd gotten a second wind. He needed to visit someone. Dressed in jeans and a sweatshirt, Sam left for Lake Arrowhead. His mom was off today, and he hoped to catch her at home. The late snow from the weekend had already melted and if he knew his mom, she'd be out trying to get her garden ready for the real spring.

He lucked out. When he pulled into his mother's parking pad, her car was there. Her house was on the hillside overlooking Lake Arrowhead. She was on a south slope and got a lot of sun, so most of the snow was gone. She enjoyed a breathtaking view from her back deck. He glimpsed her on the side of the deck in her gardening gloves with a bag of soil and a hand spade.

She heard him park and turned and waved at him with the spade.

He got out, walked to where she was, and gave her a hug.

She patted his back and spoke into his ear. "I'm glad you stopped by." Stepping back, she held his gaze. "I saw the news. I was going to call you, but I didn't want to interrupt anything important."

"You're never an interruption," Sam said, and he meant it. His mother would never be called a hover mother. She cared, but she also treated him as an adult. As a prayer warrior, she prayed for him daily, and she trusted the Lord where he was concerned. Her calm, sure faith after his accident and Rick's death helped Sam get through a hard time. It always served to remind him of the importance of prayer. He could pray when he couldn't move and when everything hurt, especially.

"Do you need any help?"

She nodded. "I do. There are a couple bags of potting soil in the back of my car." She pointed. "Could you get them out and put them on the deck?"

"You bet." Sam did as asked and ended up helping his mother with her gardening. When they were finished, Mom made lunch.

"So I'm guessing you want to tell me something. You don't stop by unannounced unless something's on your mind."

Sam nodded as he chewed his sandwich. Once he swallowed, he took the time to bring Mom up to date on how crazy his life had been since he'd seen her last. It seemed like much longer— but it was barely a week ago she gave him a ride to work. He left nothing out; his mother could handle it all. Sam's dad had been a forest ranger, and his grandfather, an LAPD detective. Leslie Gresham was used to law enforcement and the danger inherent in the job. She was never given to hysterics and Sam often relied on her counsel.

She listened without interruption as he finished. "Wow, you

had quite a week. This Long Beach officer, Jodie, do you believe she's safe now?"

"She's safe with George for the time being. But we really need to catch this guy."

"I agree. It also sounds as if you're quite taken with her."

"I'd be lying if I said I wasn't. She understands the job. She understands me."

"Unlike Vanessa?"

He hiked a shoulder. "It hurt when Vanessa left. But after the pain eased, I was glad she was honest. You know better than most how hard it is to be married to a cop. If she hadn't been honest and we'd gotten married, it wouldn't have been good."

"I agree. I'm glad you're moving on from Vanessa."

"There's more, Mom." He put his hand over hers and held her gaze. "I realized when I was under the house, facing a pile of explosive . . . I did everything I could for Rick. I . . ." He paused, swallowed, and continued. "It wasn't my fault. I just wanted you to know I've released the burden. I'm still sad, I still miss him, but I'm letting go."

"I'm so glad to hear you say so." Leslie stood and hugged Sam tight. "It really puts my mind to rest."

Sam hugged back, the healing begun when he was under the house moving further and further along. The next call he had to make was to Doc Roe, to tell him what was going on and to put his mind to rest as well.

CHAPTER 46

JODIE SLEPT LONGER THAN SHE PLANNED. When she woke up, it was almost four o'clock and she was starving. She hadn't had a good sit-down meal since Estella's. There was food in the small kitchen. She made herself what she thought would be the quickest, a peanut butter and jelly sandwich, and just about inhaled it. There were no messages on her phone, which she thought odd. She was about to call Mike when she decided to check with Upton.

She left the room and heard him before she found him, following the sound of a clicking computer keyboard.

He looked up when she entered his office. "I hope you had a good rest."

"I did, probably overslept. Have you heard anything?"

"Yes. They found out who purchased one of the trackers on your car."

"What? Who?"

"Let's call your uncle. I'll let him fill you in."

Mike answered right away. George put it on speaker.

"Yes, we got a hit on one of the trackers. You're not going to believe it."

"I'm listening."

"Two of them are not traceable. Whoever bought them covered their tracks well. The third was bought locally with a credit card. A card belonging to Ian Hunter."

"What?" Jodie's jaw dropped and she saw George watching her.

"Yep, he purchased it two months ago. That's possibly how long it was on your car."

"I can't . . ." Jodie shook her head in dismay. She might have felt a bit sorry for Ian because of the empty promise Mike made, but not now. All she felt was anger. Ian had been stalking her? And he killed the people they both worked with for years?

"I can't believe it."

"Believe it. We just served a search warrant on his residence and vehicle. We found an AR-15 in the trunk of his car. Ballistics will tell us if it's the one used to shoot at you. He was off on Saturday and has offered no explanation for his whereabouts."

"But he couldn't have been the shooter. Ian is tall, and Logan identified Collins as the shooter."

"Doesn't mean Ian wasn't helping in some way. We're sending the gun to San Bernardino for ballistics. I knew he could sometimes be immature, but all of this surprised me to no end."

"I—uh . . . I'm in shock. What does Ian say?"

"He lawyered up."

Jodie considered this, truly speechless. He murdered her team?

"There's a lot more, and the investigation is just getting started. We've also discovered a link on his computer. It appears he was the one who hacked you. He'd been watching you from his phone."

"Is there any connection between Ian and Collins?"

"We've not found any."

"Have you talked to his wife?"

"They've been estranged for two months, not her choice. She says he up and moved out."

"Wait a minute. I'm really having trouble buying this," Jodie said, as her racing pulse slowed and her thoughts cleared. "He was always intense. But I can't believe he's a cold-blooded killer."

"He was in the perfect position to know everything you were doing. Those photos on the walls in Collins's house? Ian could have taken any of them. Plus, he was shadowing you on the computer. I didn't want to believe it either, but evidence is piling up."

"I still can't see it." Jodie was aghast. "Ian is not a murderer."

"You probably wouldn't have called Collins a killer after you interviewed him," Mike countered. "Yet here we are."

"There's a difference. I've known Ian my whole career. I can't believe I was such a poor judge of character."

"We hope he'll start talking."

"Have you given Smiley and Sam the update?"

"Yep."

"Can I come home now?"

"Collins is still at large. Can you hang there for a day or so? We're waiting on ballistics. If the rifle matches the rifle that shot at you . . . well, Ian will be in a bad place. Maybe it'll open his mouth."

The call left Jodie reflecting on the totality of her working relationship with Ian.

She stood and paced, hands on hips. "I just can't see it."

"How well did you know him?"

"As well as anyone. This just doesn't fit."

"He had access to your life and movements."

Jodie stared at Upton. He was right. Was it possible to be so completely wrong about Ian?

She went back to her room. Her phone pinged with an email from Mike. It contained some of the preliminary report on Ian and explained how he sent an innocuous email to her personal account. When she opened the message, a virus installed and gave Ian access to everything on her computer. If he was watching her so carefully, he would know what she was going to do before she announced it to anyone else.

What am I missing? Jodie broke out in a cold sweat.

Her phone and computer had been checked by the Feds right after she lost her team. When did Ian do this?

There was a knock at the front door. When Upton opened the door, Jodie heard Sam's voice. She left her room to meet with him.

"You heard."

"I did. I'm sorry. I know you and Ian were close."

"I'm having trouble believing it."

"It sure doesn't seem plausible for a guy who has been a good cop for so many years to go off the rails so completely."

Jodie sat in one of Upton's chairs. "It feels wrong."

Sam sat across from her. He brushed the back of her hand with his knuckles. "Jodie, I'm sorry. If it is Ian, this is betrayal of the worst kind."

"Not only betrayal." Jodie liked the feel of his hand on hers. She noticed he wasn't wearing his glove. And he'd shaved; the red stubble was gone. "For months my obsession has been to find the man responsible, and if it's Ian, well . . . I feel so odd. I thought catching the person responsible would make me happy, bring me closure. I don't feel happy at all."

"Maybe closure will come when Collins is in custody."

"Maybe." Jodie chewed on a thumbnail. Nothing in her believed Ian was a mass murderer. She understood Sam meant to be supportive. Her thoughts weren't clear enough now to debate the issue. "Guys, I guess I'm more tired than I thought, even though I've slept most of the day. I'm going back to bed."

Sam stood as well. "I understand. I think I could sleep for a week."

"Rest well, Jodie. You're safe here," George said.

■ ■ ■

After Jodie went back to her room, George looked at Sam.

"What do you think about this person in custody? Ian Hunter."

"I only met him briefly, and I didn't like him."

"But? He was on your list, or so you said."

"True. Everything is stacking up so nicely. I mean, the killer laid low for months, not a peep. He committed a practically perfect crime and got away scot-free. The IED explosion was on the verge of going cold. This hacking wasn't discovered months ago, though the FBI looked for it. Now, suddenly incriminating evidence is falling from the sky like confetti."

"You want to keep looking at everyone even though Hunter is in custody."

"Yes."

Upton chuckled. "I trained you right. Trust no one, test everything. I have an interesting tidbit for you. I found out about Bennett. Why he was fired."

"Why?"

"It happened at an end-of-probation party; things got out of hand."

Sam rolled his eyes. End-of-probation parties always got out of hand. Too much alcohol. "What's new?"

"This was over-the-top. A woman accused Bennett of rape."

"Whoa."

"Yeah, criminal charges were never filed, but Bennett was shown the door."

"Hmm. Jodie said there were no hard feelings, and everyone was still friends, even after he got fired."

Upton shrugged. "It was a long time ago, so it's plausible. After all, Hunter's the one in custody, not Bennett."

CHAPTER 47

JODIE LAY DOWN ON THE BED, but she didn't close her eyes. She couldn't conceive of any scenario where Ian was the guy who murdered her whole team, Hayes, and Jukebox, and then tried to kill her. They'd known each other forever; Ian had been in the academy class before hers. They'd worked together in patrol when she got off probation. He was a good, honest cop or he would not have been on her team.

He's a killer?

Her phone buzzed with an unknown number. She stared at it, then realized the FBI agents often had the same prefix. Maybe it was Agent Greto. She hadn't heard how he was doing. She answered.

"Jodie? It's Agent Parker, the FBI tech. I took your laptop."

"Yes." Jodie's face brightened. He should know about the hacker. "Agent Parker, do you have something for me?"

"I've given everything I found to your uncle. The virus on your computer traces back to Ian Hunter."

"Really? There's no doubt?"

"Right now everything points to Ian." He paused and to Jodie, he didn't sound at all convinced. "Though none of this was evident three months ago. I looked over your computer back then as well. I'm embarrassed to have missed all this. It really makes me want to catch this guy." He continued. "I found a couple of other things, specifically some deleted emails."

"I usually delete emails after I read them, unless it's something I need to save. Then I put it in a folder."

"These are emails on your work account. If they were to your personal email, they would be unrecoverable. But work is different. The system the PD uses makes it difficult to permanently delete anything, basically because who knows what might be needed in court someday. Anyway, this caught my attention because someone tried hard to delete certain email files."

"What were the emails about?"

"I'll send them to you. There are two sets: the first from Gus Perkins from about a year ago, and then the most recent, someone named Archie Radio was trying to get your attention."

"You're kidding."

"No, it's right before your team went to serve the warrant in the mountains. He sent the emails from a public computer, somewhere in Running Springs, to your work account. It sounds as if there was something wrong and he tried to warn you."

Jodie felt as if a knife just struck her in the chest. "Uh, stop. Let me process this."

The line went silent. Seconds passed before Jodie could speak. "How did I not see these?"

"How did I not see it three months ago? I retraced my steps. Someone with skill tried to completely erase them."

"How could they erase emails without my knowledge?"

"The person shadowing you on the computer—Detective King believes it's Ian Hunter—saw them first. There would be no reason for you to suspect anything if you never saw the email."

"You don't think it's Ian?"

"I think there is more work to be done. This hacker, for lack of a better term, is good. I've never seen better. Is Ian a computer guy?"

"Not to my knowledge."

"Yet now everything points in his direction. I'm still poking around."

"I understand. What's in these emails?"

"I'll send them to you. You can read them and decide for yourself."

"Thanks." Jodie hung up and then opened the first email from Jukebox, the most recent set. She looked at the date and subject.

I've never seen this before.

Subject: ALERT ALERT

Jo-Jo, it's Juke. Hey, I was fed some seriously twisted information.
DON'T DO THE RAID! STOP.

In the next one, sent a few hours later, Juke was wondering where Jodie was.

Didn't you get my email? I can't call you. They took my phone. One is
a little weasel named Dennis. I don't know the other one, but he killed
Hayes. I saw him with the gun. HAYES IS DEAD! Don't come. I just hope
they don't find me.

Jodie had to sit back and close her eyes for a minute or two.
Why didn't you call 911?

She knew the answer. Juke only trusted her. He trusted her to
see the message and act. The warrant service was secret between
team members. He would have only talked to her about it.

Oh, Juke, I'm so sorry.

She opened the older emails, from over a year ago, from Gus.
Gus's only email address was work because he was old-school. He
didn't have a personal account. He hated computers, only used
them when he absolutely had to. Likewise, he wasn't much for
texting. Yet he could have called her. Jodie's brow furrowed as she
wondered why he didn't.

Subject: Baker to Vegas

Jodie, while in Vegas, I saw something disturbing. A certain person
dropped a huge amount of money at the craps table. It wasn't a
one-off. I want to run the situation by you. You know the person,
and often you have calmer insight than I do. Let's talk.

Jodie rubbed her forehead and struggled to remember last
year's Baker to Vegas. The law enforcement relay race was held
every year. Ten-person relay teams ran 120 miles from Baker,
California, to Las Vegas, Nevada. She'd competed many times,

but she hadn't gone last year. Gus had gone as a support person with Estella in their RV.

She vaguely remembered getting a call from him. He wanted to talk to her about something. But she was getting ready to accept the Sergeant of the Year award in Sacramento. These emails were dated when she would have been gone. She had never seen them. Why didn't he ask her if she'd seen the email? The next email answered her question. It was supposedly from her.

Are you certain about what you saw?

Gus answered:

100%—it's bad.

Then suddenly she supposedly knew who he was talking about.

The person you are referring to just contacted me. They assure me the situation is under control. Just let it go. This isn't something I want to get involved in.

You got it.

Wow, who was Gus trying to tell her about? Estella might know. Jodie called and got voice mail.

"Estella, it's Jodie. Hey, I wonder if you remember an incident about a year ago at the Baker to Vegas race. Gus saw someone in Vegas. I think he wanted to talk to me about the person. Do you remember? If you do, please call me back when you are able."

Now all she could do was wait. With Juke it was clear: he'd discovered the plans of Collins and whoever he was working for and it cost him his life. But what had Gus discovered? Someone with a gambling problem? Why on earth would they do an intervention?

Her phone rang again, and she answered it without thinking, hoping it was Estella. Instead, she heard a recorded message: Would she accept a collect call from the LA County jail?

It had to be Ian. Once processed—procedures that could take several hours—he would have access to the phone. He must have just cleared processing. And Jodie did want to talk to him. She said yes.

After some clicks and buzzes, she heard Ian's voice. "Jodie! Thank God you answered."

"Does your lawyer know you're calling me?"

"I don't care. I need you to know I did not do what they are saying. You know me—I would never . . . I couldn't . . ." His voice broke, and Jodie felt his pain. She believed him.

"Someone is framing me," he continued in a rush of words. "The rifle is not mine. And I don't have a clue how to hack into someone's computer."

"Ian, why did you lawyer up? Asking for a lawyer makes you look guilty."

"I was stunned. I, uh . . . I was blindsided." He paused. Jodie could hear a lot of background noise. "They claim I bought a tracker and put it on your car. Why on earth would I do that?"

She heard his voice break.

"Jodie, I can't get over not being there. I'm dead inside. I don't understand how you are still standing. I'm mad about that, yeah, but killing cops and friends? I'm not a monster. Please tell me you don't think I'm a monster."

She thought she heard a sob. Jodie swallowed. "You're not, Ian, but you need to talk. Talk with your lawyer present but talk. If someone is framing you, maybe you can figure out who if you talk to Mike and Tara."

"I will. Do you believe me, Jodie?"

"I don't believe you're a killer. And I'm still standing because I need to move past that day. I need to get justice for our team. Anger and guilt won't do that. Please, Ian, what happened was not your fault. You being there would not have changed it. Talk to Bass; try to move on."

She heard a sigh over the phone.

"Contact your lawyer, Ian, please."

"I will. He's arranging bail. Thanks—" There was noise in the background. "I have to go. I'll call Mike. I'll talk." The line clicked and was dead.

■ ■ ■

After Jodie went to her room, George and Sam spent time going over what information they had on Jonah Bennett and Tara Corson. There wasn't much on Tara, but there was a lot on Bennett. They even found an archived article from the Long Beach *Press-Telegram* about the end-of-probation party incident that eventually got him fired. Though criminal charges were never filed, it was easy to see why Bennett was fired. The article, which detailed Bennett's career, said Bennett was no stranger to trouble. He had five use-of-force complaints filed on him during the five years he was a sworn police officer. Three of them were sustained, with his punishment each time being a week's suspension.

"He was in trouble before the allegations," Sam noted.

"Things piled up. Progressive discipline with each violation . . . firing was inevitable because he never changed his behavior."

"Yet, in the last twenty-five years, he's kept his nose clean, with the exception of two messy divorces and one DUI." Public records painted a picture of Bennett's turbulent personal life. But no other arrests, just one or two speeding tickets.

"His business is strong," George said. "He's got a high rating with the Better Business Bureau."

"I found a couple of complaints," Sam said. "Some people think he's unethical."

George shrugged. "I'd be surprised if there weren't any complaints. It's hard in business to please everyone. Especially in real estate. I've got a couple of complaints in my file as well."

"Then looking over his background, he seems to have cleaned up his act, except where his wives are concerned."

"Yeah, he certainly has never been accused of anything as heinous as rape in the last twenty-five years."

Sam tapped on his hand with a pen as he considered this. "Corson is an unknown. I can't find any issues. I know she came to the task force from violent crimes. She must have had a good record, or they wouldn't have sent her. She doesn't post much on social media. Her Facebook isn't public, and I only found a couple reposted pro-cop videos on her TikTok." Sam frowned as he looked at what they had on Corson.

"Maybe I'm a Neanderthal sexist, but I can't see a woman behind all of this death and destruction," George said.

"Anything is possible. Which brings me to my next search. Mike King."

"Her uncle?"

"We need to look at everyone."

George chuckled. "Aren't you the dogged investigator."

"It's important. I want Jodie safe. She was a good cop and I hope she will be again."

They found nothing out of the ordinary about Mike King. He was what he appeared to be: a hardworking cop. It was curious Long Beach allowed him to be so involved in Jodie's investigation, considering she was his niece. Every department had their own policies concerning such matters. The only other item of note was King's marital status. He'd never married. Police work could be hard on marriages. Maybe King didn't want to take a chance.

They continued to probe, searching for anything incriminating or exonerating in their minds. Ian was an interesting issue. Sam didn't like the guy, true, but his gut told him Ian wasn't the bad guy, even though he was on the list. Who was?

He pushed on with George, ignoring the fatigue stalking him.

CHAPTER 48

JODIE INTENDED TO GO TO BED but after talking to Ian, she couldn't sleep. Framing someone was never as easy as the movies made it look. If Ian was being framed, Jodie was certain there would be holes. She didn't know much about hacking—computer crimes had never interested her—but if Collins was able to hack her email, read and erase stuff, then she wouldn't put it past him to make it look as if Ian was the killer.

How could he get the AR-15 into the trunk of Ian's car? The PD lot is gated, and Ian has a garage at his house. Another cop could have done it. All officers parked in the same lot, and Ian had been on the job long enough. People knew who he was and what he drove. *But why now?*

Jodie felt a headache starting with all the contradictions.

Collins's house being left to blow up made it seem as if Collins planned to disappear. Was that because he'd expected to kill her when he'd shot at her in the mountains? If so, when Sam saved her, it upset his plans.

Why frame Ian now? Were they trying to cover their tracks because the police were getting too close? She didn't think they were close to anything, so framing Ian didn't compute.

She checked her phone, hoping Estella would call back. She saw the red line indicating her battery was at less than 5 percent. She dug inside her bag for her charger and came across a manilla envelope with Dennis Collins's name on it. Frowning, Jodie didn't remember where the envelope had come from.

Then it came to her. This was what the man who'd purchased Collins's house had given her to give to Collins. His mail. She'd shoved it into her backpack and it had been there ever since.

Jodie opened the envelope and dumped everything out, hoping there would be some clue. Most of the mail was junk, advertisements addressed to Collins. The last thing she picked up to scrutinize was a flyer from the local gym. Jodie had enjoyed going to the gym before the IED. She and members of her team often worked out together.

"Ahh." Jodie brought a hand to her forehead as a memory started to surface. It was from a while ago, but she couldn't remember exactly when. She'd gone to the gym with Ian, Tiny, and Gail. They couldn't scan their membership cards because the computer was down. They had to show ID. Ian noticed techs working on the problem. As usual, Jodie was simply focused on getting in and getting out. She had so much going on, and she was in a hurry.

"Hey, is that Corson from violent crimes?"

"Huh? Who?" She'd turned to see the back of Tara's head. She

was talking to one of the computer techs. In her mind's eye Jodie couldn't see the tech's face.

"Flirting with a computer geek. Her efforts won't end well," Ian had said.

Jodie thought about Tara. Ian had dated Tara a couple of years before he met his now wife. She'd overheard a conversation he'd had with Tiny about it. He'd said they'd broken up because he felt Tara was too intense and she'd only dated him because she thought he would help her career. And according to Ian, the most important thing in the world to Tara was her career.

"She's a climber," he'd said, *"not afraid to leave shoe prints on someone else's back."*

I thought so as well. But my estimation changed when she was assigned to the task force. Tara really seems like a team player. What if I'm wrong?

Jodie considered this. Then something brought her to her feet, horrified. Mike had said he didn't know the safe house address, but what if Tara did? She'd made the arrangements with the FBI. Tara would have had many opportunities to put the rifle in Ian's car. She might even have been the shooter on Saturday. In the right clothes with her stocky stature, she could be mistaken for a small man. True, Logan had identified Collins from a photograph, but everything had happened so fast. What if he was mistaken?

What if it's Tara?

...

Sam yawned, finally giving in to fatigue. "I'm beat. I'll call it a night."

"Not much we can do right now anyway. We'll have to wait and see what shakes out with Hunter."

"Yep." Sam stood and stretched, then headed for the door. "Tell Jodie I said good night."

"I will. Be careful," George said. "With Collins still on the loose, you might be in danger."

Sam stopped, remembering he'd traded in his rental car because he thought he had a tail. He'd dismissed it as paranoia. The incident seemed like ages ago. Maybe he wasn't paranoid. "You think I'll be a target with Hunter in custody?"

"You're chasing a maniac—one you thwarted twice. What do you think?"

George was right, and Sam took the advice to heart. Yet, once he got in the car, fatigue hit him like a boulder. Two nights in a row without enough sleep. Bone-tired didn't cover it.

On the way up Green Valley Lake Road, he opened his window to let the cold mountain air hit him square in the face. Jodie was safe with George. Sam would sleep easy once he got home.

Canyon Drive was a loop road bisected by Spruce Street. It was a rolling road, dropping down and then climbing and curving around. Sam's home was at the end of the loop, where Canyon Drive rose and then looped back, intersecting Spruce before starting around back to the main road. This end of Canyon there were only two homes on Sam's side of the street and two across the street. His only full-time neighbor lived across the street.

Sam yawned as he backed into his parking space. He didn't have a garage, just a raised parking pad off the street like most mountain homes. He turned off the motor and climbed out of the car, stretching his stiff shoulder as he walked.

He took one step toward the front door and stopped, foggy, tired mind registering something off. His motion light hadn't activated, and the light wasn't very old.

Alert, adrenaline surging, Sam reached for his weapon as he heard a foot scraping on his wraparound porch in front of him. He drew his gun and took a step back as he raised it.

He heard the step behind him a second too late. Two assailants. Then Taser prongs hit him square in the back, and Sam couldn't fight it. He was barely conscious of his grip releasing and his gun hitting the ground as a man came off his porch.

Dennis Collins?

Sam wasn't sure because he couldn't keep his eyes open as the jolt took over and everything went dark.

CHAPTER 49

JODIE STOOD as a horrible realization dawned. It wasn't Ian. His arrest was a terrible distraction. Dennis Collins's partner had to be Tara.

She burst out of her room. "Where's Sam?" she asked a startled George.

"He went home."

"How long ago?"

George looked at the clock. It was just after 1 a.m. "He should be there by now."

"Can you call him? My phone is still charging."

George picked up his phone, but Sam didn't answer.

"Voice mail," he said with a shrug. "Sam was tired. He probably just went to bed."

"I don't think so. I know you don't know me well, but I have a bad feeling about this. Can you take me to his house now?"

"Why don't you tell me what's got you so riled up?"

"Something jogged my memory. What if Tara Corson is the one helping Collins?" She explained her concern.

"Corson?" George stood, frowning. "She was on Sam's list as well. We found nothing. Are you sure you're not just reading too much into a memory?"

She held her hands up. "How can I be sure of anything? All I know is what is possible. Sam was assigned to work with Tara. If it is her, and she gets ahold of him . . . Did he tell you he thought he was being followed? He changed rental cars because someone was following him."

"No, he didn't mention a tail. I did tell him he could be a target."

"See? Let's go."

"Why would Sam be in danger right this minute?"

"If it is Tara, she might think his guard is down because Ian is in custody."

While this felt completely plausible to Jodie, George did not appear to feel the same urgency.

"I can't explain it any better than I have a bad feeling Sam is in danger. If I'm wrong, we can apologize to him and come right back."

He looked as if he were going to object. He studied her for a moment, then said, "Okay, let me get my shoes."

Glad she got his attention, Jodie threw on a sweatshirt and grabbed her jacket.

George not only got his shoes, but his gun as well. "Going off your hunch, there's a chance we're being lured there as well."

Jodie grabbed her own gun and her phone and charger.

George had a late-model pickup truck with four-wheel drive, and in no time at all they were on their way.

"Tell me more about why you think Tara would want you dead, and by association, Sam also. I thought she was a friend." George turned onto Highway 18.

Jodie plugged her charger into the port in George's truck. "Tara and I were never friends; we were always competitors. Even in the academy, she made everything a competition. She'd say stuff like 'I'm going to beat you this time' but never did. She's a good cop—don't misunderstand me. I was just always better. I tried to tell her I grew up idolizing my uncle. I knew a lot about police work before the academy, while for her it was all new."

"She took it personal?"

"I guess. I was only competing with myself and the guys. I tried to help her. I wanted her to do well. There weren't many women on the PD. Her success would be a good thing. I thought she had the potential to be a good cop." Jodie shrugged, remembering all the times she didn't understand why Tara was so hostile, so competitive. "Maybe I'm grasping at straws and being less than charitable to Tara, but after three attempts on my life, I'm a little sensitive." *Maybe I'm missing something.* Jodie felt a cold sweat start again. Missing something would get people killed.

"I understand. What happened after the academy?"

"We went our separate ways. She stayed in patrol longer than I did. I never heard anything bad about her. You know how a PD is when it comes to bad gossip."

George nodded. "It spreads like wildfire."

"When I passed the sergeant's exam, I found out how much others gossip. Tara believed the test was fixed—it was all over the station. She thought I was promoted because I was related to Mike. I ignored it, concentrated on my job. I wanted to think we were past these petty squabbles."

They were traveling up Green Valley Lake Road now.

"Have you been up here before?"

"Not to Sam's house, but to Green Valley Lake. Mike, Gus, Estella, Levi, and I used to come up here a lot. Jonah had a home at the end of Angeles Street. It backed up to the forest. We'd come up in the summertime and hike, fish, ride dirt bikes everywhere. Jonah had a bunch of recreational equipment. He also had a boat on Lake Arrowhead."

"Had? He doesn't have the cabin or the boat anymore?"

"I don't know about the boat, but he sold the house after Jason died. I don't think Jonah comes up here much at all anymore. At one time he talked about closing his real estate office on the mountain." She frowned. "Jason's death changed so much."

"What is it?"

"I guess it took a lot for Jonah to buy a lot for the memorial. It's located at the end of Green Valley Lake Road." Jodie bit her bottom lip. So much dread hung over her. She hoped she wasn't overreacting, she wasn't too late.

"On Saturday were you going to come up here?"

"I'd thought about it. But I'm not for the memorial until Collins and whoever is helping him is in jail or dead."

"We're almost to Sam's. He lives on a loop road, two ways in. I'll try to call him again." George hit the hands-free button and told the car to call Sam.

"Could jealousy lead Corson to murder?" he asked as the call went to voice mail and he ended it.

"I would have said no yesterday. But who else would have

known about the safe house except Tara? Jealousy and hate. She didn't always like me. But lately I thought things had changed." She closed her eyes and leaned back against the seat. "I don't want to believe it. I just don't see anyone else. Tara would certainly have more reason than Ian, I think."

What is wrong with me? I was never so indecisive before.

She opened her eyes and couldn't help but notice how dark it was up here.

George slowed. "This is Canyon Drive, Sam's street. He's all the way down on the right, where the road starts to curve back the other way."

"What's behind his house?"

"A canyon. Open forest."

Jodie tensed as George drove slowly up the narrow road, a tad wider than one lane. If traffic came the other way, one vehicle would have to pull over. It was very quiet here. They hadn't passed another vehicle since the highway.

George opened his window. Typical cop move, Jodie thought. *He wants to hear what's going on.*

"Are we close?" she asked.

"Yes."

Jodie saw the rental car, parked just off the street. The house looked so dark.

"I told you—he's probably asleep."

Jodie chewed on her bottom lip, wondering what on earth to do. Her feeling of impending doom hadn't dissipated.

"Let's knock. If we wake him, I'll take the blame. My gut is telling me we just can't walk away. What if Tara has lured him away with some odd story?"

"Sam's not gullible. But since I know better than to question a cop's intuition, we'll knock."

He parked his truck perpendicular to Sam's car, effectively blocking him in, and they got out. From the parking pad they walked around the front deck to Sam's front door. Jodie thought it was odd there were no lights at all. She saw the motion light, but it stayed dark when she walked by it.

George knocked. They waited but there was no response. He knocked harder.

"Now I'm worried," he said.

CHAPTER 50

SAM CAME TO AND REGAINED CONTROL OF HIMSELF only to find he'd been handcuffed and placed in the back of a vehicle, an SUV, he thought. It was a tight space for him. There was a taut cargo net over him, and his shoulder screamed with every bump the car rolled over. He also felt what he thought was blood on his face and thought maybe he'd cut himself when he fell. Sam hated the Taser. He'd been struck with it once in training and went down like a tree.

He tried to shift around, but every time he moved, a bump threw him back in the other direction. He had no sense of time, couldn't figure out how long he'd been out. The car ride continued for maybe ten or fifteen minutes before the vehicle stopped. Sam heard the car door slam. Footsteps walking around the car to the back. Then the hatch slowly rose. A light shone in his eyes and Sam squinted. The cargo net was released.

"All right, here's how it's going to go," a male voice said. "Time to get out. You can hop down on your own and continue under your own power." The flashlight left Sam's eyes and he got a look at the speaker. Dennis Collins . . . holding a gun on him.

"Gotcha, chief," Sam said.

Sam sat up with difficulty, straining at the cuffs, steadied himself, then slid forward to let his legs dangle over the back of the vehicle. He pushed forward out of the SUV and onto his feet, grimacing as his stiffened body uncoiled and he came to stand before his captor.

Collins pointed his gun at Sam. "Now go through the door." He motioned toward Sam's left with the gun.

"Do you want to tell me what's going on?"

"No. I'm not going to tell you anything. I'm in charge. Period."

Sam studied the kid. Behind his bluster was fear, and fear was dangerous. Collins could pull the trigger by accident.

"Sure, sure." Sam turned and walked through the door. He was at another mountain cabin, but he couldn't tell where. It was on a hillside; off to the right he saw a large shed. As he entered the room, Collins stepped in behind him and turned on the light, revealing a typical cabin with a small living room and a kitchen. Straight ahead were large windows covered with drapes. Sam guessed there was a deck.

"Sit down," Collins ordered, pointing to the couch. "You're going to be here for a while."

Sam turned to look at Collins. The kid had a superior smirk on his face. All Sam could do was sit and wonder what he meant by *a while*.

. . .

"I have a key," George said before Jodie could suggest they kick the door in. "Sam gave it to me the last time I was here."

He pulled the key from his pocket and opened the front door. "Sam and I talked about security systems, but he didn't think he needed one," George said as he flipped on a light.

The place was neat—and empty. A couch, recliner, big screen, and lots of moving boxes piled in the corner.

"Sam, are you here?" she called out.

It only took a couple of minutes to go through the whole house. Sam wasn't there. It didn't look like he'd ever come home. If it weren't for the car outside, Jodie would have thought he hadn't. She fought her rising fear. She wasn't a cop anymore, but she needed to think like one.

"Let me use your phone."

George handed her the phone. "Who are you calling?"

"Mike." Jodie dialed her uncle's number.

Mike answered right away. "George, is something wrong?"

"No, it's me using his phone," Jodie said. "Sam is missing."

"What? Missing? What do you mean? What's going on?"

"Can you get ahold of Tara? Maybe she knows where Sam is. They were working together."

"I don't think she's with him. She said she'd be running down a lead off the grid for a bit."

"When did she leave?"

"This afternoon. What do you mean Sam is missing?"

Jodie explained, though it took all her strength to keep her voice calm and level.

"Everyone needs to be mobilized. Have you notified Smiley?"

"No."

"I will. You go back to George's and sit tight. I'm headed to you."

"Mike, wait. I've got a bad feeling." She told him her fears about Tara.

"What? You're kidding. No one worked harder on the IED case than Tara. I admit it's odd she's incommunicado, but . . ."

"She goes incommunicado and then Sam goes missing?"

A beat passed before he replied. "I'll try to get a line on her. I am coming up there. We will find Sam—I promise."

The connection ended.

Jodie handed the phone back to George as a sick feeling rolled around in her stomach like a spinning basketball.

"You're still banking on Tara?" George asked.

"I'm trying to think." She massaged her forehead with her fingers. She'd been convinced Ian wasn't a killer. Could she really say Tara was?

"She told Mike she was going to be off the grid for a while. What could she be doing?"

"Why would she abduct Sam? What could she be after?"

Jodie stared at George, speechless. She had no answer for him. Nothing about this case made sense, but that didn't make it any less scary.

They stayed at Sam's until Deputy Takano arrived around two thirty in the morning. Jodie paced, prayed, and tried to regain her balance. Good detectives didn't flit around like moths chasing a light. Yet that's what she was doing.

As Jodie prayed, a memory from years ago came back to her. Her father's face shone in her mind's eye. His eyes twinkled with amusement. Jodie was trying to pull some candy from a candy jar, but she couldn't get her hand out because she'd grabbed so many pieces her fist wouldn't fit through the opening.

"It's made for one candy at a time," Daddy told her. *"Let the extra go."*

Jodie hadn't wanted to; she wanted all the candy.

"Honey, when you hold too tightly to too much, you can miss out on it all."

She let the extra candy fall away and brought her hand out of the jar with one caramel.

Right now, her fist was full of conjecture. Before the IED she would have had no problem letting go of the bad, hanging on to the good. She needed to get to that place again.

Bob Takano went across the street to talk to Sam's neighbor but came up empty there. He joined Jodie and George in searching every inch of the parking pad and street in front of Sam's house. Near Sam's car, Takano found a prong from a Taser. If Sam was tased, it probably broke off when he fell.

Jodie looked up at the motion light on the corner of Sam's house. It had been disconnected. "Bob, look at this."

Deputy Takano came over and shone his flashlight. "Yep, it looks like they were waiting for him. Disabled his lighting."

"Then he was tased and taken somewhere," George said.

Jodie was silent. She folded her arms, hating the fact that there was nothing they could do until they were contacted by whoever had Sam. What if he or she didn't call?

CHAPTER 51

SAM COULDN'T RELAX on the couch with handcuffs. Staying in the same rigid position for so long was making his shoulder muscles scream in tight agony. Time was ticking by. He felt as if he'd been sitting here for at least an hour, if not more. He tried to figure out what time it was. It was after midnight when he got home. He had no idea how long he'd been out after the Taser. Or how far away from his home he'd been driven. There were no clocks in his line of view, and while he could see the clock on the range in the kitchen, it was blinking. Obviously there had been a power outage and no one had bothered to reset it.

Collins hummed to himself, swigging an energy drink, playing on his phone.

After a while, Sam told the kid he needed to use the restroom.

"I need you to take the restraints off," he told his captor.

"I don't care what you need. You're just like my brother. You think everyone is afraid of you and they will immediately do what you say."

"You have the gun. You're in control."

"I am. I'm smarter than you and I am in control."

"Not sure how it benefits you to keep me from going to the bathroom."

"Because it does." His phone rang. Collins answered, walked into the kitchen, talking low, but his eyes never left Sam.

Sam didn't really need the facilities. But his arms were cramping, and it felt as if the circulation to his right hand had been cut off. He hoped to get the cuffs removed before any permanent damage was done.

Collins seemed unhappy about what was said over the phone. Sam couldn't hear what he was saying. Then the smirk returned, and he ended the call.

"Okay, you can use the restroom." He walked over to Sam and dropped a handcuff key on the floor. "Go ahead, bomb guy. See if you can get the cuffs off."

Sam took a deep breath, slid off the couch onto his knees, then sat where his hands could reach the key, spreading his long legs out in front of him. It was difficult but not impossible to unlock the cuffs this way. Sam had worked through so many dexterity exercises while he rehabbed his hand, unlocking the cuffs would not be as difficult as Collins thought. The problem was how tight the cuffs were. There was going to be pain and blood. He sure couldn't ask for help. Collins watched him, chuckling and mocking.

After a bit, dropping and picking up the key several times,

sweat beading on his brow, Sam got the left hand free and brought his hands around in front to undo the right cuff.

The smirk left Collins's face. He stepped back and raised his weapon. "Fine. Try anything and you're dead. And if you think you can get the drop on me, just remember, we know where your mother lives."

Sam froze for a second. He wasn't going to let the little creep get the better of him. He removed the right cuff and then held the handcuffs in one hand, palming the key and resting his left arm on his knees, stretching his cramped back muscles for a moment. He tossed the cuffs toward Collins's feet, wondering if the kid would try to put them on him again. If he did, he'd have to get close and put down the gun.

"You have nothing to fear from me."

"I'm not afraid of you. And I'm not afraid to shoot you."

Sam nodded.

"The bathroom is there." Collins pointed. He made no effort to pick the cuffs up.

Sam stood, stretched again, and went into the small room and closed the door. He slid the key into his back pocket, in case, then looked around. There was no way out, no windows. No weapons, not even soap or toilet paper. Only a dirty towel on the lone towel ring.

He saw his reflection in the mirror. He'd cut his head. Dried blood was all over the side of his face. He rinsed off as best he could, wincing when he cleaned the cut above his eyebrow. There was nothing to cover it or clean it with. His wrists were sore and bleeding as well. Stretching his shoulders again, he flushed the toilet so Collins would believe he'd done what he said he had to.

For a minute he stared in the mirror and wondered what he

should do. He had no doubt that he could take Collins, but did he want to? He wanted to know who Collins was working with. Even more so because Collins had the nerve to threaten his mother. Sam saw red.

He'd hold his temper. The guy was obviously waiting for his partner. Sam needed to find out who the partner was and then he'd figure out how to end this.

He prayed for strength and wisdom, then went back out to face the armed kid and make plans to take both Collins and his partner into custody.

CHAPTER 52

BRUCE SMILEY ARRIVED with three more deputies. One deputy went down into the canyon behind Sam's house to look around. He came back with a smashed phone.

George's expression was grim. "Yeah, it's his."

Jodie showed a second deputy the motion light.

"If they disconnected it," she said, "we might get prints off of it."

"Bag it," Smiley said, jowly face wrinkled with worry. Jodie could tell he valued Sam as a colleague and a friend.

"The only thing I think we have working in our favor is that you two came up here to check on Sam and found him gone," Smiley said, sipping coffee from a travel mug.

"What do you mean?" Jodie asked.

"Think: If they wanted him dead, they would have just killed him and left the body. It's obvious they got the drop on him. They took him away—I'm guessing because they want something or someone, probably you. I'm sure Sam is alive somewhere. We must find out where fast." He sighed and held Jodie's gaze.

Jodie felt the truth hit her hard. They took Sam because of her.

"Your uncle is on his way. I gave him George's address. Go there, wait for him, and wait for a call. This revolves around you, Jodie. This guy is most likely going to call you."

"Or woman," Jodie corrected. "If it is Tara."

"Okay, whoever. Just remember, when you get the call, you are not alone in this. As soon as my deputies finish their canvass here, I'll send one to George's as well."

Jodie nodded. What Smiley said made sense. He had the what happened down: Tara and Collins took Sam in order to lure her somewhere. Why?

Hope burned in her chest. Sam was alive—she refused to believe any different. *Oh, Lord, I need my balance back. I need a clear head. What am I not seeing?*

George and Jodie climbed back in his truck. Other than the prong from the Taser and the phone, there were no other clues about what had happened to Sam. Jodie grabbed her phone and saw it was now halfway charged and there was a message waiting from Estella. She put the phone to her ear and played the message.

"Jodie, my goodness, Baker to Vegas was so long ago. And I thought it was all resolved. It was Jonah—he lost an outrageous amount of money at the craps table. Gus was concerned, but he said you told him all was well."

"I never told him any such thing," Jodie said out loud.

"What is it?" George asked.

"I don't know. I don't know how this figures into everything."

She told him about the erased messages. And what Estella had just said in the voice mail.

"Jonah is a successful businessman. Why would it matter if he gambled and lost? It's his money."

"Not exactly. Gus told me a while ago Jonah was having serious money issues. They came to light when Jason died. Mike and Gus floated Jonah a huge loan to bury his son and to stay solvent. Mike never told me anything about it. Everything I heard was from Gus. If Gus saw him losing money in Vegas, well, it would have been a breach of the agreement they made after the loan."

"The only one who would have a reason to delete those emails was Jonah," George said, and the words hit Jodie like a ton of bricks.

"George, stop the car."

"What?"

"Please, I'm going to be sick."

George pulled over and Jodie opened the door, barely making it clear before she lost the contents of her stomach.

She stayed on her knees in the darkness, smelling pine trees and vomit and trying to wrap her arms around the thought that Jonah—not Tara, not Ian—was the one with all the hate. She could hardly breathe, the crush of betrayal hit her so hard.

Suddenly she remembered what was different when her parents died—eight-year-old Jodie was powerless to do anything but trust. Now, twenty-five years later, Jodie somehow believed she had the power to handle all of life's setbacks in her own strength.

I can't handle any of it without you, Lord, and I certainly don't have the strength to deal with Uncle Jonah being the bad guy.

She heard shoes crunching on gravel.

"Are you okay?" George asked.

"No, I'm not." She slowly got to her feet. George took hold of her arm to steady her.

"I don't know what to do, George. Mike would never believe Jonah could be behind all of this. I'm having a hard time. He's family for heaven's sake."

"First things first. We need to tell Smiley about this. Someone should pay Jonah a visit."

"Agreed."

"I'll call him right now. You pull yourself together."

Jodie stayed leaning against the truck while George called Smiley. Despite the tremendous betrayal sinking in, Jodie felt her balance returning. She could open her hand and let go of everything except one truth: for some reason Uncle Jonah wanted her dead.

She stood up straight and squared her shoulders. Maybe she'd given up her badge but she still thought like a cop. The person she'd been striving to find for three months was no longer a mystery. Folding her arms, Jodie thought hard. What would Jonah do next?

While she thought, she could tell from George's side of the conversation that Smiley was a bit dubious. After all, Jodie had just told him she was certain it was Tara. Once everything was explained, Smiley understood their concerns and said he would send a deputy to find Jonah.

George ended the call and then helped Jodie back into the car.

They continued down Green Valley Lake Road. As he turned right on Highway 18 toward Arrowbear, her phone rang.

"It's Tara," Jodie said. "I owe her a huge apology." Shaking her head, she answered the call. "Hello, Tara?"

"Yeah, Jodie, are you still in Arrowbear with the retired cop?"

"Yeah."

"It might not be the best place for you. I found something huge. I'm with the FBI and the ATF. It's not Ian who was after you—"

Jodie didn't hear the rest. Someone rammed the back of George's truck hard. The phone flew from her hand when her head snapped back against the headrest. George fought to keep control of the vehicle.

He righted the truck but then came another ram. This time George lost it. The truck careened into the guardrail on the right, then jerked back to the left. It seemed to teeter on two wheels before twisting around and slamming into the side of the mountain. The airbags deployed, stunning Jodie.

Vaguely she felt George moving. He undid his seat belt, reached for the door, and shoved it open. Jodie pushed the airbag away and reached for her own gun.

Two gunshots sounded.

Jodie couldn't open her door; it was jammed by the crash. She tried to slide across the seat and exit the way George had and found a gun shoved into her face.

"Sorry it has to be this way. Drop the gun, Jodie."

She looked up to see Uncle Jonah, wearing the coldest expression Jodie had ever seen.

"Why—?"

"No time. Drop it now."

Jodie let her gun clatter to the street. Jonah grabbed her arm and jerked her across the driver's seat and out of the truck. She hit the ground on her knees, scraping them. Before she could do anything, Jonah yanked her to her feet and dragged her to his vehicle—an older boxy blue Jeep Cherokee. The front end was smoking and dented but the engine was still running.

George was on the ground in the middle of the street. Dead or alive, she couldn't tell.

"George!" Jodie tried to pull toward him, but Jonah pulled harder and slammed her into the side of the Jeep.

"You and Tara messed everything up," he muttered through clenched teeth. "I had the perfect plan."

He twisted her hands behind her back and applied handcuffs, then opened the back door, picked her up, and threw her across the seat.

"What do you mean? What does Tara have to do with this?"

"Stay still and be quiet," Jonah ordered. He tossed a blanket over her.

He slammed the door and climbed into the driver's seat. Jodie felt the vehicle turn, then accelerate, and she guessed they were headed back up the mountain on Highway 18.

"What is wrong with you?" With her hands behind her back, it was difficult to stay in one place on the seat. Sliding around only made her angrier.

"I told you to be quiet."

"Jonah, I've known you my whole life. You've tried to kill me three times?"

Jonah said nothing.

"Why? I've always considered you fam—"

"It's not about you. It's about so much more!" There was anger and pain in his voice. Jodie thought she heard a break.

"Please tell me. If this is about money, we can sol—"

"It's about payback and pain. It's about Saint Mike feeling the same kind of pain I felt when Jason died. It's about Gus and Mike getting their just rewards after they both stabbed me in the back. Maybe your uncle should explain. I've invited him up here for the

party. Until he gets here, I'm not going to say it again. Shut. Up."
He turned on the radio, loud, blasting heavy metal music.

Angry and heart broken in disbelief, wrists aching, Jodie let
her head fall back as she tried to think. Earsplitting strains of Def
Leppard did not help.

Had he already killed Sam? Was George dead?

Jodie prayed Sam and George were okay. Under the blanket she
worked to slip the cuffs. She was limber enough to switch them
from back to front but being on the back seat of a moving car
would make it difficult. And she didn't know how closely Jonah
was watching in the rearview mirror or if he could even see her.
The blanket then slipped off and onto the floorboard. Jodie sat up.
They were traveling on Highway 18 toward Big Bear, she thought.
She saw Jonah's hard stare in the rearview mirror.

Slipping the cuffs was her only chance. Handcuffed in front,
she could better defend herself. Then Jonah made a sharp left, and
Jodie nearly flew off the seat. He'd gone off road.

As uncomfortable as all the bumping and rocking was, it was to
her advantage because Jonah would not notice her moving around.
She bent her knees to work the cuffs under her feet and bring her
hands under and forward.

It wasn't long before the music gave her a headache. Jodie's
wrists ached and bled; the rough ride was making it difficult to
get the cuffs off. She bit her bottom lip, grunted, and with a final
effort, bent her knees as far as she could, squeezed the chain under
her feet, and jerked the cuffs in front of her, then lost her balance
and rolled off the seat onto the floor. It felt like her whole body
was getting beaten and bruised by the bouncing around in the
back seat of the Jeep.

She pulled herself up into the seat again, having more control now with her hands in front. Jonah had to be stopped, but how? Looking out the windshield, she saw forest and dirt road. They'd turned left. Where was he going? She thought maybe Jonah was on a road that went behind Green Valley Lake but she couldn't be certain.

She tried to yell and get his attention, but the music was insufferable. Then she realized they were slowing. The acrid smell of burning oil was strong. She could see smoke pouring from under the hood. Ramming George into the mountain probably seriously damaged the vehicle.

A minute later her suspicions were proven correct. The SUV shuddered to a stop.

Jonah cursed and banged on the steering wheel. Thankfully the music stopped and Jodie could hear her own thoughts. Jonah opened his door and got out of the car. Jodie saw the light from his cell phone, and she moved closer to the window in order to overhear.

"There's been a setback," he said. "The car died. I'm about ten minutes out."

CHAPTER 53

SAM SAT QUIETLY ON THE SOFA while Collins paced, and time ticked away. Sam had gone past exhausted a long time ago, but now was certainly not the time to sleep. Collins had had two energy drinks in the time they'd been here. It wouldn't surprise Sam if he started bouncing off the walls.

"Who helped you plan all this?" Sam asked, hoping simple conversation would reveal more than Collins wanted to.

"A very smart man. You'll know soon enough. We planned well until you showed up."

"Not really well. Jodie survived the blast."

Collins sneered at him. "Sheer luck."

"You want her dead because you didn't make it to the police force?"

A muscle in Collins's face twitched. "I don't care. I can make more money hacking, and it's all tax-free. I'm too smart to be a stupid cop."

"Then why spend so much time trying to get hired? Martin said you worked really hard—"

"Ha, Martin's a moron. He washed out after four weeks in the academy."

"But he got hired and you didn't."

"It was all an exercise anyway."

"What do you mean?"

"It didn't matter. I was learning."

Sam frowned, not certain what Collins meant. Something was off. "Learning what?"

"I'm smarter than any cop."

"You're not smart. You're a psychopath. You killed four good officers."

"To prove I could." His expression was defiant.

Yet Sam wasn't buying it. Collins was involved, he had no doubt. There was no passion in his tone of voice. Sam was not reading the drive to murder in anything Collins was saying.

He decided to try a different tack. "You hack people's accounts and steal their money? Martin told me you hacked into the bank."

"Child's play. My friend needed some money; I got it for him. No matter the security, I can breach it. I told Sergeant King that my computer skills would be a huge asset to the police department. She was too dense to see it." He smirked and looked away from Sam.

Why did any of it matter if he really didn't want to be an officer? Sam wondered. He didn't say anything because Collins kept talking. Fine as far as Sam was concerned. He wanted to keep him talking.

"Everyone's information is on the web. They think it's secure—it's not. I can peel away any layer of security and expose them. I can make people look guilty, and I can erase guilt. I even fooled the FBI. Like you—you thought you thwarted me by changing rental cars. Ha, fooled you. I tracked your phone every minute. When it comes to technology, I am god."

It was easy to clone phones; Sam never thought his had been in danger. When would it have been possible? It couldn't have been Ian. It had to be the cop, Collins's partner.

"You should realize this is not going to end well for you or your partner," Sam said. "You will be caught."

"First, you're wrong. We're not going to get caught. Second, even if they catch us, they have no proof of anything."

"They have your whole house filled with incriminating evidence."

Collins jerked toward him, angry. "You messed it all up. Jodie should have died last Saturday. My house would have exploded on schedule and no evidence would have been left!" He pointed the gun at Sam's head, eyes wild with rage.

Then he took a deep breath and lowered the gun. Rolling his shoulders and tilting his head from side to side, he said, "No matter. I can explain everything. But I won't have to. They have no direct evidence of anything. Once you, King, and her uncle are dead, we will be gone. We've committed the perfect crime."

"Her uncle?"

Collins shot him a glare.

Sam got the impression he hadn't meant to give up so much information. He moved on.

"No, your partner committed the perfect crime, because we don't know who he is. You, on the other hand, your name is everywhere. You are the number one suspect."

Collins stared at Sam. "I know what you're trying to do. It won't work."

"I'm only telling you the truth. Didn't you wonder why we found your house? Your fingerprints, buddy. They were on the bullets you left after you tried to kill Jodie."

Sam could see he was getting to the kid. He certainly didn't have a poker face.

"And at your house, all those photos. We have a map and it points right to you. He's setting you up."

"He wouldn't."

"Keep believing in the guy. How'd you hook up with him anyway? And why so much carnage just because you weren't hired?"

"People needed to be paid back. People like you who think you're so superior because you're tall and athletic. People who don't look out for their friends like they're supposed to. We just exacted a little retribution. And we have a plan. Shut up and stop trying to get in my head. If I have to shoot you, I can think of a good excuse. You're not the important one anyway."

"Who is the important one?

"Your girlfriend." Collins pursed his lips and made kissing noises.

Sam ignored him, not wanting him to see how worried he was about Jodie. He saw the anger as Collins talked about paying people back. He still didn't see the impetus for murder. He also began to believe that whoever Collins's partner was, he was using the kid. He was a gifted hacker, after all.

Collins's phone rang.

"Are you here?" he said, stepping forward to peer out the window.

He stood up straight, listening to the call. His guard was down; he wasn't paying any attention to Sam.

"What do you mean, setback?" Collins listened for a second. "Hurry up. I'm tired of watching this guy."

The man on the other end was clearly angry. Sam could hear his voice raised but could not understand what was being said. Collins's face turned bright red.

Sam realized something had gone wrong. He sat up slowly. The change in Collins's demeanor could mean dire consequences for Sam. He needed to act now.

Collins ended the call, body language telling Sam the guy was stiff and furious. He turned toward Sam a second too late. Sam got up from the couch and in one smooth motion smacked Collins across the side of his face with an open hand. Collins slammed into the front door and went down hard, the gun flying from his grasp.

Sam grabbed the gun, stuffed it in his waistband. He was about to bend down and secure Collins when, as the day brightened, something outside caught his attention.

He stepped to the window. There in the drive was a Cadillac SUV. The same one he'd seen the morning he went to Estella's house. The only person it could have belonged to was Jonah Bennett.

"King and her uncle . . ."

This was never about Jodie. It was about Gus, Mike, and Jonah. His whole body went cold as he realized a horrible truth: Jonah Bennett was someone Jodie trusted implicitly.

CHAPTER 54

"I DON'T CARE IF YOU'RE TIRED OF WAITING. Sit tight. I'll be there."

Jonah was angry with whoever was on the other side of the call. Jodie had an idea. The darkness had lifted somewhat, and the forest was visible. She glanced at her watch. It would be light soon. Back to her, Jonah stood still. Maybe collecting his thoughts. Quickly she scrambled to reposition herself.

She bent her legs and put her feet toward the door. She'd kick the door into him, hopefully knock him out and get free. Just as she got in position, she changed her mind. This was Uncle Jonah. She'd known him since she was eight. Even the realization that he killed her team did not make it easy for her to want to hurt him.

Jodie relaxed and sat back on the seat. He had to make the next move. She couldn't even run because she wasn't sure which direction to go.

Jonah didn't open the door right away. He went to the back and opened the hatch. Jodie turned and saw a backpack there and some rope. He grabbed the rope, opened the backpack, and jammed it inside. The pack was stuffed full, and Jodie wondered what else was in there. Jonah slammed the hatch and walked around to Jodie's door.

"Come on, get out. We have a ways to go." He'd slung the pack over his shoulder. Jodie had no choice but to do what he said.

She climbed out of the car.

He looked at her cuffs. "It won't do you any good. And I won't take the time to put them back the way they should be." He pointed to the road in front of the Jeep. "Walk."

Jodie did as she was told and Jonah fell into step behind her. It was getting lighter now; she could make out the terrain and guessed they were behind Green Valley Lake.

"What do you mean, Tara and I ruined things?" she asked, not looking back.

"You can't just be quiet, can you?"

"No, Uncle Jonah, I can't. I don't understand. Why are you doing this?"

"Keep walking."

"Or what? You'll shoot me?" She stopped in the middle of the road and faced him.

"You should have died three months ago. I planned everything perfectly." The words were frosty, not the words of a man she'd always loved.

"What did I do to you? Why . . . ?" Jodie's voice broke, and she swallowed, wanting to keep her composure. Now was not the time to be sentimental. Jonah certainly wasn't. "What did four awesome officers and one great CI ever do to you?"

"It's not about you, not about them. I made a point. I didn't care about your team. You and Gus were the ones who were supposed to die. Gus deserved it for his own sins. As for you, Mike would have had to suffer through the kind of loss I've lived with."

His face flushed and a tic started under his right eye. "For twenty-five years I've lived with Mike's boot on my neck. The only way for me to cut him off at the knees was through you."

"I don't understand."

"I know you don't. I've set up this finale to force Mike to face what he did to me and what it's going to cost him." He gestured with the gun. "Keep walking. Your boyfriend is waiting on the other end. I could shoot you and carry you, but I have other plans."

He was taking her to Sam. Jodie started walking. She wanted to keep Jonah talking but wasn't sure how. And shock about all the hatred he spewed toward Gus and Mike had her flustered. Then Jonah just began to speak.

"You think your uncle Mike is a saint, don't you? Always the do-gooder, the by-the-book guy. Well, he's not. He stabbed me in the back, ruined my life. It wasn't fair. All these years of unfairness. I finally had enough when Jason died."

"Mike had nothing to do with you being fired."

"Is that what he told you? Did he ever tell you why I got fired?"

Jodie glanced back.

"He didn't, did he? Because I took the fall for him. Him and Gus. The both of them pulled the rug out from under me. They did not have my back; they stabbed me square in the back."

"I don't know what you're talking about."

"Of course you don't. They covered for each other. Mike raped the woman, not me."

Jodie stopped, turned, and stared. "What did you say?"

Jonah's face was red with anger. "Right. He's a rapist. Him and Gus played dumb and let me take the rap. Cost me my career. If I hadn't been fired, my whole life would have been different. Life for Jason would have been different. He was a good kid who didn't deserve to die the way he did. What did Gus and Mike do for me? They cornered me about money."

He spit on the ground, then stepped forward, towering over Jodie, face twisted in hate and rage. "When Jason died, everything decent in this world died as far as I am concerned. He was the only good in this stinking world. I'm not going to play along anymore. Then Gus and Mike tried to squeeze me over money. They hadn't caused me enough trouble over the years—they still wanted to ruin me."

"They tried to help you. They loa—"

"They kept playing the good boys, the self-righteous ones. They didn't care about me; they only cared about themselves. Yeah, I set the IED. I wanted them to pay. Gus with his life and Mike with you dead. It went wrong, but I'm going to fix it. Your uncle will pay. Your boyfriend added himself to the list. Your life is the price. Now keep walking."

CHAPTER 55

COLLINS STIRRED and Sam bent to secure the dazed man.

Collins was groggy at first. A trickle of blood ran down his chin. Sam clicked the cuffs on him, picked him up, and pushed him back to sit on the couch. He then did a quick survey of the cabin, walking around the room, keeping an eye on Collins. The back door in the kitchen opened out to a deck, with stairs leading into the forest.

"Tables turned, dude," Sam said. He reached down again and grabbed the kid's phone. It was now locked.

Sam held the phone up and looked at Collins. "You need to unlock this."

Initially stunned, Collins gathered his wits about him quickly. "No. I won't unlock the phone for you. My partner, as you call him, is on the way. He's got your girlfriend. You both will die as planned."

"I know who your partner is. Jonah Bennett."

"What?" Collins's face was a study in surprise, but it faded fast. "Doesn't matter if you know, I guess. He's still smarter than you."

"How'd you hook up with him?"

"Why do you want to know?"

"Humor me."

"I was a student aide in one of Jason's classes. He came to me after Jason died. He wanted me to unlock his son's computer."

"Were you a friend of Jason's?"

"Just from computer work. Jason loved computers; he didn't have the same knack for them I do. He'd come to me and ask about how to do stuff. I unlocked the computer and then Jonah helped me sell my house, found me a great one, in a great neighborhood." He smirked. "I got a lot of good intel there."

Sam stared at the kid and tried to think. He claimed Jodie was already with Jonah. She trusted him; he might have talked her into going with him. Fear spiked in Sam. *They would die as planned.* What in the world was the plan? And how did Mike King fit into it? He kept his face neutral.

"If I'm not mistaken, I can call 911 even if this phone is locked."

"You don't know where you are."

"Yeah, but GPS does."

"Maybe I turned mine off."

The boy's face betrayed him. He hadn't turned off the GPS.

Sam hit emergency and dialed 911. He got a dispatcher in San Bernardino and patiently explained what was happening. While it took longer than he liked, eventually the dispatcher got the message and the GPS signal. Help was on the way.

"Keep the line open," she said.

"I have no intention of hanging up. Please, I need you to check on someone. Ask the responding officers where Jodie King is. I'm afraid she might be in trouble as well."

The line stayed open while the dispatcher took care of his request. To Sam, it seemed an eternity, but finally a familiar voice came on the line.

"Sam, it's Smiley. Glad you're okay."

"Me too. How's Jodie?"

"I wish I had better news, buddy, but she's missing. She and George were run into the mountain. She's gone and George has been shot."

Sam felt as if the floor had fallen away from his feet. "Is George okay?"

"He's critical, in surgery as we speak. We have no idea where Jodie is."

Sam took a deep breath and fought threatening panic. Clarity struck. "I think I know where Jodie is. He's bringing her here, Bruce. It's Jonah Bennett."

"Yeah, we know about Bennett. We got a message from him. You must be in his cabin on Angeles. If Jodie's not there yet, maybe we can get there first. We are on the way. He doesn't only want to kill Jodie, but you and Mike King as well."

CHAPTER 56

JODIE WALKED, Jonah a step or two behind her. She tried to think, but her mind was numb from all the revelations. Mike a rapist? Gus a backstabbing opportunist? She couldn't see it, but Jonah did. He saw it clearly enough to want bloody revenge.

Then she thought about George, lying in the middle of Highway 18. Someone would have found him by now. Surely officers were looking for both her and Sam. They'd have no idea where to look. There were several numbered dirt roads in and around Green Valley Lake, all over the San Bernardino Mountains really. She'd ridden dirt bikes here with Jason often. Jason hadn't been much of an athlete, but he was a daredevil when it came to dirt bikes. This was one of the numbered roads, but she wasn't sure which one. Recognition gave her hope. She could get away if the opportunity arose.

She thought about the Jeep Jonah had driven her here in. It was badly damaged; perhaps the fluids leaking from the vehicle would lead rescuers to her. As hard as it was to hear, she wanted to keep Jonah talking, learn more, maybe find a way to reason with him. She turned to look at him. He was studying his phone, frowning.

"You sent Collins up to the mountains to shoot me?"

He looked up, still frowning. "Hmph. No, I didn't. That was all his idea. He was trying to impress me. I wish he hadn't done it, though. He made such a mess of things. Good intentions. He's a little misfit. But he's served me well."

"He's your servant?"

"He's a means to an end. He was a friend of Jason's. He'll be good company when we both skip out." He kept looking at the phone.

"Where are you going? Checking out a map?"

Now he laughed. "I know where I am at all times. You should remember from all the hikes we took."

Jodie did remember. Jonah had an amazing sense of direction. She felt a pinch in her chest as memories of those good times flooded her mind.

"I do remember." She stopped walking. "I remember a lot. I remember good times filled with love and laughter. Why are you doing this?"

He stopped as well and looked at her, his expression stony. "I told you. It's payback, revenge, justice." He shrugged and continued. "Whatever you want to call it. If it's any consolation, I'm sorry you've become a means to an end. I remember wishing you were closer in age to Jason. The two of you would have been great together. Keep walking."

"What if I don't? Why don't you just shoot me here?"

"I'm not going to carry you. I have a big finish planned, but I can alter it. Once I finish with you and hopefully Mike if he gets here in time, I'm going far, far away." He stopped and pointed toward the left. "Go left. In a little bit, I think you'll see my car."

Jodie hesitated.

"You're prolonging the inevitable. Look, I have your friend Sam. He's been quite a nuisance. You want him to die alone?"

"All this death and destruction, why did you let Agent Greto live?"

Jonah frowned. "The guy in the safe house? He was practice. I was going to take you out the same way, Taser, then sedative. You messed things up. I had to improvise."

"Why involve Sam?"

"He keeps getting in the way."

Jodie didn't start to walk immediately, fear for Sam overwhelming her, freezing her muscles. Frustrated because the man in front of her was not the Jonah she grew up with.

She looked around, struggling to find anything familiar. It clicked that this had to be near where Jonah's cabin used to be. Would being at his cabin help her situation or hurt it? *Oh, Lord, what is the way out of this?*

Jonah's voice brought her back to the stark reality of the here and now.

"One call and Dennis will put a bullet in his brain."

CHAPTER 57

COLLINS'S FACE WAS A STUDY in anger and petulance.

"He'll be here. He's never late. He'll get here in time."

"In time for what?"

He looked away.

Sam knelt to be at eye level with Collins. "Look, Dennis, none of this makes sense to me. Okay, you're a smart kid. Did you go on a killing spree just because you weren't hired? Why even try to be a cop if you were so invested in what was illegal?"

"I could have been a good cop. Do you know how many cyber-crimes I could have thwarted? Instead LBPD said I wasn't good enough."

"So you killed four good officers?"

"They weren't as good as me, huh?" He arched an eyebrow.

Sam stood and went back to the window. It was light now and he could see they were surrounded by forest. They were still in GVL, he bet. He doubted they'd gone as far as Big Bear or Lake Arrowhead.

"It's been more than ten minutes. Where is Jonah?"

Collins said nothing.

"All this death and destruction, yet you let the FBI agent live. Why?"

"Just to prove we can do whatever we want."

"You say *we*, but Jonah calls all the shots."

Collins's face reddened. "We discuss everything."

"Well, maybe he got caught. He called the police to brag; they know where he is. Did you discuss how to deal with that?"

Collins said nothing.

Sam paced, keeping an eye on the window. "Why does he want to kill Mike King? I thought they were lifelong buddies."

"You don't stab a buddy in the back."

Sam turned and looked at Dennis. "The IED was to get back at Mike King?"

"Sure. Two birds with one stone. Gus had the decency to die when he was supposed to."

"Jodie escaped. Then you tried to shoot her last Saturday."

Dennis looked away.

"You had a line on her. Did you freeze up? Not so easy to kill someone up close."

"I got the deputy good. He never saw it coming. He thought I was small and weak. I showed him."

Sam considered Collins's bravado now. He wanted to break the facade; what would get under the kid's skin?

"Something tells me shooting Jodie wasn't Jonah's idea. I do think Jonah is smart, a lot smarter than you. He planned the IED, maybe with your help. It was sophisticated. The mess of C-4 under your house, not so much. Yeah, I'm beginning to see . . . Jonah is the brains here."

"He wouldn't have gotten nearly as much done without me."

"Whose idea was the IED at the very beginning?"

"Jonah had the idea. But I worked out the details. It would have been perfect if . . ."

"Jodie had died?"

Collins nodded.

The energy drinks had worn off and he was crashing, big-time. Lord knew Sam was tired. But he had to stay sharp.

"Jonah was so upset when she escaped. He couldn't believe it. We rigged everything so perfectly." He yawned. "I thought it would please him if I finished the job. You came along and messed it all up."

"Is that why I'm here now?"

"Yeah." He put his head back and closed his eyes, sounding punchy now. "You were bait. Then it all went wrong when the other woman cop hooked up with the ATF and started sniffing around about the C-4." His voice faded out and Sam feared he would fall asleep and stop talking.

"What about the C-4?"

Then a voice from outside interrupted.

"Dennis, are you there? Is everything okay?"

CHAPTER 58

SAM LOOKED AT COLLINS, who smiled.

"I told you so," he said in a singsongy voice.

Peering out the window, Sam could barely see the top of Jonah's head. He was behind the SUV. If Jodie was with him, he couldn't tell.

"Dennis, say something," Jonah yelled again.

"Go ahead," Sam said. "Tell him you're a bit tied up."

"I'm not saying anything until you take these handcuffs off," Collins whispered.

"I know you're in there, Gresham. You should know that I'm holding a gun to Jodie's head now. I want to know if Dennis is all right."

Sam glanced over at Dennis, then turned to the window. "He's fine. He doesn't want to talk."

"Okay, I don't have time to play games. Here's what I'm going to do."

Sam watched as Jodie was pushed to the front of the SUV. Her hands were cuffed in front and Jonah had a rope looped around her waist, entrapping her hands. His heart dropped. Bennett had a gun pointed at her head, but he made himself a small target.

"Right now, send me Dennis. Or she dies."

Sam had no choice. He grabbed Collins by the arm and pulled him up. Opening the front door, he pushed the kid out in front of him but held him in place.

"Here he is. Send me Jodie."

"Sam, stop stalling. I have all the cards."

"They know all about you. I called—they're on the way."

"I called as well. I want them to come. I want Mike King here. And anyone else who is stupid enough to get in my way. And since they're coming, as I knew they would, they're going to meet some booby traps first."

Collins giggled. "Should be boom-be traps."

As if on cue, Sam heard what sounded like an explosion in the distance, in the direction of the road he figured the deputies he called would be using. His hand closed around the gun. He had no clear shot, and Jonah had Jodie.

Bennett tossed his keys, which landed at Sam's feet. "Unlock him, Sam, and give him the gun now. I'm through playing."

All Sam could think of was stopping Jonah from shooting Jodie. He prayed, stalling, hoping the Lord would show him the way out of whatever was next.

He picked up the keys, found the cuff key, and undid Collins's hands.

Collins spun around, grin on his face. "Ha-ha. I told you he was smarter than you." He grabbed the gun from Sam's belt and the phone from his back pocket. He disconnected the call.

"Cuff him," Bennett ordered.

Sam turned and Collins slapped on the cuffs again.

Now Bennett came around the back of the SUV, into clear view. He dragged Jodie with him.

"Bring him here, Dennis. I want them back-to-back."

Before his back was to her, Sam caught Jodie's gaze. There was no fear there; she was calm and her demeanor fortified him. They would get out of this.

"Sit down," Bennett ordered. They sat, Sam with his arms restrained behind him and Jodie with her hands cuffed in front.

Bennett pulled something from his backpack and Sam's blood turned to ice. It was a suicide vest. He could make out three bricks of C-4 in the fabric. He also saw a detonator and a timer.

Jonah looped the vest around them so there was a square of C-4 in front of Sam, one at his side, and he guessed one in front of Jodie. He then looped the rope around them a couple of times and handcuffed the ropes to Sam's handcuffs.

"Jonah, whatever you think, you'll never get away with this," Jodie said.

Jonah knelt and Sam felt him whisper in her ear. "Of course I will. I fooled the FBI, the ATF, and every law enforcement agency in Southern California for months. I will get away with it—I am getting away with it."

He stood. "All right, get the bikes, Dennis," Jonah ordered.

Sam couldn't see where Dennis went. He remembered seeing a shed on the property, but it was behind him.

Bennett knelt again, this time speaking to both of them. "I wanted to hang tight, wait until everyone got here, and see the final expression on Mike's face. But I'm nothing if not flexible. I'm setting a ten-minute countdown. By my calculations, everything should blow precisely when good old Uncle Mike gets here. But my booby trap might have slowed them down too much. Sorry I can't be here to greet him properly. I have a flight to make."

With a click, he set the timer, got up, and from what Sam could hear, jogged toward where Dennis had gone. Two dirt bikes started up and were soon heading away.

In his mind, Sam was counting down the seconds—*10:00, 09:59, 09:58*—and praying for a way out.

CHAPTER 59

JODIE WATCHED JONAH AND COLLINS disappear down the trail. They were at his cabin. He'd never sold it. Time ticked away. Yet an unexplainable peace had settled over her when Jonah tied her and Sam back-to-back. The two of them working together would find a way out—they had to.

"Are you okay, Sam?"

"I'm fine. Can you move at all?"

"A little, my hands are in front." She moved and Sam with her. "I can't get my hands around to the back to take this thing off, though."

"He's got it fastened to me. I have a cuff key in my back pocket. I think I can get it out, but I need more room. We need to tip over to my right. I'll be able to move a little more then."

Sam counted to three and they fell to the side.

"Thanks, now I have more space, but this is difficult."

Jodie could feel him working. There was no way she could help him, and in her mind, she was thinking about the timer. At least two minutes had passed. Would he get it in time?

Sam grunted and pulled; Jodie's shoulder got the brunt of it.

"I got it," he exclaimed breathlessly. "It will take me too long to get mine off. I'm dropping the key. If we slide away a bit, you should be able to pick it up. Hurry."

Sam pulled her back toward him as she moved to the left. It wasn't long before Jodie saw the key and picked it up. Her cuffs were off quickly but the two of them were still tied together. She pulled the rope up over her head and then wriggled out of it.

"Don't look at the time, Jodie. Just undo all the cuffs."

Jodie saw the time anyway and almost panicked. They had less than a minute. There were four pairs of cuffs to go. Jonah had attached everything to Sam.

Biting her bottom lip, she bent to the task. One, two, three, four, and Sam was free of the vest. They pulled each other up, Sam holding the vest in his hand.

"Quick—into the house." He heaved the vest to the right and then pulled Jodie into the house, closing the door. "On the floor behind the sofa."

They'd barely hit the floor when a large *boom* sounded. Two windows blew out and the whole house shuddered, then went still.

■ ■ ■

Sam rolled to a sitting position. "You okay, Jodie?" He looked her over as he asked the question. Other than being disheveled, with her wrists cut up a bit, she looked fine.

"I'm good. You?"

"In one piece. I did call 911 before you got here, talked to Smiley. They know where we are, and they should be here soon."

"But Jonah is getting away."

"He won't get far."

"I know where he's going."

"Where?"

"Jonah is a licensed pilot. He's going to the airport in Big Bear. We have to stop him, but we don't have a phone to tell anyone."

"We both almost just died. Remember sometimes discretion is the better part of valor?"

Jodie faced him and grabbed both his hands in hers. "Yes, I do believe that, but now is not the time. Suppose he has time to set more booby traps? Suppose a cop who doesn't know what a monster he is gets in his way? Sam, he's a fleeing felon who is very likely to hurt someone else. We need to stop him."

Sam looked into those clear blue eyes, so earnest and committed. He agreed with her but he had no idea how they could stop Jonah.

"With what?" he asked.

She got up and left the house, calling out, "Follow me."

Sam jogged after her. They went to the shed. Inside were three more dirt bikes and an assortment of ski gear.

"We go after him."

"He's got a head start," he said, "but if he's heading to Big Bear, there might be a way to cut him off."

Jodie pushed aside some skis and pulled at the doors of a padlocked cabinet. "Jonah kept guns in here. This is his place. I thought he'd sold it, but everything is just as I remember it. Find something to break the lock."

Where at first Sam had been reluctant, he could tell he was not going to talk Jodie out of this course of action. And if they went after Jonah and Collins, they would need to be prepared. He found an axe and went to work on the lock.

"What makes you think he left the guns?"

"It's a hunch." She went to work clearing gear away from two of the remaining dirt bikes.

After three swings, the lock broke free. Sam pulled the doors open and found two hunting rifles, a shotgun, and a .22 pistol. The pistol was loaded, but there were no extra shells. The shotgun was empty but there was one box of shotgun shells. He grabbed the pistol, stuck it in his belt, then loaded the shotgun. He kept hoping to hear the cavalry arrive, but Jonah was right—the booby trap slowed them down.

"There's gas in both these bikes," Jodie said. "I think it's enough to get over the mountain."

Sam checked. Green Valley Lake was roughly the same elevation as Big Bear, but Butler Peak stood between them. A designated dirt road traversed the mountain and dropped down into Fawnskin, the community on the other side of the lake from Big Bear. From there it was a short jaunt to Big Bear Airport. Sam bet Jonah was on the road right now. It was twentysome miles to the airport from here on the highway, roughly forty minutes. On dirt bikes, over tough terrain, it would take a lot longer.

Sam considered the shortcut. If Jonah and Collins were on 2N13, there was a chance he and Jodie could intercept them before Fawnskin. They might just be able to do it.

"All right, this is crazy, but I think it's possible. Follow me closely."

Sam kept the handgun and secured the shotgun to Jodie's bike.

They put on helmets and started both bikes and took off after Jonah and Collins. Sam prayed for his memory to hold. This area had been his backyard growing up, but it had been years since his last camping trip. He found the road and they traversed it for a few minutes before he veered off onto the faster but rougher trail that would enable them to cut Jonah off.

Glancing back, he saw Jodie was keeping up. He pressed on, accelerating as fast as he dared. He also prayed. Confidence flooded his soul. They could do this—he was certain.

CHAPTER 60

JODIE STRUGGLED TO KEEP UP WITH SAM. She trusted him implicitly, but it had been a long time since she'd been on a dirt bike. As they climbed a rutty, rocky trail, she almost lost it more times than she wanted to admit. She prayed, asking the Lord for strength and wisdom and for Jonah to not get away. Her balance came roaring back, the barrier between her and God crumbling to nothing. Jodie felt the familiar adrenaline surge of the chase. They were on the right track, and she knew who was responsible for the worst day in her life. She'd done nothing wrong except trust someone she loved. And she could not understand Jonah's twisted logic in wanting her dead.

Her prayers were interrupted by discomfort. Unused muscles

were screaming. Just when she thought she couldn't take it anymore, they crested a rise and Sam stopped.

He took off his helmet and pointed. "Look."

Jodie did and saw puffs of dust rising from the road below
them. Two dirt bikes. Collins was quite a ways behind Jonah.

"It's them. Doesn't look as if Collins is very good at dirt bike
riding. We have a good chance to cut them off. How are you
doing?"

Jodie held up a thumb, determined to suck it up and follow
Sam into whatever awaited them.

Sam took off and Jodie accelerated after him. She couldn't keep
an eye on Jonah; it took all her concentration to stay behind Sam.
When they started going downhill, it was even harder to keep up at
what she felt was a safe speed. Then her bike began to sputter and
stall. She was running out of gas. Jodie's ride stuttered to a stop.

Sam heard. He jerked his bike around and scooted back to her.

"Grab the shotgun and hop on the back of mine."

Jodie did as Sam asked, secured the shotgun and climbed on
behind him. She encircled his waist with her arms and held on
tight as Sam rocketed along the trail. She lost track of time on the
bone-jarring ride and nearly screamed in relief when he slowed and
stopped. They were next to a bend in the road.

"I think we've got maybe two minutes on them," Sam said as
he pulled off his helmet.

They got off the bike. Jodie held on to the shotgun and Sam
pushed the bike right into the middle of the road, placing his helmet on one end and hers on the other. Jodie could hear the roar
of motors in the distance.

Sam hurried back toward her. "They're coming. Let's get ready."

Jodie racked a round into the chamber of the shotgun. They

took a position behind some rocks. Jonah and Collins would be forced to stop, and Sam and Jodie would be behind them.

Jodie ducked down as the sound of motors came closer. For a second, she froze. Was this her chance to fix things? She'd wanted to take the life of the man responsible for the IED. She might get the chance. Was it really what she wanted? The bad guy was Jonah. And she feared she couldn't shoot Jonah, no matter what he'd done.

She started to put the shotgun down. She needed to tell Sam there was no way she could shoot Jonah. But she was too late. Jonah came tearing around the corner, going too fast to go around the blockage and sliding to a stop at the downed dirt bike. He very nearly ran into it. He jumped off the bike, cursing. Collins was still some distance away by the sound of his engine. He wasn't going as fast as Jonah.

Jonah slung off his backpack and drew his weapon, looking around suspiciously. Jodie was about to stand up and make her presence known, but Sam put a hand on her shoulder and a finger to his lips. He pointed, and there came Collins. He was wobbly on the bike; he had no control. As he rounded the corner, Jonah's eyes widened in surprise. He tried to jump out of the way, but he was a second too slow. To Jodie, it seemed as if a panicked Collins had accelerated instead of braking. The bike slammed into Jonah, ramming his legs into his own bike, and the gun went flying.

Jonah screamed in pain.

"Get the gun," Sam said. "I've got Collins." He leaped from cover and headed for Collins.

Jodie sprinted to the gun. She grabbed it easily and turned to point it at Jonah. There was no need. He was on the ground writhing in pain, back against the dirt road. From what she could see, the collision had broken his leg. It was clearly bent at an unnatural angle. She turned her attention to Sam. He had Collins on the ground and pulled a gun from the guy's belt. Sweaty and breathing hard, Collins put up no resistance.

"You busted my leg, you idiot." Jonah squirmed, breathless in agony.

"You got him?" Sam asked, looking at Jodie and pointing to Jonah.

"Yep."

She watched as Sam kept an eye on Collins, then reached for Jonah's backpack. He rustled around in it for a moment and then his hand came out, holding Jonah's phone.

"Oh, get me help, get me help," Jonah begged.

"You betcha," Sam said. "I'll make sure help is on the way." He turned to Jodie, smiled, and gave her a thumbs-up.

Relief flooded through Jodie's veins, and she smiled back not only because the ordeal was over, but because she had not had to make the decision to shoot Jonah, and both he and Collins would be held to account for their crimes.

CHAPTER 61

JODIE KNELT AND TRIED TO HELP JONAH. Up close she could see a bone sticking out of the open fracture.

He pushed her away. "Leave me. Call a doctor. Moron broke my leg." He rocked back and forth, moaning.

She stood back and looked at Sam, who shook his head.

"Nothing we can do."

Collins sat against a boulder, pulled his knees up with his arms wrapped around them. He said nothing.

They waited about thirty minutes before the first members of the rescue party arrived. They were roughly in the middle between Green Valley Lake and Fawnskin. The help came from a forest ranger and two GVL deputies who arrived in a four-wheel drive.

Once the location was pinpointed, they radioed for medical assistance. By then, Jonah had passed out.

"Can anyone tell me if there was an explosion in Green Valley Lake?" Sam asked.

He was worried about the booby trap. So was Jodie.

One of the deputies nodded. "A patrol car ran over an explosive device. Two deputies were injured, but they'll be okay."

"Thanks, glad to hear it," he said, casting a glance at Jodie.

She was glad Mike hadn't been hurt, but the accusations Jonah made had her unsettled.

Jodie and Sam were taken back to GVL. In the back of the rig Jodie relaxed for the first time in a long while and leaned against Sam. He put his arm around her and she rested her head on his shoulder. It was a bumpy ride but Jodie didn't mind it a bit.

They found everyone staged at the fire station there. Mike and Tara rushed to greet them as they got out of the rig. Mike hugged her first; then he shook Sam's hand.

"George is going to make it," he said.

Jodie saw the relief in Sam's face.

"Oh, Jodie, I'm so glad you're okay. When your call disconnected, I feared the worst." Tara looked ragged and sleep-deprived.

"What were you ready to tell me?"

Tara glanced at Mike, who looked away.

"I knew it was Jonah. I'd been investigating him on the sly. I, well . . . I'd decided Mike wouldn't go for it. Detective Fenton learned about some locals who got arrested by the ATF for stealing C-4 from a National Guard facility." She turned to Sam. "The night I told you I had a spare room, I wanted to bring you in on my side invest, but away from the station."

"Really? As it turns out, I'm glad I was free for Jodie when she called."

"Good point. Anyway, the thieves sold the stuff but gave a description of the buyer to the ATF. I took a six-pack of photos to them. They picked Jonah out."

"Somehow Jonah guessed you were on to him," Jodie said. "He told me you messed up his plans."

"Yeah, we all found out too late," Mike said, bitterness dripping from his tone. "He'd cloned all of our phones. He could follow everything we were up to in real time. I want to talk to him. I'm heading up with the paramedics."

He left before Jodie could say anything. Smiley met him at the 4x4.

Jodie watched him go. Mike hurt as much or more than she did. Asking about what Jonah had accused him of would have to wait.

Sam handed her a bottle of water.

"Thanks," she said before drinking a good bit.

"The medics want to check us out," Sam told her.

"Okay, I'll meet you over there."

He nodded and walked to where a medic waited. Two had gone with Mike to get Jonah; the third had stayed behind.

Jodie turned to Tara. "Hey, thank you again. I have to admit my imagination ran away with me for a bit, and I thought you were the one working with Jonah. Sorry."

"Don't be. After seeing everything in Collins's house, well, I'd have been thinking the same about everyone. My attitude would have been trust no one." She looked toward Sam. "I was right, you know."

"About what?"

"He is a superhero."

Jodie laughed, and it felt good.

"He definitely is," she agreed, then walked over and sat next to him. They'd gone through a lot in an intensely short time. She wanted to get to know him better in normalcy. Maybe being wherever Sam was, was where she should be.

CHAPTER 62

TWO MONTHS LATER

Jodie dressed carefully. Since she was no longer a police sergeant, she couldn't attend the ceremony in uniform, but she had a professional skirt and jacket set she'd worn often to court.

Today was the day of the memorial ceremony for her team. Their names would be inscribed on a memorial monument, just not one in the mountains. The names of the RAT officers, even those who did not work for LBPD, and Archie "Jukebox" Radio—something she fought hard for—would be inscribed on the police memorial at the base of Chestnut, south of Broadway in Long Beach.

She put the finishing touches on her makeup and then checked her watch. Sam would be there any minute. The last two months had muted the pain and loss Jodie had felt for the three long months the case was not resolved. Jodie felt a pinch of pain from the loss she knew would be with her forever. Knowing Jonah Bennett, a man she loved like family, had tried to kill her and did kill five innocent people was still a point of bafflement. She'd confronted Mike about Jonah's claims when she returned home to Seal Beach.

"Jonah made some accusations about you."

"Accusations about what?"

"About what got him fired."

Mike turned away, brought a hand to his chin.

"Was what he said true?"

"Jodie, can we leave this for another time? You and Sam are safe; George Upton is on the mend; we all need to rest and decompress."

"No, Mike, I need to know. He said you raped someone."

Mike stared at her. "No, of course not. That's crazy and convoluted. Jonah has issues."

"Why would he say it?"

Hands on his hips, he held her gaze. "I have no idea. You've never asked why Jonah got fired."

"It was never important to me until now."

He put his hands together and tapped his lips, sighing as he dropped them to his sides.

"It was an end-of-probation party. Things got out of hand. I'm not perfect, Jodie. I had way too much to drink. I went into the street and discharged my weapon, shooting at the moon. So did Gus. We were stupid, drunk and howling at the moon. I don't know where Jonah was at the time. We could have been fired for unauthorized discharge of our weapons. But no one could identify us at the time and we skated when the complaint came in. Two months later my brother was killed

and you became my responsibility. It was like being dunked in freezing water." He looked away as if remembering.

"Gus had just started dating Estella. I told her I couldn't do it; I couldn't raise you. I was not father material. She agreed. I was hopeless, but she knew where I could find hope. She took me to church. It wasn't anything I hadn't heard before; I mean your dad was an on-fire Christian. I always dismissed it coming from him."

He paused, voice breaking. *"It finally took this time, because of you. You walked into my life holding a Bible almost as big as you were. I had to do right by you. All I've ever tried to do is be a good dad. For twenty-five years."*

"And Jonah? Why would he say you raped someone?"

"You'd have to ask him. Four months after the party, a woman came forward and accused him of rape. He wanted us to lie, to say he was with us, but neither of us could. To put ourselves there, where he said he was, would have contradicted our earlier stories. We thought he understood. Gus was serious about Estella by then and I had you to raise. Neither one of us wanted to lie any more than we already had. In the end, the woman never pressed charges, but it was too late for Jonah. All these years, I thought there were no hard feelings. Life went on. He did well."

"Until Jason died."

"Yeah, you're right. I don't know why he told you I was a rapist. In a way I did stab him in the back. I let him down, yes, but I'm not guilty of anything else. Over the years I only tried to help and protect him. Gus and I both did. We mortgaged our houses to help him out financially. I'm truly sorry that all he felt all these years was resentment."

For Jodie, life had resumed some semblance of normal. She'd returned to church, met with Dr. Bass, and the balance she felt returning when she was chasing Jonah was getting stronger. There would always be a big hole where her team was concerned, but she would live with it. She'd come to the place where she could accept not having an answer to the why question. Like Sam, she'd learned to live with it. "God is good, even when life isn't" was reality to Jodie, and she was sorry she'd ever forgotten it.

A knock on her door brought her back to the present. Sam was here. Macnut ran to the door first, tail wagging. Jodie had the dog with her for the day. After the memorial, she had to return him to Estella. Eventually she'd be able to keep him. She'd given her thirty-day notice and was looking for a place she could rent that would allow dogs.

"You know it's the guy who gives you the best belly rubs, don't you?" The dog sat for her, and she opened the door and felt smacked in the chest. He was so handsome in his dress tan and greens.

He smiled. "You look terrific." He bent down and gave Macnut his expected rubs.

"I was just thinking the same about you."

They'd been enjoying as much normal as they could the past several weeks. After all the interviews and debriefing, they'd shared some sweet dates. She'd met his mother, a sweet woman. Jodie really cared for Sam and believed he felt the same. But since their acquaintance had started so intensely, they decided to move slow and steady with the romance.

He stood, leaned forward, and they shared a kiss. He gripped her hands in his. "You ready?"

"I am." She looked down at the dog. "Mackie's coming. Estella will pick him up after the ceremony." Reluctantly she let go of Sam's hands and reached for the dog's leash.

Jodie hooked on the leash and handed it to Sam.

She grabbed her purse, locked the door, and she and Sam walked with Mackie between them to his patrol car.

When they arrived at the station, there was a sea of police vehicles from several Southern California law enforcement agencies already there. Seal Beach, Gail Shyler's department, and El Monte PD, Tim Evers's, were well represented. Additionally, a lot of civilians were present. As Jodie and Sam walked closer to the monument where the new names would be unveiled, she saw Juke's parents, and with them was Finn. Estella and Levi arrived. Estella took Mackie from Jodie. The ceremony was outdoors and the dog was welcome.

Jodie saw Tracy and Shannon in the audience with their husbands. Since Jodie had returned to church, arriving before everything started and not leaving until everything ended, they had reconnected, and things were back to as normal as they ever were.

Jodie and Sam joined Mike and Tara, and they were soon joined by Detective Smiley and George Upton. George looked good, if a little thin and pale. He'd lost a lot of blood when Jonah shot him, but nothing vital had been impacted.

Ian appeared as well, with his wife. Jodie had learned that they'd reconciled. Ian himself shared he'd been talking to Dr. Bass. Mike invited him to church and got a solid "Yes, I'll come." He was back at work and now wearing his dress uniform.

"Jodie, Sam, good to see you two." Looking healthier and more normal, he held out his hand and Sam shook it.

The mayor, the chief, and several other dignitaries arrived, and the ceremony began. Jodie had been asked to say a few words but she declined. She wanted the ceremony to be about the officers who died, not about the one who survived.

All three chiefs spoke glowingly about the dead, and there was not a dry eye in the place.

Jodie gripped Sam's hand and wept. She'd always miss those she loved and worked with, but it was time to move on. When the speeches ended and the names were unveiled, she hunted down Archie's parents and told them what a brave man their son had been.

"Jodie."

She looked up and saw Tara coming her way.

"What's up?"

"A group of us are going down to Parkers' Lighthouse for lunch—you want to join?"

She looked to Sam, who nodded. "I just need to change," he said. "I have a change of clothes in my unit."

"I'll show you to the locker room," Mike said, gesturing to Sam.

The two walked off and Tara turned to Jodie. Jodie counted Tara as one of the blessings to come out of all the tragedy. They had become fast friends.

"Is it true what I'm hearing? You're going to return to law enforcement?"

"I'm thinking about it. It might not be here, though."

"What do you mean?"

"I'm considering my options. I'm looking for a big house with a yard for Macnut. There's a lot of new construction out in San Bernardino." She paused and bit her bottom lip. This was the hardest decision she'd ever made. Her career had consumed her before, and she did not want to repeat past mistakes. A new start looked to be the only option.

"It would be too difficult to come back to the LBPD after

everything I've been through. But I won't make my final decision in haste. I need a change. Change isn't always a bad thing."

"I'd hate to see you go somewhere else, but I get it. Too much history here." She handed Jodie a newspaper. "Have you seen this?"

Jodie took it, saw the headline, and read the first line of the article. *Local Realtor Jonah Bennett is facing more federal charges as additional evidence comes to light.*

"The outcome of all this will be interesting," Tara said before walking off toward the parking structure.

Jodie skimmed the article. Further down, she saw that Dennis Collins had agreed to testify against Jonah in return for a lighter sentence. She already knew about the murder charges against Jonah; the article indicated charges for buying the stolen C-4, kidnapping, and attempting murder by shooting George had been added. Prosecutors initially only charged Dennis with shooting Chad Logan and left charging him as an accomplice to Jonah and a lot of the computer crimes pending, because they were hoping to get his testimony against Jonah. Looked like their strategy worked.

Despite the resolution, Jodie felt no joy or elation. Nothing would bring her team back, and a man she considered family was the cause. There was no closure in this situation, only senseless loss. It had even taken the starch out of Mike. He'd turned in his papers to retire. In spite of fractured feelings about the end, Jodie felt whole. She'd resolved to concentrate on what she knew, not on what she couldn't see or know.

■ ■ ■

Sam changed quickly and hurried to find Jodie. He caught sight of her reading a newspaper. As always, seeing her brought a smile to his lips and made his heart light. They'd been through so much in a short period of time. The first day they'd met she was lost and hurt—devastated, out of touch with life and her faith. He'd seen her fight through the pain and change. Now she was a different person, confident, in touch.

She was still wobbly in places, not certain about her career path. But she was back in church and engaged in life. The hurt and loss still dogged her at times, he knew, just like it dogged him. They were both broken people standing on a firm foundation.

God is good, even when life is not.

"Whatcha got there?" Sam asked.

Jodie showed him the newspaper article and he skimmed it.

"They got Dennis to turn. Good. Maybe Jonah will plead out and save the city a trial."

"Maybe. You ready to go to lunch?"

"I'm ready to go anywhere with you, Jodie." He smiled and leaned down for a kiss. Jodie threw her arms around his neck and kissed back. And then hugged him tight.

"Hey, you're holding on like I'm leaving. I'm going with you," he laughed.

"I know. I just don't ever want to lose sight of what's really important ever again, and right now you are one of the many unexpected blessings I do not want to take for granted."

She returned his smile and they walked arm in arm back to his patrol car. And really, into their future together.

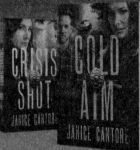

DISCUSSION QUESTIONS

1. Months after losing her team in a devastating bombing, Jodie King is still grieving. What questions does she struggle to see answers to? How effective are the people who speak into her life—Doc Bass, Sam Gresham, George Upton, Mike King, Tracy and Shannon, Estella Perkins? What would you say to Jodie?

2. Sam has worked hard to return to patrol, but his department psychologist is more concerned with his emotional recovery. What invisible scars does he have? Is Sam ready to get back to active police work?

3. With the deaths of her parents, Jodie has seen quite a bit of loss in her life. What makes losing her team different? Have you ever been surprised by the depth of your feelings following a loss?

4. Jodie is familiar with an expression: "If tragedy could destroy a person's faith, then the faith was not worth keeping." Has her faith been destroyed? How much truth is there in this idea, if any?

5. Ian Hunter lashes out at Jodie, blaming her for not including him in the ill-fated raid. Doc Bass tells Jodie, "Hurt people hurt people." Have you ever seen this play out in your own life? How have you handled those situations?

6. What drives Jodie to track down the perpetrator, the person responsible for killing her team, on her own and without a badge? What makes her decision to do so a reckless one?

7. On the same day Sam has a moment in the sheriff's department locker room, he's faced with his biggest challenge since returning to work: a bomb threat in a residential neighborhood. How does he pull through and overcome? Where do you turn when you feel overwhelmed?

8. When she doesn't know where else to turn, Jodie says a foxhole prayer but admits she doesn't think God is really hearing her because of a wall between them. Who built the wall and what is it protecting or keeping out? Are there any walls in your life that need to come down?

9. Both Sam and Estella remind Jodie of God's presence in the midst of hard times. Sam believes God is good, even when life isn't. Estella says, "Trusting God doesn't mean no trials." What makes simple belief in those statements hard? Are there other things you would tell Jodie or do for her?

10. In her zeal to identify the person responsible for killing her team, Jodie considers several people, including some very close to her personally. Were you surprised by the suspect's ultimate reveal? Do the person's motives explain his or her actions?

11. In the end, does Jodie have answers for the questions she's been asking? How does she find peace? Is this resolution satisfying? Realistic? What questions in your own life are you still awaiting answers for? Do you have peace with not knowing?

ABOUT THE AUTHOR

A FORMER LONG BEACH, CALIFORNIA, POLICE OFFICER of twenty-two years, Janice Cantore worked a variety of assignments, including patrol, administration, juvenile investigations, and training. She's always enjoyed writing and published two short articles on faith at work for *Cop and Christ* and *Today's Christian Woman* before tackling novels. She now lives in Hawaii, where she enjoys ocean swimming, golfing, spending time on the beach, and going on long walks with her Labrador retrievers, Abbie and Tilly.

Janice writes suspense novels designed to keep readers engrossed and leave them inspired. *One Final Target* is her fourteenth novel. Janice also authored *Code of Courage*, *Breach of Honor*, the Line of Duty series—*Crisis Shot*, *Lethal Target*, and *Cold Aim*—the Cold Case Justice series—*Drawing Fire*, *Burning Proof*, and *Catching Heat*—the Pacific Coast Justice series—*Accused*, *Abducted*, and *Avenged*—and the Brinna Caruso novels, *Critical Pursuit* and *Visible Threat*.

Visit Janice's website at janicecantore.com and connect with her on Facebook at facebook.com/JaniceCantore and at the Romantic Suspense A-TEAM group.

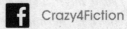
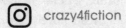
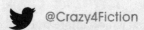